MW00614967

Back to

SS

DATE DUE		
APR 0 4 2018		
L-25-18		
MAY 0 5 2020		

Back to Business
Copyright © 2013 Ann Cobb
All Rights Reserved.

This is a work of fiction. Names, characters, places and incidents either are products of the author's imagination or are used fictitiously. Any resemblance to actual events or locales or persons, living or dead, is entirely coincidental.

Cover Art by Matthew M. Waters

Book Design & Production by WatersDesigns.com

ISBN: 978-0-9883279-3-1

First Edition: September 2013

Please visit the author's web site at: www.AnnCobb.net

Printed in the USA

To my husband, Jerry Cobb, I dedicate this book, just as I have also dedicated the last forty-eight years of my life.

Acknowledgments

Shari Waters, whose technical service is invaluable.

Matthew Waters, who listened and created the book cover.

Sandra Ray, whose knowledge of the English language is
amazing.

Margaret Newberry, who will eagerly read my words the
first time, and then read again and again... and...

Also by Ann Cobb

Bee's Business

CHAPTER ONE

I felt much like the goose at the pond with the broken wing, wounded and left behind. The other geese repeatedly flew away, leaving the injured one with the withered limb to fend for itself. I was out walking in the early morning air, absorbed in the sights and sounds of the land and the water around me, as I glanced across the cold, still water of my farm pond. I could feel that old sad ache come across my body, telling me that I was still alive, but without much to look forward to. Adjusting to being alone had been a daily struggle for the last few years, but with the changing seasons and with every new year, I was beginning to believe I could resurrect some of my old life. Life as I had always known it had changed in 1945, a couple of years earlier. You see, my husband of over thirty-eight years had suddenly died after a heart attack, leaving me alone with just my memories. I was all alone now, and time seemed to stand still. I'd really had enough time to adjust to a new way of living, and at times I felt as if I had, and other times

I knew I never would. I guess I was just feeling a little melancholy this morning.

I do have our daughter, Margaret, my greatest comfort. She lives over in Burt County and works as a schoolteacher. She really is my pride and joy. Her time is taken up most of the year with work, but she does visit quite often. I always cherish every minute we have together. She has never found the right fellow to settle down with, but we are still looking; maybe I should say I'm looking. I really don't think she devotes much time at all to it. She is a modern day woman, and it hasn't really occurred to her yet that she needs a man in her life to make her happy.

Walking is good for me; at least that's what my doctor and my sister tell me. It does give me time to reminisce and dream. Visions of my yesterdays fill my mind and heart as I plod methodically across the pond dam. I was born right here on this land sixty-one years ago and never left. Mama and Daddy raised their family in the very house I live in now. Daddy farmed the land and, with Mama at his side, carved out a good life. I have an older sister who lives just a few miles from me over in Jeffersontown. She and her husband raised a family too, and then Fred, her husband, passed away, leaving Bess alone. Their two sons live close by, but it seems they are not as close to their mother as they should be. Bess seems content on the outside, but I know she feels a little displaced, much as I do. Her main focus in life is to keep everything clean, neat, and organized. She runs a tight ship over at her house. Her houseplants are always watered and fertilized, all "thank you" cards are sent on time, her recipe file is continually updated, and a cake is perpetually baking in her oven. Her house is her domain, and it stays clean with a capital "C." She never, ever lets herself go, and she stays right on top of styles all the time. Next to my sister, Bess

Truman would probably feel dowdy and unfashionable. Lately, she has worn pants around the house, but I know she considers it shameful to be seen in public dressed like a man. Rules, neatness, and etiquette are her bible. I fall short in each category. I never really considered that I could keep up with Bess. *I really never tried. A simple life on the farm in comfortable shoes is right for me.*

Bess had a romantic fling the year before, but now she claims she's through with romance all together. I really have my doubts about that. If some eligible man gave her "the look," I'm sure she would cave into temptation and jump right back into the fire. She just loves a little bit of attention from the opposite sex.

My farm is my home and my means of support. I was able to rent the land to my neighbor and friend, Tom Wilson, soon after Will passed away. He plants cotton and corn just as Will had done. The large pecan orchard behind my house keeps producing year after year, giving me some additional income, too. I heard pecans are bringing a good price this year, and my trees are loaded. With the help of Vonion and Ora Lee, I'll harvest the nuts and sell them at market.

Vonion and Ora Lee are my farm caretakers and, more than that, my friends and family. Vonion asked my daddy for a job the first year of his and Ora Lee's married life, and they never left. Just like Daddy and Mama, they raised a family and are living a contented life right here on the farm. They are as solid as the Rock of Gibraltar. Even though their skin color is darker than mine, I consider them my equal, but they consider me their protector. Maybe that's why our relationship has endured the test of time.

Their home is the little shotgun house down the lane from the "big house" where I live. Never making much improvement to the house, but always contented with what they have, Vonion and Ora Lee live simply by earthly standards but royally in godly ways. Vonion has always been second in command, next to Daddy, and then to Will. *Now that both had passed away, he considered himself to be first. I was never even in the running.* He can do most anything if you give him enough time. He has chopped more firewood than any man alive and was on a first name basis with every cow or hog Daddy or Will ever raised. Ora Lee and I cleaned my house from top to bottom this past summer, but I suspect it could be the last time Ora Lee would be able to help. At eighty years now, her strength and stamina are waning. A little dust and dirt don't bother me much anymore, and if every peach or butter bean isn't in a jar at the end of the season, so be it.

Growing up, Mama didn't want Bess and me to work in the cotton fields, but Daddy saw to it we did. Up before dawn, with our quart jars filled with water and our croaker sacks dragging beside us, we'd work alongside the colored folks Daddy rounded up every morning to pick the cotton. Bess and I received quite an education going up and down those rows of cotton in the hot sun, day after day. Ora Lee, working alongside us, tried to protect us from every danger, but she couldn't always control what we heard or saw. We learned why Rodeena had that swollen belly that seemed to grow and grow. Information of utmost importance such as where the best corn liquor around could be found, and where to raise a little sand on Saturday night never escaped our attention. Four-letter words, common language out in the field, were heard and memorized, but never repeated in Mama's presence. We learned how to squat and pee in the woods next to the field without being noticed, and how to grab a quick nap in the middle of the cotton row with our head resting on the cotton sack.

Spiritual songs such as "Swing Low, Sweet Chariot" and "In the Sweet Bye and Bye" were sung right along with all the constant chatter. Ora Lee could harmonize along with the best of them. She couldn't read a word off of a printed page, but she knew the words to every spiritual under the rainbow. After ten or eleven hours of hearing song after song about "Amazing Grace, how sweet the sound" and "I've got a home in gloryland that outshines the sun," even as a child, I was looking forward to the hereafter just like Ora Lee and all the other colored folks.

I could outpick Bess, but that wasn't saying much. Payday was always on Saturday afternoon right there in the cotton field. I saved enough money one summer to buy my first watch. Proud, but poorer, I wore that little gold watch for years until I lost it. Bess was vain even back then. She had one of those newfangled permanent waves put in her hair with her money one summer, and it's still a standing joke with us how her hair frizzed up and burned on the ends. She was so mortified she had to wear a hat to school when we finally made it in late October that year. Those days of our youth in the cotton fields where we sweated and swore still seem magical to me now.

Other days we spent in a little one-room schoolhouse. I generally wore a dress made from flour sacks. Since I liked plaids and Bess loved flowers, we never fought over which sack our dress would be made from. I did end up with a good many dresses with little faded pink flowers because as Bess outgrew them, I was in line to wear them. A lard can was packed with lunch by Mama's loving hand every day. Most days it was a biscuit with a piece of ham or cheese. Other days Mama would slice some souse meat, or maybe spread butter on homemade bread. I can feel a hint of a smile come to my face as I remember. Oh! Those were the days!

I was beginning to tire as I rounded the edge of the trees that laced the back side of my property. The fertile soil had produced deep woods with an abundance of oak, poplar, and sweet gum. Will always said those trees would be our nest egg. "We can eventually have them harvested since hardwood always brings quite a premium," he had said. But in my heart, I hope I never have to face a day when I have to cut my trees to survive.

Over at a distance, I could see a curl of smoke disappear into the clouds. I knew it came from Foy Jackson's farmhouse over on the other side of the woods. Foy had acquired his land after Daddy settled here and had built a nice home and barn over there next to the road. He never farmed but made his living working at the cotton gin. He was retired now and had outlived his wife. Foy had been crippled several years before when his milk cow kicked him clear across the barn. Now arthritis had settled into his joints, ravaging his tired old body, leaving him dependent on a wheelchair. I had heard my lifelong friend, Vera, my neighbor on the other side of my property, say Foy's son, Walter, had recently moved back home to see about his needs. Walter was probably Foy's saving grace. He was a medical doctor now, and Vera said he had opened an office right next to our new hospital in town.

Our little community was very proud of the new modern hospital with its emergency room open twenty-four hours a day, seven days a week. Bones were set, babies were delivered, and surgery was performed there every day. Ora Lee said all that doctoring wasn't necessary, and home was where a baby needed to be delivered, but she never did go for anything newfangled.

I could barely make out Ora Lee in the distance now, but there she was, out in her yard, leaning over her washtub. Today was wash day. Ora Lee had faithfully scrubbed her laundry on an old washboard for as long as I could remember. I neared the edge of the pecan orchard and could faintly hear the sweet melody of the same hymns I recall from the cotton fields of my youth. "Hymns like prayers," Ora Lee always said. "It ain't hard to talk to the Lord. Open your mouth and just let it come. He knows what you is tryin' to say."

Change was hard for Ora Lee and Vonion. They steadfastly resisted any improvement to the place or any modernization. I had hired a painter the year before to paint my tired, old, neglected house and had offered the leftover paint to Vonion for their little clapboard house. He had stepped back as if he was offended. "What good is a'paintin'? It just be a'peelin' off again. I ain't a'doin' it in the first place." I always thought he and Ora Lee were so wise.

My steps quickened as I remembered Bess was planning on stopping by the house later this morning. She had said she had something very important to talk to me about. I could just wonder what was disturbing her mind now. It could be anything from the color of the new choir robes our little Baptist church planned on ordering to some juicy bit of gossip we dared not talk about on the party line telephone. With Nellie, our nosy, but necessary, telephone operator, anything that was said over the telephone wires became common knowledge as soon as it was out of your mouth.

As I neared the barn, I could overhear Vonion, in his old raspy voice, coaxing Hortence, our milk cow, to give just another drop or two of milk. Over in the distance, I could make out the rumble of a truck on the road, and then the sound of a car door closing. I quickened my steps since I figured it was Bess. She was early, so this must be important. You never really know what's bearing down on Bess's mind.

But I'd bet the farm it'll be of interest.

CHAPTER TWO

As I rounded the corner of the house, I noticed the butterflies and bees, with their nonstop flickering and fluttering, circling the blooming lantana bushes. I slowed my pace to glance at the colorful activity and soon saw Bess, dressed in her lavender shirtwaist with the tiny pearl buttons, impatiently waiting for me by the steps to the porch. She was leaning over pulling on a stubborn dandelion in the flower bed. The beauty of nature hardly ever escapes my notice, and Bess continually tries to improve it. That's just the way we are. I took after Mama, and Bess after Daddy. Mama could always see the beauty of the land. Daddy helped Mama with the flowers, but he never took the time to really enjoy them. It was just a necessary chore, like feeding the chickens or milking the cows.

"Bess," I said, as I stopped at the mailbox and took a breath, "you don't have to do that. I'll get to it later."

"I've got it now. The ground is hard as a brickbat, but I got the roots."

"Thanks," I said, as I pulled the mail out of the box. "I have a feeling I know what you're thinking about that's so important. I've had a feeling for a while you wanted to take a trip to visit Cousin Myrtle. I'm ready when you are."

Bess readily answered, as she rubbed the dirt from her hands and smoothed her dress. "What in the world makes you think I want to go traveling to South Carolina now of all times? You know as well as I do we have to participate in the church bazaar next month. Who on earth do you think is going to make aprons and put up scuppernong jelly if I don't? There's not another member of the church who knows a thing about ruffling an apron."

"I, uh, guess you're right about that."

"Now let's be sensible. This is not a good time of year to think about visiting Myrtle. Myrtle is probably suffering with hay fever right about now, anyway. You know as well as I do, she has it every year. She's probably as ornery as an old billy goat without a can to nibble on."

"Maybe we can get up there in the spring. You know Myrtle isn't getting any younger. If we wait too long, it might just be too late."

"I know. We want to visit with her and not attend her funeral." Bess nervously glanced at the sky. "Oh, Bee, do you see that cloud?"

I gazed out toward the morning sky as it suddenly changed from a bright blue to a dull gray. Suddenly a bright shaft of lightening appeared in the distance, and then the sound of thunder roared as heavy, deep purple clouds rolled in. "We might get a little rain out of those clouds," Bess continued, as she glanced at the sky. "I know Tom needs to get the cotton picked soon, but a little rain would be wonderful about now. I don't know when it's been this dry in October. I do remember a few years back when..."

"Okay, Bess. Quit beating around the bush. What's on your mind?" I asked, as I trudged up the steps behind her dress tail, and we plopped down in the rockers Vonion had recently painted. "I know you didn't drive out here this morning to talk about this weather. Today is your beauty parlor day anyway, and I know good and well you don't let anything get between you and your hair appointment. Is Thelma sick or something?"

Thelma, our local beautician, knows the true color of most everybody's hair roots in town. She's flighty in some ways, but she knows her business thrives only if she keeps her mouth shut concerning our beauty secrets. Other information, on not such a personal level, such as whose husband had been seen leaving a certain widow woman's house early in the morning hours, or the horrible condition of some neglectful housekeeper's home, can be discussed at will any time there is a conversation lull in the shop.

Bess and I rely on Thelma's Cut and Curl for much of our information. The beauty shop is the ideal place to gather new leads. You see, Bess and I began a small business venture last year. We even had cards and stationery printed with our company name and telephone numbers engraved on them: "The B and B Investigative Services—We go where you can't." Bess had even suggested we have matching outfits to wear when we are on a case. *Sometimes I wondered if Bess really "got it."* We had been hired a few times since our initial case involving the new preacher. That ruthless preacher imposter had actually murdered one of the upstanding members of our community, and would have gotten away with it, too, if I hadn't figured the whole scheme out. Sheriff Ledbetter never would have found them without our professional help, either. Bess and I led the sheriff right to the Resoto Hotel in Savannah where he and his girlfriend accomplice were hiding out. They are now spending life sentences in the state penitentiary, and hopefully, they'll never see the light of day again.

Working on that case wet our whistles for more challenging cases. Since then we helped Sheriff Ledbetter find the culprit who was dumping garbage next to the woods out on Route 1, found a lost dog for Mr. Lawson, our local mortician and funeral director, and we even located a long lost friend of Vera's husband, Tillman. The friend had seemingly disappeared but had actually just moved out of the state into Alabama. Each of those cases was relatively simple. The garbage was traced back to Ida Wallace. An empty Soft and Satin hand lotion bottle, a meat wrapper that smelled like beef liver, and an old printed program for a special anniversary day from the Jeffersontown Baptist Church were the only clues Bess and I needed. Nobody but Ida would think about using that brand of greasy hand lotion that smelled just like persimmons. You could smell it clear across the sanctuary. She claimed the garbage fell off the tailgate of the old Ford pickup truck she had learned to drive after her husband passed away, leaving her with no other means of transportation. Sheriff Ledbetter, Bess, and I found that story hard to believe since the garbage was at least ten feet from the side of the road. She was scolded by the sheriff, and she promised to burn her garbage from then on. The dog had been picked up by Cleo, the proprietor of the rolling store. He was keeping the hungry, lost dog in a wire pen back of his house until someone came forth looking for the mangy creature. Bess and I noticed him digging a tunnel under the fence as we drove by taking fresh eggs over to his neighbor, Mrs. Estelle Pickens, an elderly widow woman with not much of an income, and too proud to ask for assistance. Finding the lost friend had even been easier. We found him by checking the nationwide telephone directory. Now we're ready for a real case.

"Bee, for your information, I just left Thelma. You can't tell? You are so unobservant." And lifting her hand to pat her hair, Bess smugly replied, "I do have something on my mind." She hesitated then, as if she was reluctant to talk. "It's something I've been thinking about for a while. Now Bee, listen carefully..."

Just as the word *listen* came out of Bess's mouth, the telephone in the hall started ringing. Two rings—one long, one short. That's me. "Oh, Bess, I'm sorry. I'll just be a second. Whoever it is, I'll try to keep it short." I hurried into the house toward the telephone and almost tripped over the stool I use to prop my feet while talking. You never know how long you might be tied up discussing an upcoming social event or some church affair, and it's important to have some way to elevate your feet. Once I stayed on the line over an hour conferring with our church secretary, Miss Effie Belle Sweetwater, about a very upsetting development in our church concerning the printing of a weekly church bulletin. Some of us felt we needed a nice attractive bulletin to refer to during the week as a reminder of all the meetings and social activities, and others felt any unnecessary spending was absolutely uncalled for. I felt as if my ears were numb after we finally settled on a solution to the problem—let the deacons decide. They were the ones that controlled the money spending anyway. *As you might guess, we never got a bulletin.*

Moments later, I hung up—baffled, excited, and confused. *Our first real big assignment! And we were to get paid! Wait until I tell Bess...*

"Bess, you are absolutely not going to believe it, but we've been hired!" I called to Bess as I hurried back out to the porch. "I can't believe it myself! Our ship has finally come in this time! We get a hundred dollars if we can solve a mystery." Then stopping short and thinking about what I just said, I added, "Oh, dear, I hope we're up to it. Oh, Bess, this is so exciting! Exciting for us, but not for poor Molly." Molly Turner is the young wife of the school principal, Sam Turner, and a member of our missionary group. And for the next little while, Bess's news was all but forgotten as I excitedly explained our new assignment to my older, but not always wiser, sister and business partner.

"We've got to be very discreet gathering the information," I adamantly told Bess, as we mulled over what our first step was to be in solving this mystery. "We need to meet with Molly, face-to-face, and find out all the vital information before we go off half-cocked looking for clues."

"You're right. But did you tell Molly we'd meet immediately? I'm not really dressed for a business meeting. Maybe I need to go to the house and change. Did you tell Molly we have business cards and stationery? She'll be so impressed, I imagine."

"I told her I'd call back in a few minutes, after I talked to you. Oh, Bess, can you believe it? A real case! If Molly really thinks her husband is in some kind of trouble, there must be something to it. Now, we have to be very businesslike and act like real detectives. Molly doesn't need to be throwing her money around. We have to deal in facts and not get carried away. Molly said her husband is secretly spending lots of money. He's obviously hiding something from her. She said he's spending a great deal of time out of town at meetings lately too. It sounds to me that two and two add up to an affair, but let's just listen to Molly and not jump to any quick conclusions. And Bess, for goodness sake, don't worry about your dress. You look fine. You aren't going to be in a beauty contest or anything."

"I know it," Bess replied in an aggravated tone, "but you know I always like to look my best. Now Bee, do you think we'll get shot at or anything? I've told you before I'm not ever risking my life again for anything or anybody."

"Nobody's gonna get shot at. We're just gonna do a little snooping, err, I mean investigating. We aren't actually going to try to arrest anybody or anything. This is gonna be different from our last big case. Now do you want me to call Molly back and tell her to meet us at headquarters in half an hour?"

"That sounds good...but where in the dickens is headquarters? I didn't know we had a headquarters."

"Well, we do now. Headquarters is right here on the front porch. It's private, and Molly will feel relaxed out here. Nobody will see us meeting, but if they do, we can always say we're talking about the bazaar. I'll call Molly back while you make some lemonade. There are lemons in the refrigerator. And, for heaven's sake, put enough sugar in it this time."

"Okay. Bee, this is so-o exciting! You know, you might want to give the porch a little swipe with the broom before Molly arrives."

I certainly would never really admit it to anyone else, but there were times I actually admired the way Bess was always so concerned about cleanliness and appearances, but not right now. "I will, but now, where did I leave that new writing tablet? We need something to write on, and a good sharp pencil. What other tools of the trade do we need?"

"An instruction book on crime solving for one thing; but for the time being, I guess a pencil and tablet will do. Now go make that call, but don't sound too eager. We don't want to sound as if we don't have much business."

"Right! We want to act as if we hear this sort of thing all the time. And Bess, when Molly gets here, let me do most of the talking."

CHAPTER THREE

Molly arrived right on time. The rain had set in to a steady downpour, but Molly paid little attention to the weather and jumped from the car without even glancing toward the sky. With her current personal circumstances, an apparent concern for keeping dry must have totally escaped her mind. She dashed up the steps without a hood or a raincoat. Bess ran for a towel, and Molly, dripping wet, gratefully reached for it as she bounded into the porch.

"Child, you are soaking wet. Let's get you into some dry clothes. I've got an old housecoat you can throw on, and we'll hang your clothes over a chair by the oven door. It won't take but a few minutes for them to dry. I'll go turn the oven on, and you go straight in there and get that robe on," I ordered. "It's hanging on the hook on the inside of the bathroom door." I pointed toward the door as a pool of rain water puddled at her feet and began to run toward the screen door across the uneven porch floor.

"Ms. Bee, I'm really all right. My clothes will be dry directly," Molly nervously answered, as she stood, shivering. I'm making such a mess on your floor. I'm sorry. I'll wipe it up. Do you have an old towel or something I can use?" Molly timidly asked, as she untied her wet scarf from around her head and peeled off her pink sweater.

"It won't hurt a thing. Maybe the rain water will clean the floor a little. Now I'm not taking 'no' for an answer. Get in there and hand me those clothes. You can't even think with those wet things on, and besides that, you'll catch pneumonia," I said, as I gave Molly a nudge. She hesitated but finally relented and started for the bathroom.

A few minutes later, Molly, wrapped in my old robe and much less damp, walked back to the porch. Her short, chestnut brown hair was lank and damp, and a weary expression still covered her drained, sad face. She shivered as she sat down, and with emotions too powerful to hold in, she covered her face with her hands and began to sob uncontrollably. Bess reached over and gently patted her shoulders to comfort her. It was evident Molly was in deep despair. Bess glanced at me with a helpless expression and sorrowfully shook her head. I hurried to the bedroom for a handkerchief as I began to realize we were dealing with real pain and sadness here. The reality of these circumstances swiftly began to weigh deeply on my heart. Bess and I had been playing a game with this detective stuff, but this was real life. What were we thinking about, asking this young girl with the weight of the world on her shoulders to rely on us for help? She needed a preacher or a counselor for real guidance, not a pretend detective agency. We must be out of our minds!

Regaining her composure, Molly raised her head a bit as I hurried back to the porch. I handed her Will's handkerchief, and she readily took it. *Will's handkerchief...*

There are some things you just can't get rid of. "Here now. Dry your eyes. You're going to make yourself sick. Bess just made some lemonade. I'll get you a glass."

"That does sound good. I don't think I've eaten or drunk a thing today," Molly answered, as she dried her eyes.

"Well, in that case, I'm going to get you a little something to eat too. How about a nice slice of pound cake? I made one yesterday. It won't be as good as if Bess made it, but it does taste pretty good if I do say so myself."

"No thank you. I have to watch my weight. Sam likes for me to stay slim, and I do think I might have gained a pound or two lately."

"You look fine to me. A little meat on your bones is good for you," Bess declared. I thought maybe I needed to check my hearing. Even in my most sorrowful times after Will passed away, Bess always made me feel guilty as sin if one crumb of something sweet passed through my lips.

"The lemonade is real refreshing," Molly said, after she took a small swallow, and placed her glass on the little round wicker table between the rockers.

"Bess, I didn't bring any lemonade out for you. I'll get you a glass," I said, as I stood back up. "I'll be right back." A little time alone in the kitchen would give me a little time to think over this situation. Bess and I needed to be prepared to give Molly a whole lot of reassurance. These were difficult circumstances, and probably way out of our range of expertise. *I don't know if we even have any expertise.*

"Thank you, Bee. I do believe I'd enjoy some. But let me get it. I'll get both of us some." Bess jumped up and left for the kitchen, leaving me alone with Molly. Bess must be feeling a need to be alone to think about this situation, too.

"Ms. Bee, I really shouldn't have called you this morning," Molly murmured hopelessly. "I'm such a bother.

Sam would kill me if he thought I was talking about our personal problems with anybody. Maybe I'll just go on back home. I'm sure my dress is dry by now."

Molly placed her hands on the arms of the rocker to rise, and I quickly reached over and covered her hand with mine. "Molly, you came out here to talk. Now Bess and I aren't the most knowledgeable people in the world, but we certainly can listen. Sometimes it makes you feel better just to talk things over, and it's pretty evident there are some circumstances in your life that are troubling you a great deal. Whatever you say won't go a bit further than this porch, and I can guarantee that. Bess and I have all the time in the world. You take your time, and we'll listen, even if it takes all day. Now just relax and start from the beginning."

"But Ms. Bee, suppose Sam found out I had confided in you and Ms. Bess? I'm sure he'd leave me. Then what would I do? Mama and Daddy don't want me back, and my only sister lives way out in Texas. I rarely ever hear from her. She's so busy with her career and all. She works at a major newspaper out there as a big-time journalist. She's really made something of herself. Mama and Daddy were so proud of her when she graduated from college with honors. I didn't even graduate from high school. Sam wanted to get married as soon as he found his first teaching job so we ran off one weekend without my parents' permission. They eventually got over it, though. Daddy said Sam was a really good catch for me, and I could have done a lot worse. That was eleven years ago. It's a wonder Sam has put up with me this long. My housekeeping skills are terrible, cooking is a real challenge, and you can see for yourself, I'm no looker. I never have been able to manage Sam's money very well, either. If he gives me ten dollars, I need twelve. I'm really just a mess!"

"Lord, child. You're describing every woman and wife I know. Why, anybody who knows me could say the same thing about me. God didn't make perfect people, you know." Bess walked out with the lemonades and obviously overheard my observation because she gave me a look as to say that my remark didn't include her. *She just can't take herself down off that pedestal.*

"I really don't know where to start," Molly muttered, as she nervously gripped the arms of the rocker.

"Start at the beginning," Bess replied, as she sat down. "When did all this start?"

With a little more resolve, Molly hesitated, but started. "I began to realize something was terribly wrong about three years ago. Sam would lose patience with everything, especially me. He complained about everything that was going on at school, and he especially seemed irritated about the way I kept such an imperfect home. I thought the house looked all right, but Sam could always find fault. Either the house wouldn't be clean enough, or the clothes didn't smell fresh enough, or the meat I cooked was dry. There was always something wrong. I knew we had a problem, but I didn't know what the root of it was. I felt as if our home had become a prison to him. He wasn't happy with me...or really anything else. There was something troubling Sam, and whatever it was, it was stealing all the joy from our lives." Molly stopped short and stared off into space.

The clouds were beginning to pass over, and the steady downpour of rain had subsided. The sun was peeking through the last remaining cloud as Molly nervously shifted in her seat.

"Go on," Bess encouraged, as Molly nervously fingered Will's handkerchief. "We're still listening. That was three years ago. Did things get any better?"

21

"Not really. Sam came home from school one day and, out of the blue, announced he had quit his job as school principal and we were moving away from Burt County. We didn't even wait until the end of the school year. Sam found us a little apartment in Atlanta and off we went. Sam had been hired for a teaching position at a small parochial school nearby, and we lived on his small salary for the next few months. I never could understand why Sam was in such a hurry to move in the first place. All he would say was it was time to move on, and nobody at that stupid school appreciated a thing he had ever tried to accomplish."

"So Sam left a nice job with a lot of responsibility as a school principal in Burt County for a job as a teacher in a small church school? Do you have any idea what was behind the move?" I questioned. "Did you even quiz him about it, or did Sam ever come forth with a reasonable explanation?"

"Oh, I asked him time after time to explain why he felt the need to leave so abruptly, but all he would say was, 'You wouldn't understand.' It was something he said he just had to do. Sam never tells me anything about school business. He says it's over my head, and he's right too. You know I didn't even finish high school, so I really don't understand much about business or professional stuff."

Molly had already told us she didn't finish school. She seemed to have such a low opinion of herself, and I had a feeling her "superior to you" husband put her in her place quite frequently. My opinion of Sam Turner was plummeting as rapidly as my desire to get involved in this marital disaster. But we were involved, so I urged Molly to go on.

"We stayed in Atlanta just a few months, long enough to finish out the school term. Sam seemed elated when he came home one day and told me he had been hired as the school principal, and we were moving here to Jeffersontown. He was to replace Mr. Humblebee, who was retiring at the end of the term. Sam's mood changed a great deal about then, and it seemed to me we were getting along fine. I was amazed at the difference in Sam and our marriage. We started talking about having a baby, and maybe buying a house here in Jeffersontown. We had a lot to look forward to, and things stayed good for several months after that. We had settled here in our little rented house, and Sam and I began to try to become a part of the community. You know we joined the church, and I started coming to the missionary meetings. The ladies were always so nice to me, and I especially admired the two of you. Y'all made me realize what I was missing since I rarely ever saw my own sister."

I looked over at Bess and gave her a smile. She simply smiled back, and I felt that familiar connection she and I had always had. You never know when you'll be reminded of the things we possess that money can't buy.

Molly paused for a moment, but continued on. "Anyway, things were good for a while. Then, gradually, Sam started acting the same old way. He became mean and hateful again, always talking down to me and never smiling. I can't seem to do a thing right anymore. When we are out in public, we just pretend everything is fine between us. At home Sam is as jumpy as a cat. He hardly says a kind word to me, and he seems terribly preoccupied with something. I don't know what it is, and I'm just at my wit's end. I feel as if our marriage is crumbling apart, and I don't know what to do about it. If I try to talk to him about it, he just gets madder. If I argued with him, he'd probably leave, and then what would I do? I'd be out in the cold with nowhere to go. Oh, whatever am I gonna do?" Molly leaned over and began to sob again.

"Oh, dear child, you've been through so much," Bess sorrowfully replied, as she teared up also. She reached over and gave Molly a tender hug. My emotions were also welling up inside as I watched Molly limply bring the handkerchief back to her face and wipe away fresh tears. Bess humbly asked, "What can we do for you, Molly, to make things easier? We'll do what you want."

"Ms. Bess, I really don't know what anybody can do. I guess I should just go on with things like they are, but now I've discovered something I really and truly don't understand, and I really need some expert advice."

I started cringing then and realized Bess and I were way out of our league. We had stepped into deep waters, and I was beginning to think we would eventually drown. Even though I realized our limitations, we could never walk away from this poor helpless girl. "We'll do anything to help you," I adamantly added. "Now just go on. We're listening."

"I don't usually see anything about our banking or anything about money. Sam sees about all that. He just gives me five dollars a week for groceries and any incidentals we might need. I try to budget, and as long as I don't get carried away with something, I do fairly well. Anyway last week, a letter came to the house from the bank. I don't know why…I know I shouldn't have, but I opened it, knowing full well Sam would have a fit if he knew I read his mail. There are sometimes you just can't help yourself. As soon as I saw that letter, I knew I was going to open it and read it." Molly hesitated then, as if she wasn't sure she should go on.

Bess and I waited, watching as Molly fidgeted. Building her courage, she finally went on. "The letter from the bank was informing Sam that they would not cover his overdrafts any longer, and he needed to come into the bank and discuss another possible loan. I was floored. Sam had never said a word to me about overdrafts. I thought there had to be a mistake at the bank. Why on earth was Sam writing checks with no money to cover them? The more I thought about it the more I panicked. I hid the letter, and the next day I decided to find out for myself what was going on. I knew my name was on the bank account because I had gone to the bank with Sam and we opened it together soon after we moved to town. A few days ago I went to the bank by myself and asked for a copy of our bank records. I didn't want them to question me about the records, so I pretended to be getting them for Sam."

"Did it work?" I questioned as my interest grew.

"Oh, yes. It worked all right. I was so nervous in there, but Ms. Belle Pennyworth was so kind to me. She mimeographed the records, put them in an envelope, and just handed them over to me. It was so easy. Then she asked if I wanted a mimeographed copy of our loans. Ms. Bee, I almost collapsed right there on the floor of that big old bank. I didn't even know we had loans. After composing myself enough to talk, I told Ms. Belle we'd love to have those copies too, if she didn't mind and had the time.

"Well, in no time flat she mimeographed some more papers and handed them to me. She told me she was always happy to be of service. Ms. Bee, I couldn't get out of that bank fast enough. If anybody had told Sam they saw me in there, he would have questioned me until he was blue in the face, and I would have had to tell him the truth."

"You mean to say Sam has loans you knew nothing about?" Bess quizzed. She had quit rocking by this time and was sitting straight up in her chair, hanging on to every word.

"Oh, yes. I was so taken aback by what was in those records, I almost died. Sam has been periodically withdrawing big, big sums of money. Every month for the last year, he has withdrawn fifty dollars. He has been overdrawn numerous times, and several times he has borrowed as much as a hundred dollars at one time. Ms. Bess, I have absolutely no knowledge whatsoever of what he's doing with all that money. We've been doing without all this time, and he's been spending all that money on something or someone. I've got to know the truth about everything. If I asked Sam, or if he knew I had been to the bank, I'm sure he would leave me. I'm desperate! Please, please take the case! Find out what Sam's been up to. Ms. Bee, my whole life depends on it."

Bess and I sat there stunned as Molly collapsed again into an avalanche of more tears. My head said to stay out of this, but my heart told me to do anything I could to help this pathetic young girl. She didn't have another soul in the world to turn to except Bess and me.

And if you think about it, that really is a pathetic thought!

CHAPTER FOUR

Bess and I stood in the doorway of the porch, waving to Molly as her car rolled up the waterlogged lane to the road. Bess forlornly sighed and said, "Bee, we might be getting into something we can't get out of. I don't know how you do it, but trouble just follows you around like flies to a henhouse. You know good and well we don't know how to go about finding out anything about that good-looking man or what he's been up to. He really seems to be a fine, upstanding, young man, and a pillar of our society. He might be sending money to a church or an orphanage somewhere, for all we know. You've really gotten us in a jam this time if you ask me."

We sat down, but neither of us relaxed. "I've gotten us in a jam...Is that what you think?" I answered in an exasperated, irritated tone. *I knew we needed to get things straight right then.* "You know good and well it was your idea, as well as mine, to start this detective business. Don't blame this on me." Then, I added, with a little more encouragement in my voice, "Bess, we can figure it out. All we have to do is put all the pieces together. Now, where do we start?" I asked, as I looked squarely at Bess. "And what does the fact that he's good-looking have to do with any of this? You've still got men on your mind."

"I do not! I was just stating a fact. You know good and well you've noticed his wavy blond hair. You aren't blind, are you?" Bess calmed down a bit then and resumed rocking back and forth. "Okay, let's start at the beginning. Now when did Molly say Sam started acting out of sorts?"

Maybe Bess was finally jumping on board.

"Let me see," I answered, as I was reviewing in my mind all that Molly had told us that morning. "She said he had been working over in Burt County. Hey, Bess, that's the same school where Margaret teaches. We could start by questioning Margaret. See, I told you we could come up with something to start off with. All we have to do is call Margaret and ask if she had heard anything about why Sam left the school in such a hurry."

"We don't want to get Margaret involved in all this, Bee. Maybe we had better talk to somebody else."

"No, absolutely not. We can pretend to be very casual, and Margaret won't catch on that she's giving us undercover information. Now, do you want to call her or do you want me to? Either way, we've got to talk to her."

"Isn't she teaching about now? We'll have to wait until later in the day."

"Oh, that's right. Okay, in the meantime, let's review what we do know."

"Bee, let's talk about it a little later. I came out to discuss something really important with you. Are you at all interested?" Bess seemed squeamish as she shifted her weight in her rocker. She hesitated and gave a pitiful little cough, as if to put off telling me what was really on her mind.

I leaned forward in my chair and couldn't help but scold her. "Bess, you know I'm interested. Now what on earth is all this about, anyway? Are you in trouble or something? You know whatever it is, I'll understand. I know you didn't rob a bank, did you?" I kidded. "Pe-lease don't tell me this has something to do with that scoundrel, J.R. Kitchens. I thought you had that two-timing Casanova clean out of your system after what happened in Savannah last year."

You've probably figured out by now that Bess and J.R. never got back together after that stunt she pulled at the Resoto Hotel. Bess almost landed herself in jail after she pranced, without knocking, right into the hotel room he and that floozy Eunice Donaldson occupied, and started beating J.R. over the head with her big pocketbook with the Griswold frying pan in it. I followed her into the room and held her off as long as I could while Eunice ran down to the first floor. She grabbed Jasper Honeycutt, the old geezer that ran the front desk at the hotel, and together they hurried back to the room. That scrawny old man must have been stronger than anybody gave him credit for, because he single-handedly pried a fired-up Bess off that two-timing rascal, J.R. Kitchens.

Evidently Bess halted the romantic interlude before the lovebirds had gotten down to real business, but only momentarily, because word had gotten out around town that the skintight purple dress Eunice showed up wearing at that fancy hotel in Savannah got a lot tighter. After the birth of twins about nine months after their rendezvous, Eunice, or should I say the recently betrothed Mrs. J.R. Kitchens (but a little too recent) was busy changing diapers, and the proud daddy had gone back to work selling fertilizer. His late wife, Ms. Minnie Lou, had left him a little sum of money in a life insurance policy, but I expect he'd had to use most of it for pablum by now. Eunice's other children were probably calling J. R. "Daddy." Bess narrowly missed that bullet. Thank heavens.

"Bee, will you ever let me live that down? I swear, one little hitch in my life, and you'll probably never forget it and never quit reminding me of it. Men are not in my future, and I'm going to dedicate the rest of my life to maintaining good health and spreading the gospel."

Barely suppressing an eye roll, I replied, "Good, you can start by going to the circle meeting with me next week. It's at Nina's, and you know what a good cook she is."

"I'll bet she'll serve lemon pie. She really cooks the best lemon pie with that flaky crust. I can't figure out, for the life of me, how she gets that crust so flaky and light. You couldn't budge a recipe out of her with a pry bar."

"I've asked her time and again for that recipe, and she just says it's a little pinch of something special," I exasperatedly added. "She just drives me crazy. She thinks she's the only one around here that knows a thing about baking. If I had a good recipe like that, and somebody asked for it, I know I'd share it."

"I wouldn't be so sure about that. You never would tell me how to make hoecakes like Mama used to make."

"I've told you plenty of times. You've got to use plenty of lard. That's the secret."

"You know that stuff's terrible for you."

"Well, you can either use plenty of lard and make good hoecakes, or you can skimp and make bad hoecakes. That's the choice you have to make," I replied, matter-of-factly.

Then, after giving a little more thought to our conversation, I had to add, "Listen, Bess, don't go in there bragging too much about the pie. Nina will get the big head, and you know how she is. I thought we never would get through hearing about her granddaughter after she won that 'Miss Sweet Potato' contest over in Alabama. You'd have thought she won the 'Miss America' pageant."

"I know what you mean. I don't believe she's mentioned a thing about that girl since she ran off with that rodeo cowboy. I do know for a fact, because I heard it from Mildred, that she came back home alone to Macon to live with her parents the next year, and with a tattoo on her buttocks that read, 'Ride'em cowboy'."

"I don't know how Mildred finds out all that interesting stuff about people," I replied. "And you never mentioned that to me."

"Bee, I don't tell you everything I know."

* * *

A loud rattling noise filled the air. "That sounds like Vonion's pickup truck," I said, as I glanced down the lane.

"He needs a muffler on that old thing," Bess complained. "You can hear it clear over in the next county."

It was Vonion all right, and he was in a big hurry. He rolled into the yard in Will's old beat-up pickup truck and slammed on the brakes, piercing the air with a louder squealing noise. He jumped from the truck before it came to a dead stop, and without even attempting to slam the truck door, tore over to the porch, with his old spindly legs twirling like tiny whirlwinds, and waving his arms wildly about.

"Ms. Bee, Ms. Bee! You is got to come now! Come on!" he excitedly hollered, as he danced around in the yard, trying to control his emotions. "It's Ora Lee! She ailing bad. I's don't know what to do. She just laying there with her eyes rolled back in her head. I done asked her to tell me what wrong, but she don't even try to answer. She ain't dead, but she must be mighty close to them pearly gates.

31

Oh, please, Ms. Bee, come on. We's need Mr. Will rat now if'n we's ever needed him. He always know what to do!"

I grabbed Bess's hand in mine, quickly squeezed it, and in a panic, yelled back, "I'll grab my car keys and be on in a second." A fast prayer went up as I stood.

"Ain't got no time fer that. Come on with me rat now." Vonion must have noticed Bess about then because he stopped short, tipped his old straw hat, and said, "Morning, Ms. Bess." *Bess has that effect on everybody. Politeness is vitally important. Even if you're bleeding to death around Bess, you need to ask to be excused before you pass away.* "Ms. Bess, you come too. We's gonna need all the help at prayin' we's can git."

Panicking, Bess and I raced down the steps and jumped into the rattly old pickup truck. Vonion gunned the motor. Hardly noticing the rank odor of sweat and tobacco in the cab at all, Bess and I held onto the dashboard trying to keep from falling back out onto the muddy ground. With our hearts beating wildly, and the fear of the unknown pressing down around us, the three of us raced down the waterlogged lane in that ancient truck. Vonion never latched the door or ever changed a gear.

We pulled into the drenched yard that surrounded the small weather-beaten home of Vonion and Ora Lee's family. Vonion slammed on the brakes again, making that same loud squealing noise that reverberated through the cab of the pickup, leaving us almost deaf. The old truck jolted forward, but Bess and I quickly regained our balance. We slid across the worn-out seat, jumped over the running board, and dashed right behind a panicky Vonion. He stepped in the middle of a big puddle of water, splashing mud all over us as we ran right behind him and into the same puddle. I managed to keep going, but Bess stopped short, leaned over, and searched through the mud for her missing left shoe as Vonion darted on ahead of us onto the sagging front porch. As he dashed into the dark interior of the house, I could hear Vonion praying and pleading out loud with the Lord at the same time. Hoping for the best, but telling myself to be prepared for the worst, I ran in behind Vonion, and Bess, holding her muddy shoe in her hand, brought up the rear.

The dim interior of the house made it hard for our eyes to adjust, but we found our way to the back room. Ora Lee lay lifelessly on the same old iron bed where she had given birth to all their children. Her weak, small body seemed to be melted into the mattress, leaving only the slightest indention. She looked so pitiful and frail lying there under one of many quilts she had hand-stitched in earlier years when her eyesight had been clearer. My mind and heart were clouded with fear as I looked down toward my "other mother."

"Thank Heavens! She's alive," I thankfully announced as I noticed a slight movement. "Let's get her to the hospital. Vonion, do you think we can move her?"

"That horspital..." and he paused, "hit just fer white peoples, ain't it?" Vonion questioned in a humble voice. "We's can't go there, Ms. Bee. You knows we's ain't welcome." Vonion was saying one thing, but I knew he was really pleading for help.

"That's nonsense," Bess indignantly replied. "Ora Lee is as welcome there as anybody. Now wrap her in the quilt and pick her up as gently as you can."

Quickly consenting, Vonion tenderly said, "Ora Lee, we's is gonna move you rat now. You be all right. You listen to me now, fer once in yor life. It ain't no time fer dying today."

We gently wrapped Ora Lee in the tattered old quilt, and Vonion, with all the strength he could muster, carried his lifelong companion out to the truck where I had gone on ahead and slid in. He placed Ora Lee beside me and rested her head against my shoulder. After making sure she was securely positioned, he ran around to crank the truck. Bess had run out into the yard behind us but was left standing by the door of the truck.

"Hey, what about me? I want to go, too," Bess shouted, as Vonion slammed the truck door.

"Jump on the tailgate, Ms. Bess! You's can ride back there!" Vonion already had the truck in gear, and as it began to move forward, Bess knew she didn't have much of a choice. Without thinking, *I'm sure,* she jumped up on the tailgate. I figured she'd jump off as we raced through my yard, but she hung on all the way up the lane.

We slowed down at the intersection for a truck hauling chickens to pass before entering the main road. I was holding onto Ora Lee as Vonion drove up the road toward town behind the slow-moving poultry truck. I glanced back through the back window and marveled at my high society sister, clutching the chain of the tailgate with one hand and pressing her hairdo down with the other. We sped right up to the back of that chicken truck, but Vonion wasn't able to pass since Cleo's slow-moving rolling store was taking up most of the other side of the road, going in the opposite direction. The wire pen in the back of the truck holding the chickens bounced around when the truck hit a hole in the road, causing the trapdoor to fly open. A mass of chickens exploded from the pen, filling the air with feathers and squawks. Chickens began to crash into our windshield, roll over the top of the cab, and flop into the bed of the truck.

"Lord have mercy!" Vonion exclaimed, as he skillfully held the truck in the road after hitting the same hole. "Ms. Bess might not make it to the horspital with us. She's really a'fightin' a chicken storm back there!"

"Keep going, Vonion. We can't slow down now. Bess'll be all right. She might have a feather or two in her hair and a little gunk between her teeth, but she'll get over it. *I knew that wasn't true, but we had to keep on rolling.*

We proceeded on up the road, never even slowing down for the stop sign, weaving around Vera and Tillman, my neighbors, as they crept along in their car. Even from the front of the pickup, I could see the astonished expression on Vera's face as we flew around them. I imagine she never in a million years expected to see Bess riding on the tailgate of Vonion's old pickup truck right in the middle of Jeffersontown with a chicken under her arm. Under normal circumstances, Bess wouldn't have been caught dead at night riding in the front of the truck, much less on the back tailgate. Tillman stayed close behind all the way to the hospital.

Vonion kept one hand on the horn, honking it at anything that got in our way. We had to slam on the brakes as Earnest Lee Black, the slower-than-Christmas mailman, plodded across the street, right in our path carrying his mail sack. With her hair flying in the wind, Bess, with that chicken under one arm and holding onto the tailgate chain with the other hand, yelled for him to get out of the way or we'd knock that sack right off his scrawny backside. He stumbled over to the side of the road and yelled something that I really shouldn't repeat. By that time Tillman must have become aware that something was terribly wrong, and he laid on his horn, too. The old truck finally rattled up to the hospital, Vonion slammed on those squealing brakes again, and we came to an abrupt stop. Tillman, just a few feet behind, had to swerve his car to keep from ramming right into the rear of us. Bess, sensing danger, had already pulled her legs up to her chest. Clutching that chicken with one arm and waving frantically with the other, she looked victorious. *She's really a trooper when it comes right down to it.*

Vonion looked at me as he grabbed the door handle and pathetically asked, "Ora Lee ain't left us, is she?"

"She's hanging on right now, but let's hurry and get her into the hospital," I reassuringly answered.

The old truck door sprung open, and Tillman peered in. He had obviously sensed the dire situation and steadfastly said, "Just turn her a little toward me, and I'll get her." He tenderly picked Ora Lee up in his arms and struggled toward the big emergency room sign. Vonion ran ahead and pushed open the heavy door.

I glanced back toward Bess. She had not moved a muscle, and she was still holding that chicken. "Bess, we made it. Let's go inside," I said, as I walked around to the back of the truck. "You did great."

She seemed frozen to the tailgate, and her eyes were glazed over. She finally shook her head, held on to the chicken, but pointed a finger right at me. "Don't you ever, ever let on to anybody how I got here today! I'll never be able to show my face around this town again."

"For pity sake, quit worrying about how you got here. You got here! Now let's go in and see about Ora Lee. You know Mama would never forgive us if we let anything happen to her."

Still holding on to the chicken, Bess scrambled down from the tailgate and began picking feathers out of her hair. As she attempted to straighten her dress, she said, "I need a comb and a little lipstick. I look a mess. And what about this chicken? I saved its life. It could have easily gotten run over. What are we gonna do with it?"

Aggravated, I said, "Leave it out here. Maybe somebody will come along and catch it. It'll make a good supper for somebody."

"After I saved this chicken's life, you want somebody to eat it. You are so inhumane," Bess sneered, as the chicken cackled and attempted to spread its wings. She immediately dropped it, and the chicken flew off to perch on a high limb in a sycamore tree across the street.

"Well, it's gone now, so you don't have to worry about it anymore. And, for pity sake, don't worry about what you look like. We've got to get in there and make sure Ora Lee's getting all the attention she needs. Now come on." I pulled Bess behind me through the big door into the brightly lit emergency room. Vera, Tillman, and Vonion, all with worried expressions plastered on their faces, were standing in a little semicircle halfway across the room.

"They've already taken her in," Tillman said softly, as we walked up to them.

"Thank heavens, we made it in time," I answered, as I glanced over toward Vonion. Knowing he was in an unfamiliar, strange place, he stood still, stiff and fearful, as if he was pondering a whole graveyard full of lost hopes and dreams.

The room was clean and smelled sanitary. The walls were painted bright white and the white linoleum floor was polished to a high sheen. A sign, with the word "Quiet" printed in large letters and an illustration of fingers pressing against lips, hung over an unattended desk. Crooked rows of metal chairs lined the walls on the far end of the room, where a heavy, dark-skinned woman, jiggling a small sick child, sat under another sign that indicated that area of the room was reserved for colored people.

Vonion's expression told the whole story. His firm jaw was clinched, and his old bloodshot eyes showed more fright than if he were being attacked by a rabid dog. He didn't move a muscle as Bess and I joined the group. I was gripped with fear as I asked everyone in the small cluster to pray for our loved one. Tillman started with a lot of dignified rhetoric, and Vonion finished with a simple, pitiful plea. "Lord, look after my's Ora Lee. I's ain't ready to give her up just yet. But, Lord, I's know you is the boss man." Then, in a pleading voice, he added, "Lord, Ora Lee be my angel. Can't you wait a little longer fer her to be one a' yor angels? Amen."

I silently "amened" that.

We waited out in the waiting room for what seemed like hours. Vonion paced back and forth from one side of the room to another. The rest of us fidgeted, sitting in those hard straight chairs. I did my best to think positively. Ora Lee would have balked at us for bringing her to a hospital if she had been in her right mind. As it was, she didn't know anything about it, so I suppose that was a blessing.

Having Vera and Tillman with us was a mixed blessing. Vera continually complained that they didn't tell us a thing that was going on back there. She waved her handkerchief back and forth and tapped her foot on the floor as if she were waiting for a late train. "We might as well be strangers, for all they care. They haven't told us one single thing since we got here. They've probably left Ora Lee by herself, strapped to that rolling bed, for all we know. I think we all need to go back there and demand to know what's going on. Why, those people that took Ora Lee are so young they probably don't know the difference between a toothache and a toe ache!"

Tillman kept patting her arm, trying to calm her, but he never could do too much with Vera. I could tell Vera was getting on Bess's last nerve. Bess told Tillman several times that she wouldn't blame them a bit if they wanted to go on to do their errands and check back with us later. I got her full meaning, but Tillman was so used to Vera's complaining and bad attitude, he didn't catch on.

Just as I thought Bess was about to blow up—*I can always tell when Bess's had enough by the veins popping out on her neck*—the finest specimen of manhood I have ever in all my years laid my eyes on walked through the big doors in the back of the room. He was dressed in a white coat with the words, "Dr. Walter Jackson" printed across the front pocket where a fountain pen had leaked, leaving a dark blue stain. A big smile covered his handsome, unshaven face. He quickly looked around and walked directly toward Vonion.

He reached out and grabbed Vonion's big, gnarled hand, and announced in a friendly voice, "I presume you're Vonion Washington, and your wife's going to be just fine."

Sighs of relief flooded the room as our prayers were answered!

Thank you, Lord!

CHAPTER FIVE

I can't believe Ora Lee asked Dr. Jackson if he was a married man," Bess said with a giggle, as we walked back into my kitchen later that day. "She asked him everything from his religious beliefs to what size shoe he wears. Why, she found out just about everything we need to know about the man. I tell you, she might be a sick woman, but she wasn't about to let the doctor out of her room until we knew all his particulars."

"Wasn't she just great? We really got a whole lot of vital information. Now we've got to get Margaret here before Dr. Jackson releases Ora Lee to go home." Letting my imagination go completely haywire, I excitedly added, "He would be just perfect for Margaret. I can just see it now. They could get married...and live nearby...and I could babysit the children, and..."

"Don't get too carried away, Bee. We've got to give it a little time; it might take six months or more, but I can see it too."

"If they have a boy, we can name him William or maybe Willie. If it's a girl, Beatrice. I know—Beatrice Elizabeth! Then she'll be named for both of us."

"Well, I don't know," Bess thoughtfully replied. "Actually Elizabeth Beatrice sounds a little better. We could call her Lizy."

"That sounds a little cumbersome to me. I guess we'll have to let the parents work that out when the time comes. We're getting the cart before the horse, anyway. We have to plan the wedding first."

"You're absolutely right. I really hate to think about Margaret getting married in that drab church sanctuary of ours. Everything in there needs either painting or refinishing. It's downright embarrassing when we have visitors. When Vera and Tillman brought their sister-in-law from Macon to church a week or two ago, I couldn't concentrate on a word the preacher was saying for thinking about how awful that stained ceiling must have looked to her."

"It does look pretty bad," I agreed.

Bess shook her head and scoffed. "Half the paint's flaking off, and the other half's the color of mud. We have got to do something about that sanctuary. We girls might have to get together and override the deacons about a sanctuary facelift. If we wait much longer to update it, we'll all be funeralized in that drab, dingy place. I'd hate to think about any of our distant cousins who might make the trip here for our funerals, sitting on those splintery pews, looking at those grimy walls and ceiling, and listening to that noisy, outdated, clunking furnace." *Now I knew for sure, Bess didn't have enough to worry about.* "They can take my body straight from the funeral home to the cemetery and bypass the sanctuary, for all I care. Ina's Florist would have a hard time distracting everybody's attention away from those stained, faded walls and scratched up floors with those puny arrangements that she concocts. I noticed one of those sprays she put together for Floyd's funeral last year didn't have but three little old dinky carnations stuck in it. Whoever paid for that thing certainly didn't get their money's worth."

"I don't see how you remember something that far back, Bess. You've got a memory like an elephant."

"I'm not the only one who remembers those flowers. Mildred mentioned it to me not too long ago when she was thinking about having Ina put special flowers in the church sanctuary in memory of Horace." Horace, who was Mildred's dear departed husband, had died of cancer some time back. Then, as if it had just occurred to her, Bess interjected, "Oh, Bee, we haven't even thought about the most important thing regarding Margaret's nuptials! We could get free medical attention if Margaret marries Dr. Jackson. Wouldn't that be just wonderful! Every time I have to see my doctor, it costs three and a half dollars, and that's absolutely highway robbery. Just think of the money we could save! You know, it really would be just heavenly having a doctor in the family."

I nodded in agreement. Then turning my mind back to Ora Lee, I added, "I don't think it's going to take too long for Ora Lee to get well now that they're giving her fluids and working on her blood pressure. You know, I stay on her all the time about her health. She just will not take care of herself. She has absolutely got to take her pressure medicine and keep herself hydrated, or she's gonna get sick again, and maybe die next time. Now we've got two reasons to call Margaret. We've got to make that call right now. Who's gonna do it?"

"I will," piped up Bess. "You know I've got more influence over Margaret than you do. She'll come if I tell her Ora Lee's in the hospital. I'm gonna tell her Ora Lee is asking for her, and she needs to come before it's too late. And that really is the truth. She did tell us to get Margaret Girl to that hospital before she goes home."

"Well, don't be too dramatic. We don't want to scare the child to death. Did you find out what time Dr. Jackson makes his daily rounds? We've got to time her visit precisely so that they run into each other."

"He comes by early in the mornings and again about six thirty, right after he closes his office for the day. Let's see if we can get her over there by six o'clock, at the latest, tomorrow afternoon. We'll sit right there with her and Ora Lee until Dr. Jackson makes his appearance," Bess answered firmly. "You know, I had forgotten about Foy Jackson's son being a doctor. He's so fortunate to have that boy back here. Now that Foy's in a wheelchair, he's probably pretty helpless. I heard Nellie say they've recently hired somebody to come in to take care of his personal needs, but don't you imagine that's really expensive?"

"Oh, I'm sure it is, but Foy has it. His wife's family had plenty of money, and I'm quite confident she left it all to him."

"We need to stop by and check on old Foy. He's fairly harmless, if you know what I mean."

"Bess, he is not completely harmless. I didn't mention this to you, but the last time I was over there visiting, he reached out and pinched me on my leg, just above my knee. At first I thought I had been bitten by a mosquito until I saw the gleam in his old roving eye. I swear, I don't believe men ever get too old to forget what they used to have. Whatever Foy had is gone, except in his imagination, I expect."

"Heavens, Bee, he did the same thing to me when I dropped by with a sweet potato pie a week or so ago. If he hadn't been in that wheelchair, I probably would have reached over and pinched the tar out of him."

"You talk mighty big, Sister." *I knew my sister didn't have a violent bone in her body.*

"Let's call Margaret. She's probably home by now. Come on, and let's get this show on the road."

"Okay, let's review. We want to know why Sam Turner left school in such a hurry a year or so ago, and if there was anything fishy about it. Tell her about Ora Lee, but wait until we know about Sam first. She's gonna be very upset about Ora Lee's condition and won't be able to think straight about Sam's departure. Now, Bess, stay focused, and get all the information out of Margaret you can, but don't let her get too distraught. Oh, and tell her to make sure she looks her best tomorrow. Suggest that she wear her new blue suit with the pale pink blouse. It makes her complexion look so pretty. Do I need to write all this down? Can you remember everything?"

"Maybe I do need an outline. Now where did you put that tablet?"

We jotted down a few notes, and Bess picked up the telephone. I could overhear Nellie, our meddlesome telephone operator, ask how Ora Lee was doing. She said she had heard about Ora Lee being in the hospital and, of course, she mentioned to Bess that she had heard all about her triumphant ride through the streets of town. *If Nellie knew, everybody knew. Bess might as well get over it.*

Margaret answered after two rings. Bess chitchatted a minute but soon got down to the nitty-gritty. With Nellie listening in, Bess really couldn't get too much information about Sam without sounding too inquisitive, but Margaret did say that they really liked him at school, and she really didn't know any details about his departure other than he left suddenly. After Bess told Margaret about Ora Lee's condition, she said she would be home as soon as she could after school tomorrow. Bess casually mentioned that she had heard me say how pretty she looked in her blue suit and pink blouse, and she knew Ora Lee would love to see her in it.

As soon as Bess hung up, it hit me all of a sudden that I was to have very persnickety company. "I haven't done a thing around here today, and Margaret's gonna be here tomorrow. I better start cleaning and put a ham in the oven. If you're gonna stay, you can make yourself useful and sweep the porches while I clean the bathroom." Before Bess could answer, I was out the door, headed for the smokehouse.

Bess stayed on into the night helping me with the cleaning. We never slowed down long enough to have much more conversation. Just as Bess was reaching for her purse and car keys to leave, I said, "Bess, you never did tell me what was on your mind that was so important. Stay a few more minutes and let's talk."

"Not right now, Bee. I'm bushed. This has been one hectic day. I can't even think straight right now. We'll have to talk tomorrow."

I nodded and gave Bess a big hug. "We have had a big day today. We'll talk tomorrow. Drive home safely, and call me in the morning."

* * *

I could hear rain hitting my new tin roof the next morning as I opened my eyes. I was reminded how thankful I was to have that roof over my head. My old roof would have been leaking by now, and I'd be grabbing buckets. Now all I had to worry about was that this one didn't rust.

After a short prayer, thanking God for all His blessing, I threw the covers back and struggled into my old, faded housecoat. Soon I was standing at the window and gazing across my drenched yard. It was obvious Vonion had been up to the house earlier from the deep tire ruts out by the barn and lot. He had apparently gotten up early this morning, finished his chores, and already left for the hospital. I walked into the kitchen and opened the door to the icebox. The fresh milk was strained and stored. Brown eggs, collected this morning, were in a bowl on the top shelf. As I made coffee, I began to think about my day. Taking my coffee cup out to the hall, I put in a call to the hospital. I was told by someone with a very official-sounding voice that Ora Lee had rested well during the night. That was a relief.

I was soon peeling a few sweet potatoes for a pie and rolling out the crust. Margaret loved my sweet potato pies. I always added a little cinnamon and nutmeg. *That's what makes them so good, along with those fresh brown eggs. When anybody asks about the recipe, I never mention the nutmeg. That's my secret.* I planned on getting all my cooking done that morning so I could devote myself to Ora Lee that afternoon. I couldn't help but smile as I thought about yesterday. *The indelible mental image of my fashion plate sister rolling into the hospital parking lot on the back of Vonion's old beat-up truck with feathers in her hair, and a chicken under her arm, flooded my mind.* What a memory!

I really wanted to look my best today; after all, we needed to make a favorable impression on Dr. Jackson. I knew Bess would probably wear something real nice, so I decided to iron my blue and green striped dress with the big pockets. Everybody said it makes me look slimmer. I'd add Mama's pearls. A little rouge and lipstick wouldn't hurt a thing, either.

Bess and I arrived at the hospital at the same time that afternoon. With our strategy in place to make sure Margaret and Dr. Jackson met, we hurried down the hall to

Ora Lee's room, only to find her fast asleep. It was still a little early for Dr. Jackson or for Margaret, so, to pass the time, Bess and I decided to stroll around and admire the new hospital.

Bess stuck her head into a few rooms as we walked around to see if anybody we knew was hospitalized. She said she considered it neighborly to speak. I kept telling her that people needed their privacy, but, as usual, she didn't pay me a bit of attention—that is until she got her eyes full of some old man's rear end in Room 6, as he bent over to put on his bedroom shoes with his hospital gown gaped wide open a full twelve inches across his broad backside. Bess automatically jumped back from the room door into the hall, her high-heeled shoe piercing the top of my big toe. I silently winced and swiftly hobbled behind Bess as we scurried down the hall, trusting we had been unnoticed.

Since neither one of us had seen the interior of the hospital, we were amazed at what a nice facility it really was. All the walls and floors were sparkling white, just like the emergency room. Two long corridors were connected by a nurses' station. Back of the nurses' area were big heavy doors with "Do Not Enter" printed across the front. We were sure the surgery area and labs were back there. Metal chairs were placed up and down the hall for visitors, so Bess and I set up vigil right outside Ora Lee's room.

After settling down, I asked Bess if she was ready for that big discussion she had been putting off. A look of dread came over her face as she began to wiggle and squirm. She opened her pocketbook and reached for her compact. After powdering her nose and patting her hair, she inspected her teeth. Then hesitating a bit, she stammered, "Bee, if you don't like this idea of mine, all you have to do is say so. And don't answer until you've heard me completely out. But I've been thinking about this for a long time...and, uh…what would you say…uh…about me moving out to the farm to live with you? You're out there right by yourself, and I'm all by myself. We're keeping up two households. I'm lonely in that house all by myself, and I think you are too. We could share the bills, and that would make it easier on you and me. You've got plenty of room, and I just know it would work."

Without even considering it, I answered, "Why Bess, I think that is the best idea you've ever come up with. I would consider it a great pleasure for you to live with me. I don't know why we haven't thought of it before now. I'm just flabbergasted that you would even consider it. I mean, you know I don't keep house as good as you, and things are not always that well organized." *There must be more to this than meets the eye,* I thought to myself as I questioned Bess. "Are you sure about this? You'll have to make quite an adjustment moving out of your house into mine. What would you do with your house? Sell it?"

"I've thought about that. Bee, you know how crowded Freddy and Jean are in that little cracker box they live in. The children are all cramped up in one little bedroom. I'm going to give my house to them. They would enjoy all the extra room. Besides that, it's so much nicer than theirs. I've made up my mind, so don't try to change it."

"Bess, I think that you're right on target. Freddy and Jean will love living in your house."

"I think so too. Now, how long will it take to clean and paint your house? We need to weed out some of your furniture and replace it with mine. Oh, Bee, I can just see it now! When we have the missionary meeting, everybody will just rave at the transformation."

With that remark, I flinched a little. I had answered Bess so readily, I had not even thought about all the changes she would want to make. I sheepishly answered, "I guess it shouldn't take too long.   But Bess, do you think you can lower your standards a little?"

"No, Bee. I'm not lowering my standards. We'll just raise yours."

CHAPTER SIX

Bess and I had already investigated practically the whole hospital, but after discussing Bess's exciting new idea, we were a bit antsy and needed a little exercise. With Ora Lee still asleep and resting very comfortably, we decided to check out the rest of the place. We sauntered back down the hall toward the nurses' station. Since no one was around to tell us not to go any farther, we ventured around to the back of the desk and opened the doors into the "Do Not Enter" corridor.

"They haven't done anything to make this area very attractive," Bess commented, as we opened another big swinging door and walked right in just like we owned the place. We were half-heartedly admiring the room with its bright lights and gleaming white cabinets when we were approached by a large, buxom woman who resembled a dark mahogany wardrobe with a bad disposition. She grabbed Bess by the sleeve and quickly escorted us out. Actually, you might say we were run out of the room by a fat, over-bearing woman wearing a face mask and an outfit that looked like something she might have slept in. *Some people can be so rude. She could have calmly and politely asked us to leave instead of pushing us out.* I did notice, as we were being ushered out, a group of people wearing clothes that reminded me of unmade beds, and with surprised expressions swiftly spreading across their faces, gawking at us. They were standing in a cluster around a long narrow rolling bed where some poor soul lay under a white bed sheet. The door sign that said "Off Limits" was practically hidden behind a coatrack covered with white gowns, so we had just walked right in. You can bet your bottom dollar, we wouldn't make that mistake again. You would have thought we had broken into the White House by the welcome we received. Some people have such bad manners. It makes you wonder if their mamas ever taught them a thing about politeness and dignity.

After being so rudely reprimanded by the hefty woman who evidently thought she had authority over us—and evidently she did—we hurried back to Ora Lee's room. As we neared it, we could hear gales of laughter. Hurrying in, we discovered Dr. Jackson giving Margaret a big bear hug, and everybody had huge smiles across their faces, especially Ora Lee.

"Where the blue blazes you two been? We's is havin' a fine reunion, and you two is nowhere to be found," Ora Lee announced, as if she were on cloud nine. "We's didn't speculate Dr. Jackson and Margaret Girl be so well acquainted. We's ain't got to do no introducin' after all. They already knows each other."

Still reeling from our prior incident, I hurried over to give my pretty young daughter a big hug. "Well, glory be...Oh, Margaret, I'm so glad to see you! You and Dr. Jackson already know each other?"

"Oh, Mama, it's good to see you too. Dr. Jackson's several years older than me, but we remember each other from school. I believe you were four, or maybe five, years ahead of me," Margaret added, as she glanced toward the doctor. "Oh, Aunt Bess, I'm so happy to see you too. We were about to send a posse out to look for the both of you." Margaret gave Bess a quick hug.

"Glad to see you ladies again." Dr. Jackson extended his arm out to shake our hands. "You know, I think I was at least five years ahead of you, Margaret. I graduated with your son, Freddy, Ms. Bess. Don't you remember?"

"You know, I believe I do, now that I think about it. My, how you've changed. I remember a short, skinny fellow with freckles and big ears."

"That's me all right. I've grown a few inches, and my head finally grew to match my ears."

I was so excited to see that Margaret and Dr. Jackson already knew each other, and Bess was beaming like a proud peacock strutting around in the barnyard. *We couldn't have planned it any better.* I hoped the subject of being single would come up soon. If it didn't, I was prepared to take matters into my own hands and tell Dr. Jackson that Margaret was free as the wind. I soon realized Bess was thinking faster.

"Dr. Jackson, our Margaret's a single girl, but she's had plenty of opportunities to marry. We would just love to see her settled down with the right fellow. He just hasn't come along yet," Bess blurted. *I'm sure without thinking. Lordy! Was Bess gonna get a scolding.*

Margaret moaned and rolled her eyes as she looked toward the doctor. "Walter, you'll just have to ignore my aunt and my mother too. They've been on a manhunt for me for years and years. They'll probably have you hog-tied and at the church altar before the night's out. They can be very annoying, but really, they're completely harmless."

"It sounds to me as if they have pretty good ideas. I'm available, but I'm afraid I never have a lot of time to socialize or do anything else. Between the office and the hospital, there aren't enough hours in a day. But I'd love to take you out to eat at the diner in a while, if you're available?" Walter glanced at his wristwatch as if he had an appointment. "That is, with your mother's approval."

"Mother, do you approve?" Margaret asked, with a little jest in her tone.

"Oh, I approve all right. You two young people go on out and enjoy yourselves. Dr. Jackson, by the way, how is your patient? Is she going to be okay?"

"My patient is going to be fine. I'm sending her home tomorrow, that is if she promises to take better care of herself. She had a close call yesterday." Then turning his attention toward Ora Lee, he sternly said, "Ora Lee, you are to get plenty of rest, and, by all means, take your medication. I'm telling you this in all seriousness. You absolutely cannot forget your blood pressure medicine! That medicine is what keeps your heart pumping properly. Do you promise me you'll do what I say?"

"I's'll do what you say. But I's think you needs to check up on me ever day or so. Me's and Margaret will be waiting on you tomorree evenin' at my house, say 'bout six thirty."

"I, uh, think that can be arranged." Dr. Jackson grinned, glanced at Margaret, and winked. "Margaret, you sure have a crowd of folks looking out for your welfare."

"Don't pay any attention to any of them. Every time they see a single man between the ages of twenty-five and fifty, they start dreaming about wedding bells. I just hope they won't scare you to death."

Dr. Jackson laughed and walked out with a big grin across his face. As soon as the door closed behind him, Margaret started fuming. With fire in her eyes, she exploded. "Mama, you and Aunt Bess have got to quit this. I'm tired of you two chasing around after every man you think would be halfway suitable for me. I've told the both of you until I'm blue in the face—let me find my own man!"

"You're absolutely right, dear," Bess sheepishly replied. "Maybe we can stop looking now anyway. Dr. Jackson might be just the one we've been waiting for."

Ignoring that comment, Margaret replied, "Well, now that y'all have thoroughly embarrassed me, let's sit down and have a nice visit." Bess and I settled into a couple of grey metal chairs that had been placed in the room for visitors. I was hopeful our scolding was finally complete when Margaret turned toward Ora Lee and sternly said, "Ora Lee, you better mind what the doctor says and take better care of yourself from now on. You know the lord doesn't give you but one body. After it's worn out and not properly taken care of, you die. Is that what you want? You know you don't want to leave Vonion alone with no one to care for him. You know how he depends on you."

"He find somebody else before the sun set. But you right, child. I is gonna do better from now on."

"By the way, where's Vonion?"

"He done been to the horspital today. I 'spect he missin' me puttin' supper on the table 'bout now. Hit be good fer him to do fer hisself from time to time. He be able to do around, he just don't want to. Hit tickles him fer me to wait on him hand and foot."

Not wanting to appear too anxious, Bess and I never brought up the subject of Sam Turner. Tomorrow would be soon enough. After a little more chitchat, I was thinking about getting around to the subject of Bess's sudden idea to move out to the farm with me when Dr. Jackson stuck his head in and asked Margaret if she was ready. Since Bess needed to run by the drugstore to check on a beauty lotion they had ordered for her, Ora Lee and I were left by ourselves to talk.

Working up my courage, I sheepishly said, "Ora Lee, I know this is gonna take you by complete surprise, but Bess has asked me if she could come out to the house to live with me."

"What did you say, chile?"

"I said Bess wants to move to the farm. She wants to give her house to Freddy and Jean."

"Lord have mercy on my soul! I's can't believe what I'm a'hearin'!" Ora Lee fervently shook her head in disbelief. "You two can't get along one hour, much less all's the time. You knows how she can be, and she most always get on your last nerve. I's just don't know 'bout this. She be wantin' to make a bunch of changes to the house, and upsetting yo' routine. You think you can bear up under her bossing you's 'round?"

"Ora Lee, I'm not real sure about any of that, but I'd really like for it to work. You know yourself I've been lonesome. The house is so empty and sad now without Margaret or Will. Maybe Bess will bring fresh life to the old place."

"I 'spect you right about that, but if'n thangs get too hectic, you can always go out to the barn and talk to Hortence. She listens real good, and she don't talk back."

* * *

Margaret slept late the next morning. I had eaten and was busy penning a belated letter to Cousin Myrtle when she walked into the kitchen with a sleepy expression across her face. "How about some coffee and a little breakfast?" I asked, as I lay my pen down. "I've got some fresh sweet rolls. I know how you love them."

"Mama, that sounds great. It felt so good to sleep a little later. I believe I could have lain there in my old bed all morning, but I've got to get ready. Walter asked me to go on a picnic. He's picking me up in about an hour." Margaret reached for a roll and took a sip of coffee.

"My goodness, he is a fast worker. Did you have a good time last night?"

Margaret readily answered, as she continued to munch on her roll, "Mama, we enjoyed each other's company so much. At least I enjoyed his. Now, Mama, don't jump to any wild conclusions, but it feels so natural to be with him." Margaret had a glow about her that I hadn't seen in a while. I was so excited, I could hardly think straight. *This was IT! I just knew it!*

"Margaret, he seems to be a fine young man. I'm sure you could do a lot worse. You know I like him too. Just let nature take its course. *I couldn't believe what I was saying.* Then after a sigh and a pause, I said, "I've got something else on my mind to talk to you about this morning." I really dreaded to start. "What would you say if I told you Aunt Bess has asked if she could move in to live with me? I, uh, told her I would be delighted, but now," and I hesitated, "I might be having second thoughts about it. You know, sometimes I speak without really thinking about the consequences."

"Mama, oh my stars! I'm almost speechless! I can't believe Aunt Bess would want to leave her immaculate home to come out here." Margaret waved her arms in the air. *Are things THAT bad?* "Does she really know how you keep house? She'll drive you absolutely crazy organizing everything. Why, she'll probably want to vacuum the barn and have Vonion color coordinate the feed sacks with the slop buckets. She'll have you using fine china for breakfast and listening to highbrow music on the radio instead of *The West Family Gospel Hour*. Mama, please tell me, you haven't already encouraged her to come?"

"I did. I guess I'll have to live with it. I can't tell her not to come now. It would hurt her feelings, and I simply cannot do that. Anyway, she needs me."

"Yes, she needs you all right. She needs to have somebody to boss around." Margaret put her head down on the table and muttered a quick prayer. "Dear Lord, help my mama. She's gonna need you now more than ever. Life on the farm will never be the same again! Amen."

* * *

It seems I had missed another opportunity to talk with Margaret about Sam Turner. She had finished her breakfast and was already out the door with Dr. Jackson. *Now I guess I better start calling him Walter*. I had not even had time to quiz them about where they were going or when they'd be back. It really didn't matter. Margaret looked so happy and relaxed, it made my heart sing. My problems seemed to disappear as I put a chicken on the stove to boil and began to prepare vegetables for a big pot of soup. Ora Lee would need something nourishing to eat now that she was coming home from the hospital.

Bess drove up soon after *The West Family Gospel Hour* signed off the radio. The soup had been delivered, and Ora Lee was already at home. She was snoozing away when I left the thick soup warming on her old wood-burning stove. When she felt like eating, it would be ready for her.

Bess was soon marching into the dining room with me trotting behind at her heels. She had a measuring tape in her hand and was eyeballing my china cabinet. "You know, I believe my china cabinet will fit here if we move yours over by the door. We really do need to think about refinishing yours and maybe add new pulls. This room could be quite attractive if we painted the walls a nice shade of pale green, and a new set of curtains wouldn't hurt, either. I could whip some up in no time flat. You know we'll be entertaining in here a good bit, and we want to put our best foot forward. I can just see Mama's sterling tea service sitting on her sideboard again."

My head was beginning to spin. Bess was out of control, and I didn't know one way on God's green earth to stop her. "Bess, all your ideas sound so exciting," I lied. *You know sometimes it's easier to join the army instead of fighting it.*

"Where's Margaret? What did she have to say about my move?"

"Bess, she thinks it's fine," I lied again. *The more you fib, the easier it gets, and I had had a lot of practice in the last year.* "She's out with Walter on a picnic. She didn't say when they'd be back."

"Bee, this romance is moving faster than we anticipated. We really might need to start planning a wedding. If we could just get that deacon board to get off their sorry behinds and start work on that sanctuary. You and I have enough to think about without worrying about the condition of the church. Now Bee, do you have any idea what color the bridesmaids will probably wear?"

"Bess, really. Let the poor girl get engaged before we start planning the wedding. We could jinx the whole thing just by talking about it ahead of time." *I had already thought about pale yellow.*

"You're right. Time will tell. But I think they're a perfect match."

"Bess, I never had a minute to ask Margaret about Sam Turner. As soon as they return, I'm going to find out something or bust. Stay around and help me pry some information out of her."

"Oh, I was planning on staying awhile. How's Ora Lee? Do I need to go down there and do anything to help out?"

"Ora Lee's resting now. Vonion brought her home early this morning. I took some soup and left it on the stove. I'm sure Walter'll check on her as soon as he and Margaret return."

"Good. Now let's get back to our plans. Bee, that old hall rug looks a little tattered and needs to be replaced, and—Oh! What do you think about having new shutters put on the house? And, Bee, Mama's old cook stove is so-o outdated...and what do you think about..."

CHAPTER SEVEN

M argaret and Walter were laughing and holding hands
as they strolled into the kitchen to put up the picnic
basket later that afternoon. Bess and I had depleted all
other conversations and were sitting at the kitchen table
looking through the Sears and Roebuck catalog at some of
the new dress styles. Bess kept saying she could make
anything she needed but needed a little inspiration. I knew
I'd never make a thing, and with my finances as tight as the
waistband on some of my dresses, I suppose I'd keep
squeezing into the same old things. Vonion would have
referred to my bank account "as empty as a Monday
morning pocketbook," and he'd be just about right. There
was one dress on page fifty-two of the catalog that really
caught my eye. It was a soft pink with a lace collar—just
perfect for church. At five dollars and ninety-five cents, it
was a little out of my price range. What I really needed was
one of those foundation girdles on page seventy-five. The
advertisement claimed they would take ten pounds off as

soon as you put it on. *Did I ever need one of those!* I thought it was downright disgraceful the way those young skinny girls in the catalog stood around talking to each other, baring all, except what a little scrap of underwear covered...*but...I wonder...hmm...would I look anything like those models if I bought one of those foundation girdles? That might be something to seriously consider...*

"Mama, Walter and I are going to walk down the lane and check on Ora Lee. Do y'all want to take a chance that Ora Lee's in a good mood and join us?"

"No, you two kids go on. Bess and I'll stay here and start a little supper. Walter, won't you stay and eat? We have plenty to go around."

"Ordinarily I would love to, but I need to spend a little time with Pop tonight. I've been so busy at the hospital lately, I've neglected him. Maybe some other time, though."

That man was so handsome!

"Margaret, go on with Walter, and tell Ora Lee to behave." I walked them to the door, and as they started down the lane, I stood and watched in delight as my daughter happily walked hand in hand with a handsome young man. I called out, "Bess and I'll be waiting for you."

As soon as the door closed behind them, Bess swooned. "Bee, just think, we might have that good-looking man in the family soon. It's just too good to be true." Then in a much firmer voice, Bess continued on, "Now when Margaret gets back, we don't need to act too interested in Sam Turner. Try to act nonchalant while we're prying information out of her. Let's pretend we're just remotely interested. You know, as if we're really indifferent, just casually asking about a friend's husband."

"Bess, I know what you mean. Now remember, we don't want to rush into the subject too soon, either. Let's talk about the weather or maybe something about Ora Lee's health first. We don't want Margaret to think we're quizzing her. You know how touchy she can be."

Margaret soon bounced back into the house with that same glow on her face, as well as sunburn. Bess was taking golden brown biscuits out of the oven, and I was stirring the ham gravy. "Mmm, supper smells so good. I'll wash up and be back in a sec," Margaret called, as she bounded into the back of the house to the bathroom. It made my heart sing with joy to see how happy my daughter seemed.

We finally settled around my kitchen table, and Bess said grace. After devouring her first biscuit, Margaret reached for another one and boasted, "I don't know how the two of you do it. Those biscuits are so-o good, and the fried ham is just out of this world. You two are absolutely the best cooks in the county." *Flattery can get you anything.* "I wish I could cook like this. I wouldn't know how to feed a man if I had one."

"Well, when the time comes, you'll learn. Cooking is easy; it just takes a little practice," Bess replied, with a little spark of pride. "We'll teach you everything we know. I've tried to teach Jean to cook, but she claims she just doesn't have an aptitude for it. I'm sure she just doesn't want to learn; that's all there is to it. All they ever eat around there is peanut butter and jelly sandwiches. It's a wonder my grandchildren don't have rickets. I try not to say anything, but it's hard."

"Those boys don't have rickets or anything else, for that matter. They are as healthy as can be," I replied. "Don't worry about them. Worry about something that needs to be worried about."

I knew I had held my tongue about Molly and Sam just about as long as I could. Just as I worked up my courage to mention them and opened my mouth to speak, Bess abruptly interrupted me.

"Margaret, you know Sam and Molly Turner are members of our church now. Molly goes to our missionary meetings and is such a lovely young woman. Your mother and I were wondering if you remember much about them. Sam was the principal at your school a few years ago, wasn't he? Was he good at his job and, uh, do you happen to remember why he left?"

Margaret stopped eating abruptly, put her fork down, and frowned. "I know there's something behind these questions about the Turners. I don't know what it is, but I imagine it's absolutely none of your beeswax." Then, with a little more kindness in her voice, she went on. "I do remember Sam very well, and he did a great job at school. I never knew why he left or what happened, but I suspect it might have had something to do with his man-chasing secretary. She was always flirting around with him. You know yourself that a man can only take so much before he yields to temptation. I know one thing, and that is I don't need to be talking about it. Why are y'all so interested anyway?"

Now we're getting somewhere. As pitifully as I could, I answered, "Margaret, we've noticed that Molly is a little sad, and we'd like to help her. She seems to be distracted about something, and we're very concerned about her happiness, that's all. We thought you might tell us something that would help us relate to her in some way. We simply want to help her to deal with her emotions. It's kind of hard to sympathize with somebody if you don't even have an inkling of what's wrong with them. You know we wouldn't ever let on that we knew something that was none of our business. We just want to be of help to the poor girl." I took another sip of my coffee, and trying to look as innocent as I possibly could, waited to hear Margaret's reaction.

"Well, you can probably help by staying out of her business, if you ask me." Margaret took another bite of her biscuit and chewed thoughtfully. After washing it down with a few swallows of Hortence's sweet milk, and just like a strict schoolteacher talking to a misbehaving child, she finally relented. "The only way I'm going to tell you two another thing is for the both of you to promise that if I tell you something, it will become privileged information. Do you know what that means? It means that you can't ever, ever, ever repeat a word about what I say to another living soul. Now can I get a promise from the both of you? I never should have said a thing in the first place," Margaret remorsefully added, as she stared me down and then glared at Bess. "I must be out of my mind for saying another word!"

Bess and I both nodded and spoke up at the same time. We crossed our hearts and simultaneously promised we hoped to die if we ever repeated a word. *We were really desperate!* Everything would be considered strictly privileged information. Sitting on the edges of our chairs, we must have appeared a little too anxious because Margaret backed away and said, "I don't know. Maybe I'd better not say another thing. Teachers are not supposed to gossip about any of the other teachers, and most assuredly, we aren't supposed to talk about the principal's private life. Y'all are way too eager for information."

"Now Margaret, you can't just stop in midstream," I pleaded. "Tell us what you meant about that secretary. Do you think Sam and she could have been carrying on behind closed doors or something like that?" Bess sat up straighter in her chair and nodded her head in unison with mine.

"It's really nothing that we should be talking about, but I know y'all are gonna drive me crazy until I tell you what I know. You two aren't doing any investigating, are you? Because if you are, I'm not saying another word."

"Margaret, you know we aren't doing anything like that," Bess replied, as if Margaret had hurt her feelings. "We're just interested in a motherly way." *Somewhere along the line, Bess had become a better liar than me.*

"Do you really think I believe that bunch of hogwash? I know you two are up to something."

I began to plead. "Just tell us what you know. Nobody will ever know you told us a thing. You know you can trust us, Margaret." I must have really looked pitiful by then because Margaret continued on.

"The only thing I really know is that a few days before Sam left school for good Lightening, the janitor, came running down the hall from the direction of Sam's office, all in a panic. Something must have frightened him or really upset him. If he's drinking, which he normally does, you can't believe a thing he says. But this time, he wasn't drinking. He was as sober as a judge. He just clammed up when some of us teachers quizzed him about what was wrong. Finally, after a whole lot of persuasion from all of us, he mumbled something like, "I ain't seen notin', and I ain't heard notin'." It could just be a coincidence that all that happened right before Sam left school, but Lightening must have seen or heard something in the vicinity of Sam's office, but he never let on what it was."

"My, my, that is strange," I thoughtfully replied, as Margaret picked up another biscuit. *Molly's troubles could be much more serious than we ever imagined.*

"Mama, do you have any of that good cane syrup Mr. Tom Wilson always makes? It would be so good on this biscuit."

"I've got plenty. I'll get it." I jumped up from the table and quickly returned. "Now Margaret, is there anything else that happened around that time, or before, or even after, that seems unusual?" *I needed to keep Margaret talking, and if I had to make another whole pan of biscuits to keep her going, I would.*

Margaret shook her head and poured syrup over her biscuit. "I don't know what he saw, but I suspect Dixie, Sam's secretary, might have been flaunting herself in front of Sam, and Lightening might have seen a little too much. Dixie's notorious for running after any man that draws breath. Lightening definitely saw something."

The biscuits looked so tasty I decided to eat one too. Bess frowned at me, making me a little uncomfortable as I ate one biscuit and pinched off a little from another one. If she thought she was going to change my eating habits after she moved in, she certainly had another think coming. Well, all her good intentions apparently rapidly caved in because she was soon sopping syrup right along with us. *Sister Bess might be checking out those foundation girdles in the Sears and Roebuck catalog before long too if she intended to sit at my table three times a day. And I did say, MY TABLE.*

* * *

After a quick kitchen cleanup, the three of us plopped down in the front room and moaned. We had all eaten way too much. Bess's imminent move was soon our topic of conversation. Bess said she wanted to bring her bedroom furniture that Fred's parents had given them for a wedding present, and she wouldn't think of leaving her tiger oak sideboard with the little cherubs that grace the sides. Her Duncan Phyfe settee had recently been re-covered in a tapestry fabric, and of course, it could not be left behind. I agreed that her settee was much better than mine. She said she absolutely could not part with her marble top tables or her hall bench. She would give Freddy the rest of her furniture since "they didn't have a thing that was decent." It was decided that Margaret would get a few odd pieces of furniture from the house, and Ora Lee would be delighted, we were sure, to get my old settee. The house would be a little more crowded, but Bess didn't think she could leave another thing. All her good silver, china, crystal, nice sit arounds, and fine linens would definitely be coming along with her too. We decided that Bess's porch furniture could replace mine on the front porch, and we'd put my old rockers on the back porch. We knew Ora Lee'd be tickled to get my old cane-bottomed straight chairs that had resided on my back porch since Mama and Daddy had put them there before Bess and I were born. I could live with that decision since I reckoned I wasn't really getting rid of them; they were just moving down the lane a piece.

Everything was happening so fast, and my mind was reeling. It suddenly hit me what all these changes would mean to my life. I would never really think of the house as being only mine and Will's again. It was going to be Bess's home too. Did I really want to share my home with my only sister? Was I being selfish? Bess seemed to be so excited about the changes. *She must be much more lonesome than me.* I began to believe she had been thinking about this for quite a while, and it really did make sense. After all, now I'd have Bess to share the expenses with. We would also share all the chores. *It was time for the pecans to start falling. Can't you just picture prissy Bess picking up pecans with Vonion, Ora Lee, and me?* Bess was a hard worker, though. Duty before pleasure was her motto. *But not necessarily my motto.* I just wondered how clean she was planning on keeping things around here. How many times a week does she think we'll dust the furniture or vacuum the floors? How clean can you really keep a house? All I really knew was I wasn't going to spend the rest of my life chained to a broom and a mop or waving a feather duster.

More than anything, I knew my solitude was going to be invaded. I know I complain a good deal about being lonely and isolated, but maybe I really liked it. You can't have it both ways, I thought. Bess was coming, so I might as well get ready! Bess seemed to have everything under control too. She had already hired a painter, obtained a promise from Freddy to do most of the moving, figured out a furniture arrangement at the house, and instructed Vonion to be available at a minute's notice to be at her beck and call. *You know, Vonion might be in much hotter water than me. His lackadaisical days on the farm might be numbered!*

"Mama, what are you thinking about? I asked you a question. Where is your mind?" I heard my daughter say, as I snapped back into reality.

"I'm sorry. I was just doing a little daydreaming. Now what did you say?" I asked, as I realized my mind had wondered far away from the conversation.

"I asked you if there was any way Vonion could help move the furniture and things I want to my house. Maybe the three of you could drive over and help me rearrange my furniture."

"I'm sure we can arrange something. I guess we need to move out the furniture you want before we paint or move more in. What do you think, Bess?"

"Margaret, let Bee and me think about it, and we'll let you know what day we can come. We'll have to line up Vonion, of course, but surely he doesn't have much of a schedule."

"Well, it's all decided then. What a relief," I said, with a sigh. *Bess was right on target too. We needed to get over to Burt County and talk to that Lightening as soon as possible. Now we had a real reason to go. Wow, the Lord does work in mysterious ways, and he had already figured a real excuse for Bess and me to journey over the county line. We could also make a quick run over to Dixie's house for a speedy search. Our investigation could officially begin! Vonion would just have to tag along. He might even come in handy when we interrogate old Lightening.*

CHAPTER EIGHT

The decision was made that we'd move the furniture to Margaret's on Tuesday. Sunday was a day of rest, and I intended to rest, *if I could find the time.* After church services in the morning and lunch on the porch at noon, Bess stood up and lazily walked down the steps to leave. She said a nap was calling her by name. Margaret waved her final farewell around four, leaving me all alone with all my good intentions of visiting Ora Lee awhile before Sunday evening church services, then early to bed. I wanted to be rested up for whatever came my way on Monday.

* * *

"Get plenty of good stout rope, and I'll find some blankets," I instructed a reluctant Vonion the next day. "And get a'move on it too. We want to have the truck loaded and ready to leave first thing in the morning. Oh, and tell Ora Lee to rest all day long and for her not to do a single solitary thing while we're gone. We don't want to worry about her falling and hurting herself. Make sure you tell her we'll be gone all day long too."

"I's done told that hard-headed woman she better jest lay in bed all day and not even git out, but she say, 'Folks die in bed,' and she'll do whatever comes to her mind. We's might ought to just take her with us. Dat way we won't have to be bothered with worrin' 'bout her."

"Vonion, you know good and well we can't take her with us. There's hardly enough room for the three us in the cab of the truck, much less Ora Lee. Now, do I need to speak to her? I believe I can make more of an impression on her than you can."

"No'um, that ain't necessary. She got enough sense not to do too much a'notin'. Ms. Bee, what all we gonna move anyway? We's ain't moving that 'hope' chest of Margaret's again, is we? I's said after me and Mr. Will move that thang the last time, I's 'hope' I's never has to move that heavy thang again. We's might better start referrin' to it as a hopeless chest anyways."

"We've got more hope now than ever before," I laughingly replied. "I hope we don't have to move it either. We might have to move a few things around in Margaret's house, though. You know yourself we can't bring in all that furniture and expect it to fit. Now as soon as you get the ropes, come on back to the house, and let's start piling furniture onto the truck. Bess should be here in a few minutes."

Vonion left grumbling. I could hear him cussing and saying something about that thar hopeless chest were the heaviest thang he ever did try to lift, and Margaret need to leave hit it whar hit were. I hurried to find the blankets to pad the furniture for the trip. All the decisions about which pieces of furniture Margaret would get were made, and now all we had to do was move them. I knew that was easier said than done.

Bess arrived a little after three that afternoon. "Were you able to get Dixie's address?" I asked immediately, as she entered the house. Bess had been assigned the task of finding Dixie's last name and where she lived. We were planning on making a quick call to her house before going by the school to speak to Lightening. It was going to be a busy day.

"It was so simple. Bee, this detective business gets easier and easier. All I had to do was call the school and pretend to be a census taker for the county. Dixie answered the telephone, and I got her last name and her address. She even told me she was single, and if I happened onto a single man as I conducted my business, would I let her know. She said it didn't matter what he looked like or how old he was, but if I could find out anything about his income, that would be helpful. She even filled me in with Lightening's last name and address. You never know, we might need it too."

"You are really getting good, Sister. Now, let's make our plans for tomorrow. First, we'll swing by Dixie's place and let ourselves in. After a quick search, we'll try to find Lightening at the school and question him. That might prove to be a little more difficult. I was thinking, Vonion might be able to quiz him more thoroughly than you or me. You know, he might give Vonion information that he wouldn't dream of telling us. I guess we'll have to fill Vonion in on our investigation and swear him to secrecy."

"Well, don't tell him anything yet. He might decide to buck and not go with us, and you and I can't unload the truck without him. We need to wait and mention our sideline mission to him after we leave."

"You're absolutely right," I readily agreed. "Good thinking."

We heard the old truck rattle up to the side of the house and then the truck door slam. Vonion was here in body, but I imagine, not totally in spirit. He'd probably be dragging. He never did like to move furniture around, and "all this movin' business was totally unnecessary," he had said earlier, when I filled him in on the task. It would suit him just fine for everything to stay just as it was. I think he had already figured out that Bess's move was going to inconvenience him enormously, and permanently. *His reckoning was probably right on target too.*

Will had always hated to move furniture around. I used to rearrange the furniture in the house every once in a while, and I always waited until I knew Will would be out of the house for several hours before I'd jump into action. In my younger days, I could singlehandedly slide a settee from place to place or move an entire bedroom suit from one room into another. I could move rugs, china cabinets, and anything else that wasn't permanently tied down. Those were the days—days before I knew better, and when all parts of my body worked on time and every time.

"I's here. Now what we gonna do?" Vonion irritably asked, as I heard the screen door scrape and then slam.

"I figure we have about seven pieces of furniture to move," I answered, as he lethargically sauntered into the room as if he were entering the jailhouse for a yearlong stint. "We've got three side tables, one dresser, a bed, a chest of drawers, and a chair. Margaret also wants this pile of books, these two milk glass lamps, and both of these framed floral prints." I knew I'd be reprimanded by Bess about the dust behind each piece of furniture as soon as we started moving it out. The only consolation I had was that this would probably be the last time the dust would be allowed to accumulate. After Bess's move, she would stay way ahead of the cleaning.

"Let's get busy," Bess quickly snapped. "There's no time like the present to get this show on the road. Now Vonion, grab that end of the chest, and I'll handle this end. Bee, go and open the door. Vonion, I hope you swept all the dirt out of the back of the truck and checked those sorry patched-up tires. We don't have time to be stranded beside the road tomorrow with a flat."

Vonion gave me a defenseless look, and I returned it right back at him, then ran to open the door. "Bess, I should have rounded up Roscoe to help us with this furniture. Put that thing down, and I'll run over to Tom Wilson's and find him right now." Roscoe was Vonion's grandson who had moved from Atlanta last year to live with Vonion and Ora Lee. He was now gainfully employed by Tom Wilson, our neighboring farmer.

"Don't be ridiculous, Bee. We've got to unload this stuff, so we might as well load it. I can easily handle this end if Vonion will just do his part." Vonion stiffened and gave me another helpless look. *Poor Vonion!*

All I can really report is we loaded the whole truck. Everybody had a different opinion on the way the furniture should be stacked, and everybody gave their opinion. I finally decided to keep my mouth shut. If any of the furniture blew off or fell off, I didn't want it to be my fault. With not an inch to spare on the back of the truck, we stood back and sighed. "Hit's on there. Now if'n we's don't have no bad luck, I's 'spect hit'll stay there for the duration of the trip. Now, you's both knows I's got to milk and feed up a'for we can get on the road in the mornin'. I's say let's meet up rat here 'bout seven. You's women think you's can manage that?"

"I certainly can, and I know Bee can. Now, don't be lollygagging around in the morning, Vonion. We need to leave punctually. And we have a lot to do tomorrow so make sure you're all rested up."

"We's ain't got that much to do, jest unload this here truck. I's don't know why y'all so eager to leave at first light anyway, but I's'll be ready. Don't know how rested, though. Soon as I get's home from you two, I's got another woman demandin' on my time, on top'a all my regular chores."

Vonion left, muttering something about having more bossy women in his life than Carter had liver pills. Bess and I soon collapsed on the porch. My back was aching, and Bess, looking like something the cat might have drug in, said her whole body was throbbing with pain. Hopefully, we would have enough strength left for tomorrow. Unloading the truck would be just as difficult as loading it.

* * *

Even in her misery, Bess enthusiastically began telling me all her plans for the house redo. She said she had Melvin Norton all lined up to start painting. "I picked out a beautiful pale green for the front room and the dining room. I'm having my bedroom painted 'Blush Pink,' since it goes so well with my complexion. And, Bee, if you decide to paint your bedroom or the kitchen, just let Melvin know when he gets here. He said he'd be available as long as we need him. Oh, and I hired him to sand and varnish the floors in the dining room and front room too. We might consider having him do the hall floor too. Bee, we have so much to do, and to solve this mystery too? We probably shouldn't have taken on extra business right now. You know there's a limit to what one can do in a day."

"Hush, Bess. You know we can't turn business down. If word got out we were picking and choosing our cases, nobody would ever call us again. And besides, you know we can't let Molly down. She's depending on us."

"I know you're right, Bee. This detective business means a lot to you, and it's beginning to win me over too."

Cautiously, I said, "Now, Bess, I'm not so sure about all this painting and such. I really can't afford to spend too much money right now. You know how tight my budget is. Aren't you going a little too far?"

"I am not. And, Bee, you aren't to worry about these expenses at all. I'm paying for everything. Fred left me with enough to live on nicely, and I am going to live nicely. I want to share it with you. After all, you're sharing your home with me."

"Bess, I want you to think of the house as your home too. After all, you were raised in this house, same as me. But are you sure you want to spend Fred's money on painting and such?"

"I'm absolutely positive. It's my money now, and Fred wanted me to live comfortably. Now, let's think about what we want to do with Mama's old wood-burning stove in the kitchen. You hardly ever use it anymore since Will bought you the electric one. Let's ditch it. It just takes up room."

"No, I'm going to put my foot down at that suggestion. That was our mama's stove, and I want it left right where it is. Suppose the power went out. How would we cook? Bess, don't even think about modernizing the kitchen. I happen to like it just the way it is. I do have one suggestion since you seem to think you can afford a few changes. Why don't we add a bathroom at the far end of your bedroom? It's a big room, and I think it's feasible to squeeze one in. That way, we won't be bumping into each other getting ready for church and such. I know it would be expensive, but think how nice it'd be for each of us to have our privacy. Now if you don't like the idea, just say so."

"Bee, I wanted to say something about that before, but I was afraid you'd think I was going overboard. Let's do it! I'm so excited about all this, I could just bust!"

"I think we've both already busted a blood vessel loading all that furniture and stuff, so don't bust anything else," I laughingly replied. "You know, Bess, I'm getting excited too. We'll be fine living together. The more I think about it, the more it appeals to me." I reached over and gave Bess a big bear hug before we walked back to survey the guest room, soon to become Bess's boudoir.

Later that afternoon, I offered Bess an egg salad sandwich for supper. We carried our plates out on the porch and sat munching as we complained about our aches and pains while the sun completely disappeared into the horizon. Happiness reigned down upon us as we anticipated our new life together, but eventually thoughts of "breaking and entering" Dixie's house tomorrow began to invade our thoughts, filling us with dread and excitement. We were totally aware that what we contemplated doing was completely illegal, but we knew that would never stop us. Hopefully, we would spend our last years here together in Mama's and Daddy's house, and not on the chain gang. I'm quite sure Bess and I would have to share a bathroom with all the other lady criminals there...and it wouldn't be painted "Blush Pink."

CHAPTER NINE

We were all a little irritable the next morning as we rode along. I never did like to hurry around early in the day since sitting on the porch for a quiet spell with my coffee was an ideal time for me and the Lord to get together and talk. Get me out of my routine, and I can be a little ornery. Vonion wasn't any better. He kept saying something under his breath that I dare not repeat. Bess, huddled next to the truck door, was all tensed up like she might inflate at any minute. Vonion was just plain out agitated and out of sorts about having an early morning trip. Bess and I were more than a little nervous about our intentions to break in and investigate Dixie's house.

"So, Vonion," I asked, trying to break the tension, "how was Ora Lee doing this morning?"

"She a little touchy. She feel good, but her feelin's a mite hurt. She say we could've squeezed her into this here pickup truck. I told her she just be in the way, and she acted real out of sorts. Women! I's got too many, and now another one's a 'comin'. Ms. Bess, you sure about all this here movin'? Once we's move you one time, we's ain't gonna re-move you back home."

"Ump, my mind is totally made up. You'll just have to get used to me around the place again. I won't bother you a bit. We'll all work together to keep the place up like it's supposed to be, for a change. We'll all get along fine."

"Somethin' tells me I's in fer a whole lot'a trouble, but I's'll keep an open mind just the same. Just you keep rememberin', there be two a'you and only one a' me to get thangs done."

"Ump!" *I guess you've already figured out who said that.*

There's really no way to get onto the Burt County road other than to go right through the middle of downtown Jeffersontown. It didn't bother me a bit for anybody to see me riding in Will's old beat-up pickup truck next to Vonion, but Bess, however, seemed more than a smidgen embarrassed. She was slumped over in her seat like a sack of potatoes, holding a handkerchief over her face in a make-believe attempt to blow her nose, as we rounded the corner at the post office. I noticed several early morning shopkeepers and business people going in and out of the building, greeting each other along the way. Earnest Lee Black, that same mail carrier we almost hit just days ago, unexpectedly stepped out into the road right in front of us again, without so much as a glance.

Vonion slammed on the brakes and veered the truck to the left to keep from barreling right over his skinny hide. That loud squealing noise from the worn-out brakes that I've already told you about pierced the air, causing everybody around to stop and stare. Thank heavens, as luck would have it, we narrowly missed Earnest Lee again. He evidently thought Vonion was trying to direct the truck right toward him because as soon as he regained his balance after his diving performance toward the shoulder of the street, he yelled those same curse words we had previously heard—this time a little louder and with a little more animation—before hoisting his bag back over his shoulder. Bess, with her handkerchief completely covering her face by now, was slumped over even farther into the footboard in an attempt to hide from the view of anybody who had seen the incident.

"Vonion, that Earnest Lee thinks everybody ought to stop and give him the right-of-way all the time. That's the second time we've almost run right over him. Is he blind or something?" I asked, as we kept going right on up the road as if nothing had happened.

"He ain't blind. Maybe he just be half asleep this morning."

"Oh, no. That scallywag thinks just because he's got a good job with the post office, everybody ought to yield to him all the time. He thinks he can do anything he wants to. He infuriates me every time I look at him, with his holier-than-thou attitude," Bess indignantly replied, as she lowered her handkerchief from her face.

"What's he done to you?" I asked Bess, thinking she was overreacting a little.

"Oh, I had a little run-in with him a few months ago. I don't think I ever mentioned it to you, Bee, but remember when the missionary society held the new preacher's wife's 'Get Acquainted and Lemonade Party' at my house last March? Well, I let the time slip up on me, and I thought it was a little late to be mailing the invites, so I figured it wouldn't hurt a thing for me to ride around town and personally put the handwritten invitation in everybody's mailboxes, without the benefit of a stamp, of course. I didn't see any need for a stamp since I was the one delivering them, not the federal government, for heaven's sake. I never thought for one minute there would be a bit of harm in it. Well, anyway, the next morning, every single one of those invitations was back in my mailbox, tied together in a bundle, along with a handwritten note telling me that it was a federal crime to use the mailboxes for anything other than mail that had gone through the post office with the benefit of a stamp, and if I ever abused government property again like that, I would be charged with 'Tampering with Federal Assets' in a court of law. That note was signed by, none other than, Earnest Lee Black. That old goat had collected every one of those invitations on his route that day and put them back in my mailbox. He has a lot of nerve, threatening me like that. He thinks he's so important because he gets to tote that bag all over town and get a big paycheck that, mind you, we, the taxpayers pay. Vonion, next time we get a chance, let's come a little closer, and scare the living you-know-what out of him. It'll do him good to be taken down a notch or two."

"Lord, Bess, you do get yourself into more trouble. I don't even remember that party."

"That's because you weren't able to attend. Don't you remember? You were at Margaret's that weekend. I ended up having to call every member on the telephone to invite them to the get-together since it was way too late to re-mail the invitations. I thought I never would get off of the telephone that day. You probably don't remember this either, but that was the day after Old Man Hodges went streaking through the streets of town, and every member of our group had to tell me a different version of what they had heard or seen."

"Oh, my, Mr. Hodges went streaking again? He is so senile now. You didn't tell me about that. I leave town for one weekend and miss all the action."

"Well, it was nothing that hadn't happened before. That old man will not keep his clothes on."

Vonion gave a little chuckle, and we all ended up laughing as we visualized Mr. Hodges escaping Mrs. Hodges again and running around town without the benefit of clothes. "Mrs. Hodges and Sheriff Ledbetter trailed him all the way through town," Bess went on. "The sheriff finally caught up with him as he entered Shorty's barber shop, asking for a haircut. He got one too. Mrs. Hodges said since he was already there, Shorty might as well throw the sheet over him and give him a trim."

We laughed even harder. *There's nothing like a good laugh to get the day started.*

Bess, fingering her handkerchief, finally regained her composure. "And, Bee, I forgot to mention to you that the preacher's wife actually showed up for that party wearing a pair of trousers. After all the trouble I went to, making everything so formal and all, with all Mama's good china and a flower arrangement from Ina's florist—by the way, bought and paid for by me, and only me, and not a single solitary soul offering to pay a penny—she showed up in pants! I don't know what this world is coming to! Young people have lost all their dignity! I gave her a corsage too. Now, don't you know I felt like a fool pinning that carnation on her while she stood in front of me with her legs stuck in a pair of trousers?"

"Ms. Bess, the way you go on! You's just a mess, that what you are. Now don't you's ladies go a'tellin' Ora Lee 'bout all this 'citement we done had this here mornin'. Hit just make her mad, she missin' somethin', and hit'll just get her's dander all stirred up," Vonion teased, as he tightened his grip on the steering wheel. I thought to myself, *if Vonion thinks that is exciting, just wait till we get into Burt County.*

I wish I could report that the rest of the trip over was uneventful...but unfortunately, I can't. We did have that inevitable blow out. Our left back tire must have had too much weight directly over it because about halfway over, we heard a loud noise that sounded like a gun being fired, and then the truck started shaking and wobbling. Vonion immediately slammed on the brakes, let out a few cuss words I haven't heard since I accidently let the hogs out in the garden a couple of years ago...*just thinking, maybe I heard them again when Vonion had to slam on brakes to keep from hitting that chicken truck the other day when we took Ora Lee to the hospital. Oh, and maybe when I asked Vonion about washing the windows a few weeks back...and maybe...*

"All that heavy weight's back there imposing on them tires, I's 'spect," Vonion grumbled, as he pulled the truck over to the side of the road.

Bess and I stood by and watched Vonion as he methodically removed the old tire and replaced it with another one that looked to be just as beat-up and patched. Vonion told us not to be concerned, he had the sit'ation under his control; hit was just an inconvenience, and we'd be back on the road in no time flat. He was right too. *Vonion had probably changed the tires on that old truck as many times as most people had filled their car with gas.* Bess complained that Vonion ought to keep better tires on the truck, but Vonion told her he hadn't used up all the mileage on these here ones. "Anyway," Vonion knowingly added, "you's women don't need to worry 'bout no'tin'; I got a spare fer the spare, and hit's better than the spare." *What a consolation!*

Just as Vonion was putting up his tools, I told the others that I might visit the woods on the side of the road. "Bess, would you care to join me? We might not have another chance for a while."

"No, thank you very much. I wouldn't go into that thicket for all the gold in Fort Knox. I imagine there're snakes and poison ivy all about in there."

"Suit yourself. I'll be right back."

"I's thank I's'll visit the other side der road, myself," Vonion muttered, as he ambled in the opposite direction.

Bess waited for us by the truck. I could see her impatiently adjusting the pleats on her dress and looking from side to side as I walked back through the little pine thicket toward the truck. Just as I reached the edge of the woods, a black convertible car whizzed by. Even with it traveling at a high speed, I could still hear the young female driver hollering at Bess, "Hey Granny, why don't you catch a ride on a billy goat? It'd be faster!"

"We've wasted enough time to go to China and back this morning," Bess scoffed, after we finally loaded back into the truck and closed the doors. "Let's go."

Vonion revved up the motor, and we took off, soon to reach our top speed of thirty miles an hour.

"At this rate, we might get to Burt County by noon," Bess complained, as she looked out the truck window toward a mule pulling a wagon loaded with hay across a field. "Look. That old mule's moving faster than we are."

"Can't push the truck too hard with this heavy load," Vonion replied, as he eyeballed the rearview mirror to check the load. "We's'll get there when we's gets there, and no sooner and no later."

And we did get there. Just as we passed the city limit sign, Vonion asked, "Now, which a'way is Miss Margaret's house? Just tell me the short way. I can't be drivin' this here rig all over this big ole city."

I knew the time had come to tell Vonion we weren't going to Margaret's house right away, but our immediate mission was to check out Dixie's house. Honestly, I felt as if he totally overreacted as I filled him in on some, but not all, of the details.

"Nobody tells me notin'!" he exclaimed. "Here I's thought we's was just deliverin' furniture, and we's fixin' to break into somebody's house. I's ain't ready to spend my last days in the clinker. What you thank them po-lice will do to us if'n we get caught? Mercy!"

"Vonion, it'll be all right. You can wait in the truck over on the next street. If we get caught, you just ride on back home like you don't even know us," Bess replied, trying to calm him down a bit.

"And who you's thank gonna bail y'all's out? The Queen of England, or maybe President Harry S. Truman?" Vonion dramatically asked. "I's is responsible fer you'uns. Lordy, how did I's get tied up with these two foolish old women?"

"Don't worry about that right now, Vonion." Then, glancing down at the scrap of paper Bess had given me with the address, I uncomfortably added, "We need to get to 24 Fourth Avenue. Turn left at this next stop sign. I think it's down that way about two or three blocks. When we get there, just drop us off, and then go on around the corner and wait for us over there."

Vonion irritably muttered, "I's should'a stayed ta home and tried to get a little more milk out'a Hortense this mornin'. She be the onliest female I's knows that'll co-operate with me. I's aint figure out if'n we is fightin' crime or if'n we's be the criminals. Lord have mercy on me!"

I didn't know either. I think there is a fine line between the two; at least it is when it comes to Bess and me. But our intentions were usually good!

CHAPTER TEN

We found Fourth Avenue fairly easily after we determined the town had avenues and streets. They crossed each other. It seemed a bit confusing that it was laid out that way, but I guess it worked for them. Bess ordered Vonion to let us out at the end of Fourth Avenue and to wait for us over on the next block.

"I'll be a'guardin' the furniture. Just give me enough time to get a little shut-eye whilst you is gone. I's tossed and turned thinking about drivin' this here truck on such a long haul this mornin'. My brain worried overtime most all night," he complained pitifully, "and with Ora Lee snoring like a freight train rat by me in that bed, hit were most impossible to close one eye, much less two." We groaned, but I sympathized and said we'd give him plenty of time for a nap.

We left Vonion with his complaints, and Bess and I walked down the street as if we were having an early morning stroll. The houses on Fourth Avenue were mostly narrow row houses with small front screened porches and dirt driveways that led to small garages in the rear. A few tiny flower beds were scattered about, but most of the yards were plain and unkempt, many with children's toys cluttering up the lawns. Each house did have one thing in common: a mail box between the sidewalk and the road, with a house number painted across the side of the box. Bess was chatting about the sorry condition of the yards in the neighborhood when I noticed she was carrying her huge pocketbook. "Why on earth did you bring that big old thing for?" I asked. "Don't you know it's gonna get in the way with everything we've got to do?"

"It might come in handy, Bee. We might have to confiscate evidence or something; you never know what we'll have to carry. Anyway, if we get caught breaking into Dixie's house and have our mug shots taken at the police station, we need to be prepared with a little lipstick and a comb. You'll be glad I have it."

I suppose I could understand her reasoning, but I hardly ever thought about things the same way Bess does. "Listen, we're almost to Dixie's address. Let's just walk on by her house like innocent bystanders and case the joint before trying to get in," I whispered, even though, as I glanced around, I didn't see a single soul around near enough to hear.

"I thought about that too. Now, when we get past the next house, let's turn around and hide in the bushes between Dixie's house and the neighbor's. We can wait there a few minutes and see if anybody's stirring around."

"Good idea."

With Bess at my heels, we sneaked around to the rear of the house next door and hid in the tall nandina bushes that separated the two properties. A big, tan dog, the size of a small pony, suddenly appeared from around the corner of the neighbor's house and began barking at us just as we crouched down. We immediately froze in total terror.

The back door of the neighbor's house swung open. An overweight woman, weighing considerably more than two hundred pounds, with short brown hair and dressed in a raggedy bathrobe, hollered, "Shut up, Biscuit, or I'm gonna throw hot dishwater on you. You're driving me crazy with all that barking this morning. Now leave those squirrels and birds alone, boy. They ain't bothering you none." She took another bite off the chicken leg she had in her hand and threw the bone toward Biscuit. Biscuit caught it in midair and gobbled it up like he hadn't eaten in a month.

Bess and I held our breath.

"Now don't bother me no more, dog. I'm busy." The big dog cowered a bit and whimpered. The woman turned around and went back into the house, slamming the door and muttering something under her breath that sounded like "stupid old dog."

Biscuit stood still, looking toward the back door. After a few seconds, he seemed satisfied that the woman was gone and turned his attention back to us. A loud, angry growl later, and we shrunk back into the bushes as far as we could get. Biscuit stood his ground, and with hair standing up on his back, began hissing through large teeth. *I counted eight sharp ones from a distance of about ten feet.* Another growl and a hiss, and I was convinced we were in deep trouble.

"Bess, quit pushing on me." Another growl, and this time louder. I whispered, "Bess, throw something at him. He's gonna tear us apart if we don't do something pretty quick."

Biscuit took another step closer, put his face closer to the ground, and gave out the meanest hiss I've ever heard in all my fifty-eight years. *Upps, sorry, if I'm gonna die from a dog attack, I might as well be truthful—sixty-one years.*

"Bess, get something out of your pocketbook to throw. We've got to divert Biscuit's attention with something. Throw that Milky Way candy bar you've been hiding in there and hurry up."

"How do you know I have a candy bar?" Bess asked, as she nervously rummaged through the contents of her purse. "I have absolutely no privacy with you around."

"Because you always have one. This is no time for chitchat. Just throw the thing and hurry up."

Bess pulled out the Milky Way, unwrapped it, took a bite, and threw the rest across the yard. Biscuit jumped into the air and caught it just as it flew over his enormous head. He landed even closer to us, and with his mouth full of gooey chocolate, managed another growl.

"Good dog, Biscuit," Bess called, as she trembled and cowered behind me in the bushes. "Good dog."

"Throw one of your shoes, Bess, and this time throw it way across the yard, and hurry. Biscuit probably thinks you've got another candy bar, and he wants it too."

"I do, but I was saving it for this afternoon."

"Throw your shoe, for pity sake, Bess! Biscuit's getting closer, and he looks madder," I snapped back, as Biscuit took another step closer.

"I'm not throwing my shoe. You throw yours. If I lose these shoes, I'll never be able to coordinate this outfit again. I thought I never would find shoes to match the green stripes in this dress."

"I can't reach down low enough to untie mine. Now, throw one of those green high-heeled shoes of yours as hard as you can across that yard, and do it now! You might not live long enough to ever wear that dress again if you don't! Now for Pete's sake, hurry up!"

"You can be so-o bossy. I don't know how you manage to get us in so much trouble all the time," Bess muttered, as she unwillingly pulled off her shoe.

As soon as the shoe flew through the air, Biscuit ran to fetch it, and Bess and I quickly scampered under the hedge and into Dixie's yard.

With our heads held down, we ran. No, I take that back. I ran, and Bess hobbled with one high-heeled shoe on and one in Biscuit's mouth, as fast as we could to the back door of Dixie's little house. Without even thinking, I grabbed the doorknob and pulled the door open. We dove in, heads first, and found ourselves between a cute little red dinette set and a kitchen sink full of dirty dishes.

* * *

"We made it," I whispered, as we lay on the floor right inside the door. Careful not to move or breathe too loud, we waited. Frozen in one spot, but sensing nobody was home, I whispered, "That was close. I think we're alone, but I've got to rest a minute. All this exercise and excitement is about to get the best of me."

"I hope Biscuit doesn't eat my shoe. Do you think we'll be able to get it back?"

"I don't know, but maybe we can find it when we leave. In the meantime, just take the other one off and go barefooted."

"What size shoes do you suppose Dixie wears? Do you think she would miss one pair of shoes?"

"Maybe not. Why don't you go look while I start checking around for something that ties her to Sam. He's doling out money to somebody, and if I'm right, I'd bet money it's Dixie."

Cautiously, Bess crept into the next room. I glanced around the room. The small kitchen was sunny and bright with a shaft of sunlight coming in through the window over the sink. Obviously, Dixie had not had time to clean. Dirty dishes were waiting in the kitchen sink to be washed, with the exception of two empty coffee cups that had been carelessly left on the dinette table, one with purple lipstick around the rim. A pink sweater had been thrown across one of the metal dinette chairs, obviously forgotten to be put away.

I quickly made my way into the narrow center hall and checked out the drawer of a little drop leaf table that stood by the bathroom door. Nothing in there but an old grocery list and a fingernail file. But it didn't take us long to figure out that Dixie had a night job with a sizable second income. Bess called from the other room, "Bee, I've never seen anything to compare with this place. Come here and look at this unmade bed! Purple sheets and a purple bedspread! Heart-shaped throw pillows! This place is a den of iniquity if ever there was one! Do you really think Sam would frequent this gaudy place?"

"That would be my guess," I said, as I turned to walk into the bedroom. "But we don't know anything for sure yet. Let's give him the benefit of the doubt before we condemn him." I stood in the doorway of the bedroom and glanced around. "Oh, my stars! Just look at all this purple."

"And look at all these housecoats and gowns," Bess exclaimed, as she looked inside the closet. "I've never seen so much silk and satin and feathers in all my life. And what do you suppose Dixie does with these whips?" Bess was now on her hands and knees looking for shoes in the bottom of the closet.

"I really don't know for sure, but I've heard they can be tools of the trade," I sheepishly answered, as I opened one of the dresser drawers. "There's more lacy underwear in here than in the whole Sears and Roebuck Catalog." I quickly noticed a girdle lying between a purple nighty and a black brassiere. "Look, Bess. I believe this is the same girdle that's on page seventy-five of the catalog." Holding it up so I could see it better, I thoughtfully mumbled, "I wonder if it really works."

"Bee, put that thing down." Bess, still on her hands and knees looking at the shoes in the bottom of the closet, exclaimed, "You aren't going to believe this, but Dixie has a pair of shoes exactly like my green ones, only her pair is blue. I wonder if I could wear them." She examined one of the shoes a little more thoroughly and said, "Dixie wears a six, and I wear a seven, but maybe I can squeeze my foot into it."

Bess was soon sitting on a little footstool trying on shoes. "Really Bess, you know you can't get your big foot into a size six shoe."

"I can try," Bess answered, after she stuffed her feet into the shoes and was attempting to walk across the room.

Bess soon sat back down and reluctantly pulled the tight shoes off. As she struggled to cram her number seven feet into another pair of size six shoes, I glanced around at the total disarray of the room. Clothes were thrown in piles everywhere, along with shoes, coats, scarves, and pocketbooks. "And you thought I was the messiest person in the world, Bess. Now you see how most people live."

"We are not most people, Bee. We take pride in being orderly." *I'm not quite sure why she included me in that statement.*

I felt a lecture coming on, so I hastily changed the subject. "I think I'll check out the desk." A cute little curly maple secretary sat directly under double windows, windows that were completely concealed behind venetian blinds and heavy panels of deep purple fabric. No light was allowed in or out for very obvious reasons. Sitting on the top of the desk was an empty candy jar, a watch, and a book on etiquette, of all things. I guess Dixie had a few saving graces, after all. I noticed a piece of writing paper stuck between the pages of the book. Of course I pulled it out and read it. It was a typed mimeographed letter:

> Please return a certified check for one hundred dollars to the post office address listed below. In the event that you ignore this demand, a letter will be sent to your superiors and to your wife, explaining your regular visits to a certain residence. Please remit immediately.

"Bess, come here," I said. "I believe Dixie has been moonlighting her moonlighting job." I handed the paper to Bess after she hobbled over with her feet stuffed into another pair of size sixes. "What do you think? Do you think Dixie's been entertaining and then blackmailing the same man?"

As if expecting a mouse to jump out, I cautiously opened the desk drawer as Bess read the note. Stuck under a stack of bills and some loose note paper, I spotted a ledger. Curiosity won over again. I picked it up and thumbed through the large book. A man's name was listed on each page, along with a date and a considerable amount of money. Sam Turner's name was on page five. All the dates and sums by his name indicated he must have been a very frequent visitor.

"It's easy to tell what Sam's been doing with his time." I handed the ledger over to Bess. "And all that money. Obviously this kind of fun comes with a pretty hefty paycheck."

"This is serious business, Bee. We need to get out of here before we get caught. I think we've seen all the evidence we need. Poor Molly! She's going to be devastated when we tell her about all this. Do we have to tell her everything?"

"I don't know. Let's don't think about that now. Just get out of those shoes and let's go. Hey, wait a minute. I think I'll check out the front of the house before we leave. You never know, there might be something interesting up there." I picked up the mimeographed letter from where Bess had laid it down and stuck it into my dress pocket.

"Go on ahead. I'll put the shoes back."

My curiosity always seems to get me in trouble. You never know what you're going to run into, but I never thought I'd have the shock of my life that morning when I opened the door to Dixie's front room. It was immediately apparent to me that a struggle had taken place. Broken lamp pieces were scattered across the floor, and a small chair was turned upside down. And there between a tilted end table and a broken ashtray was Dixie, clad in a purple satin nightgown, lying sprawled out across the hardwood floor of the small front room. With a small indention on her forehead about an inch wide, a clean, but deep, gash across her cheek, a few scrapes and scratches on her arms and face, and her body in a contorted position, I knew immediately Dixie was as dead as a doornail. I instantly choked back a scream. Scared to keep looking at her, but scared to look away, in case I might miss an important clue, I tried to call out to Bess, but my voice failed. Several attempts later, I whispered, "B-Bess, c-come here. You need to see this."

"What's wrong with you? I can't hear a word you're saying," Bess answered, as she pranced in wearing a pair of purple bedroom shoes. "I think I found some shoes I can actually wear. They don't really match my dress, but maybe nobody will notice. What do you think?...Oh...Oh...m-my gosh, w-what's that?" Bess stopped and stared at the dead body on the floor before stepping backward and almost tripping over her own feet. "Is she dead? I mean is she really dead?" Bess whispered in shock, as she threw her hand to her frightened face.

"She's dead all right. I don't think she's pretending. I didn't check her pulse or anything, but I, uh, don't think she's breathing, and she looks pretty dead to me."

"Is she cold?"

"I don't know. Do you think I touched her? Her eyes are open. I've heard all dead people's eyes are open."

"I never heard that. Who told you that?"

"Listen, Bess, I can't remember where I heard it, but I do remember when one of Will's bulls got struck by lightning, his eyes were open when we found him."

"I hardly think you can compare Dixie to one of Will's bulls, but I believe you. Now let's get outta here," Bess pleaded, as she backed farther out of the room. "I think we've overstayed our welcome. We're definitely in the wrong place at the wrong time again."

Glancing around to see if I had missed any other evidence, I noticed a small wad of paper near the front leg of the settee. I grabbed it before leaving the room and stuck it in my pocket along with the other note. Bess kicked off those bedroom shoes, picked up her one green high-heeled shoe and her pocketbook, and I grabbed the ledger. We dashed out the back door without another backward glance. A thought that we might be removing evidence from a murder scene or the fear of a ferocious Biscuit waiting for us never crossed my mind as we fled across the neglected backyard.

Hopefully, no peering eyes witnessed our swift escape that morning from Dixie's house on Fourth Avenue where a tragic event had recently unfolded. The tragedy was, more than likely, the consequences of a life not so well lived, but a life, none the less, not deserving of such a cruel and tragic ending.

A trip to question Lightening was totally out of the picture now. I handed Bess the ledger, and she tucked it into her pocketbook. She gave me a look that says everything when she knows she's right. *Her pocketbook really did come in handy to conceal evidence.* We headed back toward the truck with our hearts beating wildly. Outwardly, we appeared to be taking another morning stroll just for our health, but inwardly, we were terrified.

CHAPTER ELEVEN

We've just found a dead body! A real live—upps—I mean a really dead body!" Bess nervously said as we walked along. "My Lord, that was the most awful sight I've ever in all my years seen. Oh, and Bee, now you see why I brought this pocketbook along. I knew you'd find a use for it, and I guess you realize I'm ruining a perfectly good pair of hose that cost me thirty-nine cents…oh and…"

"Just keep walking, Bess. We've got to get outta here. We don't want to be spotted leaving a crime scene," I answered breathlessly, as we bustled up the street.

"My Lord, I just can't get the sight of that pitiful dead woman out of my mind. You know we've just committed another crime, don't you? Leaving the scene of a crime *is* a crime. Maybe we should call the sheriff over here or something."

"Oh, no, we're not. We're not getting mixed up with the law. We haven't done anything wrong except unlawfully going into that house, and really, we could have been just selling beauty products or something door-to-door and just happened to get in unexpectedly. We really could come up with an easy explanation if we had to. We're good at that."

"Bee, this detective business is not what it's cracked up to be. I never thought we'd be breaking into houses and encountering dead bodies," Bess whined, as she suddenly grimaced in pain but hobbled on until she abruptly stopped and rolled her foot over to the side. "Oh, that hurt! I think I've stepped on a rock. Hold up a minute."

She grabbed my shoulder for support while she examined her throbbing foot. "I've seen plenty of dead people in coffins after Mr. Lawson pinned sweet expressions on their faces, but I've never seen one laid out on the floor like that," I said, as I waited for Bess to rub the bottom of her foot.

"You know, Mr. Lawson does do a good job," Bess answered, as we walked on with Bess carrying her big pocketbook in one hand and her green shoe in the other. "Mrs. Mae Blossom never looked so good in her life as when she was lying in that casket last month. And that gardenia Mr. Lawson pinned on her dress smelled absolutely heavenly. I got a good whiff of it when I leaned over to see if Mae's hair really was that nice ashy brown color. I figured Thelma dyed it, but now I know for sure. I always had my suspicions about that color but could never really get close enough to check out the roots. I just hope old Mae made it to heaven."

"She was one cantankerous old gal all right. Remember when she walked through town with her hound dog a few months ago, waving that sign about Sheriff Ledbetter stepping out of line for giving her a parking ticket. She knew better than to park in front of that fire hydrant, but she thought she could do anything she wanted.

I'd bet she probably died just to keep from paying that ticket...Well, was her hair dyed?"

"Oh, yea, it was dyed all right. And I'm definitely going to ask Thelma about that color. Now that Mae's dead, Thelma'll probably let on to what color she used on her hair. I don't think she'd consider it to be divulging a confidence anymore. Bee, my feet are just killing me. Slow down a little."

Without the benefit of shoes and carrying that big ole pocketbook, Bess looked pretty ridiculous as we traipsed up the street toward the end of Fourth Avenue. We waved casually to a pretty young woman sitting in her yard watching her children as they played in a sandbox. A milkman slowed his truck and stopped a door or two ahead of us. We nodded to him as we passed by, and he nodded back as he carried two quarts of milk around to the back of the house. We hurried on, trying to be as inconspicuous as possible, but without shoes, Bess's efforts to walk naturally were wasted. One little towheaded boy, playing at the end of the street, asked her what happened to her shoes, and she told him she had bunions, and shoes hurt her feet. The answer seemed to satisfy him, and he went back to playing with his ball.

I spotted Will's truck as we rounded the corner. Vonion had parked it under a big shady oak tree in an empty lot over on the next block. "Tell Vonion you gave your shoes to a beggar, or tell him you lost them in some tall grass. He might believe that. I don't know, make up something, I don't care."

"Why don't I just tell him the truth? A dog got my shoe. He's not going to believe what I say, anyway."

"I'm sure you're right," I said, as I opened the truck door.

Snoring peacefully, Vonion was reclining with his head against the back of the seat, his mouth gaped wide open, and his cap perched over his eyes. The creaking sound of the door opening must have startled him because he jumped straight up when I announced, "Wake up, Vonion. We're back."

"I hope you got a good long nap while we were gone because we've got serious work to do, and you're gonna need all your strength and energy," Bess snapped, as she slid into the seat and slammed the truck door. "Let's get out of here. We're wasting good daylight."

"I's ain't wasted no time t'all. I's been ready since we driv' into town. You two a'holding things up, not me."

The reality of what we had just seen hit me as I settled in my seat. I was really as nervous as a cat but determined to act natural in front of Vonion. "Let's unload the truck and get on home," I casually said, as I patted my dress.

Vonion just grunted and didn't quiz us about what we had been up to, but more than likely, he suspected something. He could generally read me like an open book.

I held my breath as Vonion choked the stubborn truck. It finally fired up and we were off. A minute or two later, we were chugging into Margaret's neighborhood.

* * *

Margaret lived in a cute little duplex apartment in the backyard of a big Victorian home owned by a well-known superior court judge, Judge Samuel Harmon, and his wife, Livonia. Margaret lived in one side of the duplex, and the other side was occupied by the judge's caretaker and his wife, Eli and Safronia. Eli, a faithful and loyal servant to the judge, was actually his distant cousin. Eli and Safronia had worked for the judge and his high society wife for many, many years, according to Margaret. Eli took care of many of the personal needs of the judge, as well as the property and the grounds. Safronia worked as cook and maid. Judge Harmon and his wife were very social and entertained a good deal, which kept Eli and Safronia very busy most of the time. Margaret had helped Safronia serve several times in the past when the judge and his wife were putting on the dog with one of their big shindigs.

We pulled into the long gravel driveway that curved through the large gardens that surrounded the enormous white house with its wide wraparound porches. I always noticed what a wonderful job Eli did of keeping the large expanse of flower beds and shrubbery plots manicured. Few times had I driven down the wide driveway through the yard with its fountains and ornate iron benches and not seen Eli hard at work, with a rake or a grubbing hoe in his hands, or maybe pushing a wheelbarrow around, full of compost or grass cuttings. His everyday uniform was a faded pair of overalls. A wrench and a screwdriver were always in his pockets, and a hammer was usually handy, hanging from a tab on his overalls leg, ready to repair a lose piece of tin on a roof or a rotten board from the barn or the fence. It wasn't unusual at all to see him replacing and painting porch railings, scrubbing windows, or sawing firewood.

The little duplex was hidden from the street by trees and large shrubs. Nestled between the old barn, where Eli kept yard tools, and a large oak tree, the duplex added to the charm of the backyard. The clapboard exterior was painted white, with dark green front doors and window shutters similar to the big house. Next to Margaret's front stoop was a small plot of zinnias she had transplanted from my zinnia bed soon after the little plants had broken through the ground early in the summer. A few metal yard chairs under the oak tree sat empty now, but I knew, when the weather permitted, Margaret loved to sit out there in the afternoons to check spelling papers or arithmetic tests with her red pencil.

Margaret always locked her side of the duplex, but I had a key. Vonion untied the ropes from the truck, and Bess looked for a water hose to give the flowers by the door a drink of water. *She cannot walk by flowers without watering them or pinching at them; they did need it.* I unlocked the door and went right in. Sitting on a little marble topped table in the little foyer was a note telling us where she wanted everything placed. The note went on to say she regretted she wouldn't be able to get home that afternoon before we had to leave, but unfortunately, the principal had called a teachers' meeting right after school, and she would be detained until at least six o'clock.

We were disappointed we'd miss seeing Margaret, but actually it might have been for the best, since Bess and I were as skittish as two old hens with the barnyard rooster in heat. Eli was nowhere to be found that day so the three of us, two old women and one older colored man, unloaded all the furniture from the truck and carried it through the door. We followed Margaret's specific instructions as best as we could and spent the rest of the morning shoving tables and chairs around, some pieces more than once. Margaret's old bedroom suit was loaded on the truck for us to haul back home where we would store it in the back of the barn, probably never to see the light of day again. With the last piece of the bedroom furniture loaded on the truck and the small house looking a good bit more crowded, but very homey, if I do say so myself, we were totally exhausted, but I believe Bess's and my nerves were improved by all the exercise. (By the way, Vonion didn't utter one complaint when I asked him to move Margaret's hope chest from one wall to another. He did gasp for more breath when we finally set it down, and he did mention he might be close to having a major heart attack.)

Margaret had left cold ham for sandwiches and a jar of pickled peaches in the refrigerator for us to lunch on. We sat in the yard chairs out under the big oak tree at noon as we stuffed ourselves and rested. Soon Safronia appeared at the back door of the big house and briskly walked over to greet us. Usually she is so nice and pleasant, but today she was all in a dither. "The neighbor from down the street just called on the telephone," she excitedly called out, as she neared us. "A dead woman's body has been discovered in a house over on Fourth Avenue. She was brutally murdered!"

"Oh, how awful," I answered in a shocked voice and threw my hand over my mouth, *and I was shocked the body had been discovered so soon.* "Do you know who the woman is...or was?"

"I don't actually know the girl, but I do know she was the secretary over at the schoolhouse. Somebody must have broken into her house, and she was evidently beaten to death."

"Oh, my stars!" Bess gasped, in her most astonished tone of voice. "Why would anybody do such a horrible thing?"

"I'm not sure. I've never heard too much good about the girl, though. She has a reputation of being pretty forward with the gentlemen, if you know what I mean."

"Is that right?" Bess gasped again.

"Anyway, when she didn't show up at work this morning, the school janitor went over to check on her and found her stone cold dead, sprawled out on the floor. He called the law, and I guess they're over there right now, investigating..."

"The scene of the crime." Bess finished the sentence.

"Er, oh yes. The neighbor that called said the sheriff did have one piece of evidence, a woman's green shoe found in the yard."

My heart stopped abruptly, and I could feel my skin start quivering uncontrollably.   I could clearly see my whole life pass by in the matter of the next few seconds. Trying not to tremble too noticeably, I attempted to ask Safronia if there were any witnesses, but sudden panic had completely stolen my voice. I glanced at Bess and could see the blood had swiftly run from her face.   She sat frozen...thankfully, with a borrowed pair of Margaret's shoes on her feet.

Safronia waited for us to respond to the news, but when we didn't utter a word, she continued on. "A dog had chewed up the shoe, so I presume it was lost by someone coming or leaving.   The neighbor said the sheriff told another neighbor that it wasn't a match to any of Dixie's shoes in the house, and it wasn't even her size. They did say it was an odd color of green and not very smart looking." *Bess grimaced.* "I guess that could mean something, I don't know.   It just gives me the willies to think something that horrible happened just a few blocks from right here."

"Yes, it certainly does," Bess agreed, as she was beginning to overcome her initial shock and shaking her head sadly, as if she were hearing all this news for the first time.

"I need to tell Eli the news, if I could only find him. Have you seen him around? He might have gone into town to help the judge at his office. Sometimes he helps out over there with the cleaning and such." She turned to head out toward the barn just as Mrs. Harmon stuck her head out the back door and looked around. She waved to us as she called to Safronia.   "Safronia, I need you to finish the cleaning. It's about time for my guests, and we haven't finished washing the crystal or chipping the ice."

"I'll have to find Eli later, I guess. I've got to go now. Have a good trip back home, and I'll tell Margaret I saw y'all." Safronia walked over to the clothesline, grabbed a couple of tea towels that were sunning, and walked back into the house.

Just as the back door closed, Vonion stared at us in his old quizzical way. "Does either one of you'uns have anything you's want to say, cause I's feels a real heart attack a'comin' on rat about now."

We both sat there silently, and that was enough to make even the least suspicious person doubtful. Finally, Vonion laid his sandwich down and said he just wasn't hungry any longer. "I's having a lot of 'no luck' today," he grumbled, as he focused his old red eyes directly at me. A very uncomfortable feeling of being reprimanded without another word being said swiftly overtook me.

I knew we had to tell Vonion the truth about everything, but I had hoped we could put it off until we were headed back toward home. We were still sitting in the judge's backyard a few minutes later when the back door opened again. Safronia stuck her head out and hollered, "Oh, yoo-hoo! Mr. Vonion! Ms. Livonia asked if you wouldn't mind moving that piece of junk…oh, err… I mean, the truck, to the back of the barn. Her friends are due any minute."

"Why, that high society frump! She is actually ashamed of our truck. I think we should park it right outside her front door and pretend we're out of gas. That would fix her. The very idea!" *You already know who said that.*

"Tell her we'll move it right away," I called back. Bess and I hurried back into the house to give it a second look of approval. Bess left Margaret's shoes exactly where she had found them earlier and left barefooted again. We certainly didn't want Margaret jumping to any conclusions about shoes.

As we rode along toward home, we filled Vonion in on our untimely excursion. His old red eyes got bigger and bigger, and the old truck went faster and faster as we unfolded the tale of the earlier events. We made it back home without another blowout. *Of the tires. Vonion personally had a big blowout, and we, unfortunately, heard a few of those four-letter words again, as a cloud of uncertainty swiftly moved across our future.* By the time we were rolling down the lane toward home and, we hoped, security, Vonion knew the whole story, and I'm afraid he realized he was as much an accomplice to a crime as we were. The "B and B Investigative Services" had just added a reluctant new executive board member. Vonion lamented that he'd be thrown off the deacon board at church and probably be asked to leave the church altogether after today. We assured him that nobody would blame him for a thing. He was only doing what we asked.

"That won't account fer notin'," he grumbled. "Ignorance don't count in a court of law or to the church deacon board. I's is supposed to know right from wrong, and I's did wrong the minute I's let you's out of the truck! The good Lord knows I's suspected you's two was up to no good. One day I's minding my own business down on the farm, and the next day I's ridin' all over creation breakin' the law. Now what you think Ora Lee gonna do when we all go to jail? She can't run the place rat by herself! We is in a peck of trouble!"

I had a strong feeling he was right...again.

CHAPTER TWELVE

Let's put the ledger aside until tomorrow, Bee. I'm exhausted, and I'm sure you are too. Hopefully, tomorrow will be less stressful, and we can concentrate on it a little better." Vonion had put us out of the truck at my front door after giving us a lecture that lasted halfway home. I think he knew it went in one ear and out the other, but he had to get it off his chest anyway.

"I's never got in no trouble when's I's worked fer yor's daddy and Mr. Will. We's did our work on the farm and didn't get all involved in this here crime world. Mr. Will ain't been dead that long, and here we is, in all kinds of trouble." And he went on and on. We had been told, in no uncertain terms, we could go straight to jail if the law discovered we had left the scene of a crime with ev-i-dence, and besides that, we had broken into a private res-i-dence. Y'all's just amazes me. Trouble follows y'all's like hogs to a trough. And now, I's got one more thing to worry with, as if

Ora Lee ain't enough. She gettin' better now, and that mean more and more complainin'.""

Our ears were still ringing from our scolding as we watched the old truck pull over to the barn. Vonion had to feed up before going home to hear Ora Lee grumble about being left alone all day. "Let's meet here at headquarters in the morning to go over the ledger, Bess. I'm so thankful we grabbed it before the sheriff got in there. If he had discovered the ledger, Sam Turner would probably be held for questioning by now, and everybody would know his secret. I'm not convinced he had anything to do with all this, except making very bad choices about the company he kept."

"I'm sure you're right, and I am tired. I can't even think straight right now. I guess we'll have to talk to Molly tomorrow, and she's going to be mighty upset about all these developments. Do you think we can make something up about what Sam's been doing? I hate to hurt her any more than she's already been hurt."

"I don't know. Let's sleep on it. In the meantime, give me that green shoe. I'm going to burn it right now in the barrel with my trash from the house."

"That was a good pair of shoes," Bess grumbled, as she handed over the shoe and the ledger. "It's hard to find a pair that feels so good. By the way, do we have an expense account journal? If we don't, start one, and put me down for five ninety-nine, plus tax. That's what the shoes cost...no, wait, they were on sale from six ninety-nine. Put down six ninety-nine, plus tax...oh, and add in a pair of hose at thirty-nine cents, plus tax."

I hesitantly agreed. *I thought four ninety-nine was adequate since, I'm sure, Bess had already gotten at least a couple of dollars' worth of wear out of the shoes, but I knew better than to argue with Bess.*

Bess left that evening—weary, upset, and barefooted as the day she was born.

After gathering all the trash from the house, I started a fire in the barrel with the green shoe placed right on top. As the trash and the shoe burned, I stood there watching the flames, contemplating the day. *It was a day I'd never forget.* A melancholy mood gradually enveloped me. A day that would probably change the way I perceived life and death. Dixie's life was far too short. How terribly sad, the way she had lived, and especially the way she had died. As I stood by the hot barrel, watching the last flame flicker into grey ash, the sky began to fade away, leaving me in the cool darkness of dusk.

Later that evening, after I had said my nightly prayers, and since I still hadn't heard a word from Margaret, I decided to put in a call. Margaret should have already called, but something must have come up. I sat down in the hall, put my tired feet on the stool, and picked up the telephone. How could I dodge the truth about today's happening, I asked myself, and still be totally honest. *There's no way around it; I might as well keep on* fibbing.

* * *

Nellie sounded a little down that evening. Trying to be considerate, but hoping not to get into a full-fledged conversation, I reluctantly asked if anything was wrong. She said her tailbone was tired from sitting all day, and she felt like a bird in a cage, trapped to the telephone switchboard. I suggested she find someone to relieve her for a while every afternoon, but she said that would cut too deeply into her budget, and she was trying to cut down on her spending. "It's hard out in this cold world without a man," Nellie grumbled. "I'm considering buying myself an automobile. The price of a car is bad enough, but I've heard the price of gasoline is nineteen cents a gallon, and..." on and on...and...on...   After a lengthy account about   Cleo's brother-in-law over in Alabama who had just died from drinking bad moonshine, and news about Mildred's new porch furniture from Sears and Roebuck that had been delivered on a big moving van Monday afternoon, my endurance was about used up. I felt as if I had commiserated long enough when Nellie started in about Mae Blossom's inconsiderate family having Mae's old hound dog put down. I interrupted with a fake sneeze and asked if Nellie would go ahead and make the call since I was overdue taking my cold remedy.

Margaret sounded breathless as she answered the call. "Hello, Margaret Martin speaking." I could hear a man's voice in the background and knew immediately I had recently heard that same voice.

"Hello, dear. I hope I'm not catching you at a bad time."

"Oh, no, Mama. We're just coming in. The place looks great. Thank you so much for everything. Please tell Aunt Bess and Vonion how much I appreciate everything."

"Oh, I will, but it wasn't anything. I hope we placed everything where you wanted it."

"Mama, it's fine. Walter came over to visit, and we're just coming in from supper. We went out to the restaurant near the river and had spaghetti." *My heart gave a thump.*

"Oh, well, I won't keep you then. I'm glad you've had a little fun."

"We did! Oh, Mama...I really hate to tell you bad news, but somebody broke into Dixie's house, and evidently there was a struggle, and anyway, Dixie was murdered. Isn't that terrible! We've all been in shock about it at school today. Do you recall she's the one I mentioned to you and Aunt Bess this past weekend when we were discussing Sam

Turner. You know, the school secretary. Anyway, she was brutally murdered in her own home. I thought you'd want to know."

"Oh, no! I'm so terribly sorry. What a tragedy! I know she'll be missed. Have you heard any more details? Does the sheriff have any leads?"

"I haven't heard about anything in particular, and I know no one has been arrested yet. Somebody did say that the neighbor's dog had chewed up a woman's green shoe and left it in the yard. Apparently it didn't belong to anybody around there. I don't know if that has anything to do with the murder. Probably not. " *My heart missed a beat.*

"Margaret, please be cautious, and keep your doors locked. I'm so worried about your safety with a murderer on the loose."

"Oh, I definitely will. Don't worry, Mama, I'll be careful. Judge Harman has already talked to Eli about keeping an extra eye out over here."

"Good. Now remember, you can't be too careful. Check in with Eli every morning and every night. Margaret, I'm glad you're seeing Walter."

"So am I, Mama. Listen, I need to go now. Walter has to leave shortly, and I want to offer him something to drink before he leaves."

"All right, dear. Tell Walter I said hello. I love you, and good night." *I didn't fib the first time. That was a record for me.*

I placed the ledger in the bottom of the wardrobe where I wouldn't see it, or hopefully, think about it until tomorrow, and readied myself for bed, but sleep didn't come quickly that evening. I watched the clock most of the night, counting the hours, one by one until I finally lost count about one a.m.

* * *

Knock! Knock! Knock! Where on earth was that noise coming from? Maybe I was dreaming, I thought, as I sleepily pried my eyes open.

Knock! Knock! "Ms. Bee! Are you home? It's Melvin! I'm here to start painting."

I thought my ears had to be deceiving me. Why is somebody named Melvin here at my house at...Oh, Lord! I glanced at the clock. "It's only six a.m.!"

"Ms. Bee!" The words rang out as I heard a clanging noise and the porch door scraping against the floor. Bump! Bump! More bumping! "Ms. Bee, I'm here! Where do you want me to start?"

That's when it hit me. Bess's painter, Melvin, was here. I've never heard of a painter that starts before nine in the morning. Mercy me! Most painters are still drunk as skunks at the crack of dawn. Why does Melvin have to be different?

Dragging myself out of the bed and grabbing my robe, I called, "I'm coming! Hold your horses!" I sleepily staggered up the hall to the porch to find Melvin maneuvering a long ladder through the screen door. I hurried over to hold the door open before he completely tore it off the hinges. "Good morning, er...Melvin? You sure do start early in the morning. Don't you want to go home and come back around nine?"

"Oh, no ma'am. I start early every morning. You know what they say, 'The early bird catches the worm'."

"Who said that?"

"I don't know, but I've always heard it, and I believe it too. You can expect me every morning about six."

"Good grief," I moaned.

"What's that you say?"

"I said *good*!"

Melvin and I didn't start off too well, but we soon warmed up to each other. I fixed coffee. He drank his black, and I drank mine with cream. Not wanting Bess to feel left out of Melvin's first morning at work, I decided to call and give her a report on how things were progressing...at six thirty a.m. Nellie yawned loudly and put the call through. *Thank heavens; she must have been too sleepy to protest.*

Eight rings later, Bess sleepily answered. "Hello, Bess Johnson speaking." I could detect a yawn.

"Good morning, Sister," I cheerfully announced. "I thought you might be interested to know Melvin is here." The telephone sounded as if it had been dropped, and suddenly it went dead. *Misery loves company is my new motto.*

Melvin hummed or sang while he worked. I tried to drown him out with *The West Family Gospel Hour*, but the louder I played the radio, the louder Melvin sang. Along with the crows and the roosters and the hogs, we had quite a chorus. Vonion stuck his head into the house on his way out to the barn and declared the harmony sounded better than the church choir on his preacher's anniversary day. "And that's a'sayin' a whole lot," he cheerfully added, as his face broke out in a wide grin. Maybe that was his way of saying the trials of yesterday were forgotten and forgiven. You see, Vonion never held a grudge too long. Hopefully, we had a truce.

Bess arrived around eight thirty. I could immediately tell she was going to be a little touchy this morning. Bess needs her beauty sleep, and I had interrupted it with my impromptu telephone call. "Bee, I want to check in with Melvin before we sit down with the ledger. Just give me a minute."

"Go on ahead; I'll get the coffee. Ask Melvin if he'd like another cup."

ANN COBB

Bess's distressed shriek reverberated from the front room just as I reached for the coffee pot. "*Oh, no!*"

"What in tarnation is the matter?" I gasped, as I rushed into the front room to find Bess standing in the middle of the floor, hands on her hips, glaring at the wall.

"Melvin, where on earth did you find that horrible shade of green? I told you I wanted the color of mulberry leaves in the early spring sunshine. This won't do at all!" Stubbornly shaking her head, a perturbed Bess turned to walk out to the porch to inspect the paint cans.

"I ain't never heard of that color she's a'talking about. They's dark green, green, and light green. This here is light green," Melvin mumbled dryly to me, as he went back to painting. "Women! You can't satisfy none of 'um!"

Bess cooled off a little but not until Melvin added a little white paint into the green, giving the color a lighter tone. "Now, that's much better," she admiringly said, as we watched Melvin paint. He would have to paint over all he had already painted, but Bess seemed satisfied.

Melvin asked if it was all right if he smoked on the job. He said he could paint with one hand and smoke with the other. "I do it all the time. Keeps my hand steady."

Bess's vehement reply was, "Absolutely not. I'm paying you for the use of two hands, not one. Besides we don't want smoke in the paint. It'll smell up the place. Smoke on the porch if you must smoke."

"Suit yourself; hit'll just take me longer. I ain't got nowhere else to go anyhow." I suggested he chew his tobacco, and he would have the use of both hands. His ready answer was that a chaw made his stomach queasy. He better keep with his smokes. I suddenly cringed as I was beginning to realize redecorating was going to be as stressful as detective work.

116

With the battle of the paint color resolved, Bess and I finally sat down in the kitchen for coffee. I had fished the ledger out of the wardrobe earlier that morning and had placed it squarely in the middle of the table. "This is positively privileged information," I cautioned Bess, as I tapped the gray fabric-covered book with my finger before opening it.

Bess quipped right back at me, as if she was offended. "You know I never gossip, Bee. I consider the ledger to be sacred information too; after all, we practically risked our lives getting the thing."

"We didn't risk our lives."

"Oh, yes we did so. Biscuit wanted to tear us to shreds."

"Oh, yes, with everything else that happened to us yesterday, I completely forgot about that dog."

"I don't know how you could forget that shoe-eating dog. I'll probably never find another pair of green shoes."

"I hope those green shoes of yours don't come back to haunt us, Bess. I don't know why you can't wear regular shoes that look like everybody else's."

"If it will make you feel any better, I'll start wearing brogans," Bess snapped back. I suppressed another eye roll and opened the ledger.

A new chapter of our lives lay before us as I began turning the pages.

CARD: FL.D.L.E.D)

CHAPTER THIRTEEN

We really weren't sure of anything until that morning as we sat at my kitchen table. Bess pulled her chair closer to the table and reached for her coffee. "Let's get this show on the road and check this ledger out. We can't put it off any longer. You haven't been peeking, have you? I knew you'd look."

"I certainly have not," I indignantly replied, as I put my coffee cup down a little too hard, and coffee splashed on the ledger. "Now look what you made me do," I said, as I wiped the book off with the kitchen towel. "I told you I wouldn't open this thing until this morning, and I meant it."

There it was before us, a chronicle of appointments: names, dates, charges. Unbelievable! Dixie had used the ledger to record her unsuspecting visitors' sessions. Her fees were logged according to each guest's allotted time.

The first notation was made in February, nineteen forty-three. Obe Jordan had arrived at four p.m. and left at six p.m., February fourth. Her fee for services was six dollars. We decided to go through the ledger and find each visit by Obe Jordan and document it on a separate list. While I searched for a notepad, Bess checked on Melvin. "How's he coming?" I asked Bess, as she hurried back into the kitchen. I could tell she was agitated.

"He's slow as molasses in the wintertime, if you're asking me. He actually asked me if I happened to have a package of Lucky Strikes on me. When I told him I didn't smoke, he asked if I could run into town for a package. Can you believe that? He hasn't worked but a few hours, and he's already out of cigarettes."

"Well, when are you going to get them?"

"I told him I'd go directly. Bee, I've never bought a package of cigarettes in my entire life. What will Elmo say when I go into Floyd's Station and ask to buy those filthy things?" (For those who may not know, Floyd was murdered the year before. Elmo, his able assistant, bought the station from Floyd's son soon after. He decided to keep the name "Floyd's.")

"He'll probably say, 'That'll be nineteen cents, plus tax.' Don't worry about it now. We'll go later. Right now let's check out the next name. Now sit down, and get your mind back to business."

The next name was Sam Harmon. "Bee, can that be the same Samuel Harmon we know and respect? Why, I can't believe it! Judge Samuel Harmon? Our Judge Harmon! I mean Livonia Harmon's judge, I mean husband? That can't be possible! What would he be doing over at Dixie's?"

I was as mortified as Bess, and I knew the answer to her question. "I won't even answer that, Bess. You know what they were doing, and I grant you they weren't playing checkers or reading a book together. Let's don't think about that right now. Let's just think about what's in this book."

"All right, but I never in a hundred years would have believed he…"

"I know. Me either. But let's keep lookin'. His first documented visit was June tenth, nineteen hundred, forty-three. Her fee for services was six dollars."

"How long do you think he stayed, Bee?"

"However long it took, I suppose, but I would guess about two hours. Dixie charged Obe Jordan three dollars an hour, so I'm assuming that was her regular charge."

"I never heard of *that* lasting two hours."

"Listen, we said we weren't going to think about that right now. Anyway, they probably did something else part of the time. Maybe Dixie cooked something for them to eat."

"You really don't believe that," Bess replied sarcastically.

We continued to pour over the ledger and documented visit after visit. Notations went on and on. The pages revealed that Dixie had a total of seven regular visitors over the time that she kept records. Other than those of Obe Jordan and Samuel Harmon, there were regular recorded visits from Silas Jernigan, Zeniss Coleman, Henry Lee Spears, E. N. Frost, and Sam Turner. Notated along with each name was a date and a charge for services.

All in all, we documented over two hundred visits. Dixie had been a very busy lady over the last five years. She had regularly supplemented her secretarial pay with dollar after dollar of illegal income. We were coming up for a little air as Melvin walked into the kitchen with a paint brush in one hand and a rag smelling like turpentine in the other.

"Hit's almost lunch time, if'n y'all ain't noticed. I'm gonna take a little break out on the porch. I hate to trouble you'uns, but…"

"I know, you need your smokes," Bess replied in her exasperated tone of voice. "I'll run into town and get a package. You know you've got paint on the bottom your shoes, and you're tracking it all over the house."

"Oh, sorry." Melvin reached down and wiped the floor with the rag and then gave his shoes a couple of swipes. "Paint's a little runny today. Don't worry; I'll check the rest of the floor."

"See that you do," Bess answered a little too sternly. "Bee, do you need anything in town?"

"Thanks, but I'm fine. Melvin, did you bring your lunch? I could fix you a little something."

"My old lady packed me a couple of pork chop sandwiches and a big hunk of coconut cake. Just need my smokes, if'n it ain't too much trouble."

"I'm going, I'm going," Bess said, as she stiffly stood. "I'll be back shortly."

Without offering a red cent to pay for his smokes, Melvin nodded and disappeared through the doorway. Bess picked up her pocketbook from the counter, pulled out her compact, powdered her nose, and haughtily rushed out. I knew Bess was aggravated with Melvin, but I suspected she better get over it. More than likely Melvin had women running for his cigarettes everywhere he ever worked.

I sat, contemplating all the notations Bess and I had made by the seven men's names on our tablet. I reached for the threatening letter and the wadded up version, read them again, and laid them alongside the ledger. How long had the wadded paper been on the floor of Dixie's house? Had the murderer thrown it down? Had each of these men been blackmailed by Dixie? How long had Dixie's scheme been perpetrated? Were the men paying blackmail money to Dixie and then paying for her other special services at the same time? So many unanswered questions…but I was sure the answer to Dixie's untimely death was right here in this ledger. I only hoped Bess and I had time to pursue all this evidence before Sam Turner was implicated and arrested for murder...or before somebody figured out it was Bess's green shoe that Biscuit had been munching on. We owed Molly some sort of explanation, but for right now, we might as well tell her as little as possible. Right after lunch, a quick trip to visit Molly was to be next on our agenda.

* * *

Melvin was busy repairing cracks in the overhead plaster of the hall ceiling as we gathered our purses to leave for Molly and Sam's house early that afternoon. Bess, I'm afraid, was overseeing Melvin a little too closely. I could see the look of relief spread across his face as we started to leave. "Now if you need us for anything, we'll be back directly. I believe you've missed a little crack over in the corner, and check that little crevice over there," Bess instructed, as she pointed in one direction of the ceiling to another.

"Yes, ma'am. You sure have eagle eyes."

"Well, I do pride myself with my eyesight. Oh, and what about that little tiny gap over by the door and..."

"Come on, Bess. We've got to go now if we want to catch Molly at home by herself before Sam returns home from school."

I'm sure Melvin was greatly relieved to see us leave, but Vonion certainly wasn't. He glared at us from a distance as we left in Bess's car. He was under one of the many pecan trees out in the orchard, crawling around, picking up pecans off the ground. I suspect he was thinking we needed to be helping, and I really did feel guilty leaving him with such a big chore.

Vonion knew the importance of gathering the nuts off the ground quickly after they fell. As well as the price falling, we had to deal with the squirrels stealing them and the birds cracking them and pecking out the insides. We shared our bounty with all of God's creatures, or maybe I should say, they shared with us.

I had every intention of helping Vonion later that afternoon, after our visit with Molly. "I'll help with the pecans this year, Bee," Bess promised, as we drove up the lane. She must have been having guilty feelings, also.

Molly and Sam's little rented house was two blocks from downtown and three blocks from the school. Either Sam or Molly could have walked almost anywhere in town. We knew Sam had a car, and we also knew Molly, on occasion, kept the car to use during the day for errands. Today the car wasn't in the driveway. "Sam probably drove the car to work this morning," I said, as I looked out of the car window as Bess drove by. We were casing the house before actually stopping in for the visit.

"Let's park the car at my house and walk over. It's only a couple of blocks." Bess was finally, at long last, catching on to the detective business. "We need the exercise, and there's really no need for everybody in town knowing our business. I'm sure Molly would want us to be very discreet in all our meetings with her."

"That's a good idea," I answered. "I hope Molly's at home. Now, remember, let me do most of the talking."

"Okay. Okay. I know! For Pete's sake, you'd think I didn't have a brain. I'll let you do the talking, but remember, don't say more than is absolutely necessary. Just tell Molly that Sam's been visiting another lady, and let that be it. That gives her enough information to confront Sam, and that's all she needs to know from us. We did what we were supposed to do; we found out where Sam's been going and what he's spending money on. I'm sure Molly will be devastated with the news, but she probably already suspects something just as horrible. Molly can make up her mind if she wants to dig deeper or let bygones be bygones, and forgive Sam. Maybe he'll make some sort of amends, and they can go on with their lives. I'm sure Sam has learned a valuable lesson from all this."

"I certainly hope you're right." We drove on over to Bess's house and left the car in her driveway. "You know you're going to miss living in your nice house here in town, don't you?"

"I probably will some, but I'll be satisfied. Knowing Freddy and Jean and the children have a good roof over their heads and plenty of room will be so comforting. I hope you don't have any second thoughts about me moving in with you."

"Oh, no, of course not. I'm looking forward to it." *I had my fingers crossed as I answered so I didn't consider it to be a fib.*

We briskly walked the two blocks to Sam and Molly's house. *I had really been getting my exercise lately.* "Look at the condition of this place, Bess. It looks as if nobody really cares about it anymore." We immediately noticed an old bunched-up blanket and a stained, stiff dishrag hanging on a sagging clothesline to the rear. Overturned in the weed-infested, uncut grass was a large metal trashcan, surrounded by cans and bottles. "Some stray dog must have made that mess," I said, as we surveyed the mess. "I just can't believe Molly would let this place go down like this. It looks so neglected, doesn't it?"

"It certainly does. What this town really needs is a dogcatcher," Bess answered as we stood out in the front yard. I keep telling them down at city hall. I've had to resort to using a BB gun to keep dogs out of my trash. Stray dogs are running all over town and breeding like houseflies."

We walked on up to the forlorn-looking front porch, where chairs should have been placed around for a friendly afternoon conversation. A potted plant or two would have cheered up the small drab porch, but none was there. "Molly certainly doesn't go to any great lengths to make the outside of the house very attractive," Bess said, as she glanced around.

"But she did tell us she didn't have any money for extras, and it does cost money to paint a house and buy porch furniture," I had to add in Molly's defense.

We knocked and waited. Nobody seemed to be stirring around in the house. We knocked again. "Looks like nobody's picked up the mail today. The mail's still in the mailbox," Bess casually commented. I glanced over at the little metal box hanging on the side of the house and noticed a couple of letters sticking out at the top. "Nobody's home. Let's go," Bess said, as we waited on the porch.

"I guess you're right." I reached over to the mailbox and grabbed the mail. "Nothing but a couple of bills—one from the power people, marked 'overdue,' and another from an insurance company," I said, as I scanned the envelopes. I quickly put them back into the box.

"Bee, I can't believe you would look at another person's mail. You must have forgotten Earnest Lee's warning to me about tampering with federal mail. We could go to jail just for touching those letters. Now come on and let's go." Bess turned to leave, and I nervously grabbed the doorknob. *Maybe it was just a reaction to a closed door—I don't know—I just couldn't help myself.* The door wasn't locked, and it opened with just the slightest push.

"Bess, come on. Let's go in. Nobody's home."

"No!"

"We might not have another chance to investigate Sam's house. We need to find some evidence of some kind to keep him from becoming a murder suspect. It's our duty to investigate. Now come on." I grabbed Bess by the arm, pulled her in, and closed the door behind us. "Do you think anybody saw us come in?"

"The Lord saw us, and we certainly aren't making any brownie points with Him these days. We can't keep doing this, Bee."

"I don't mean the Lord, for heaven's sake. Did anybody else see us?"

"I didn't see anybody on the street, but Mrs. Ricketson, across the street, was probably peeping out of her window. You know she doesn't have anything better to do than to snoop on people."

"Maybe she missed us. Anyway we're in, so we might as well look around."

"Well, let's hurry. If the Lord comes back while we're in here snooping, I'm sure we'll miss the boat to heaven, and you know we'll never get another chance. What are we looking for anyway?"

"Anything to tell us what Sam's been doing for the last few days."

"Oh, Bee, look how drab this place is. That chair over there looks like my old chair I took to the junkyard a few weeks ago...*Hey*, that *is* my chair! Poor Molly doesn't have a decent thing in this house. The deprived child has done without while that lusting, two-timing husband of hers has been carousing around like a dog in heat. I'll bet that stove over there in the kitchen was purchased in nineteen twenty-five, and it was probably bought used back then."

"Bess, look for clues, for heaven's sake. We aren't in here to redecorate. Now look!"

"Well, he nor Molly washed the dishes this morning or last night. Look at all those dirty dishes in the sink."

"Bess, that's a real clue. There's only one plate with crusty eggs on it. One coffee cup and one juice glass.

There's a plate with—let me see—I don't know what that is. Look in the garbage can."

"There's an empty can of corned beef, some egg shells, and some coffee grounds in here."

"Sam must have been eating by himself," I quickly assumed. "Wait! There's another plate in the sink with something smeared on it. Maybe that's catsup or something. Whatever it is, it's turned black."

"Maybe Molly ate the corned beef, and Sam ate something else."

"No, she would have washed the dishes. Definitely, Sam ate alone, more than one time. What else is in that garbage can?

"A wrapper for some kind of meat is in here," Bess answered, as she tried to hold her breath and talk at the same time. "Sam must have cooked a hamburger or something. Whew, this thing stinks to high heaven!"

"Look in the oven. I'll bet there's a greasy frying pan in there. That's where I keep mine before I wash it."

"You're right," Bess answered, as she opened the door to the oven. "There's a greasy frying pan in here and a boiler with something black in it."

"I told you!" I adamantly replied. "Sam's been by himself for a day or two. He's cooked and stuck the pots and pans in the oven instead of washing them."

Bess opened the refrigerator door and smelled a milk bottle that was sitting on the shelf beside a piece of unwrapped, dried-up cheese. "Yuck, the milk's sour, and somebody didn't even put the top back on the bottle. Men don't know how to do a thing. They are all alike. I had to stay on Fred all the time about putting the lid back on anything before putting it back in the refrigerator."

"Let's look around in the bedroom, Bess."

"Bee, I'm not going one step farther. We need to get out of here. Sheriff Ledbetter won't think too kindly of us snooping around in the school principal's house... Hey...Where are you going?"

"I told you—in the bedroom. Now come on. Don't be such a scaredy-cat."

"I *am* a scaredy-cat, and I don't have any ambition to be a jailbird."

"Look, Bess. Only one person slept in the bed last night. Only one side's messed up. And there are Sam's pajama bottoms on the floor. Molly has definitely not been here for a day or two. I know she would have picked up Sam's pajamas. Look in the dirty clothes hamper. How many pieces of clothes are in there? Molly probably keeps the clothes washed up."

"There are two pairs of Sam's pants in here, and two dress shirts...and two...oh Bee, I'm not looking through Sam's dirty underwear. You can look for yourself. This detective business has gotten out of hand when you want me to count dirty drawers. Why do I always get the dirty jobs?"

"You are so-o finicky about what you touch. You've handled lots of dirty underwear before; after all, you raised two boys and were married years and years. Are there any of Molly's clothes in there?"

"No, but there are a tablecloth and a couple of handkerchiefs in here," Bess answered, after she dumped the contents of the hamper on the floor to keep from touching anything and began kicking the clothes around with one foot. "What do you think dirty clothes mean, anyway?"

"It means that Molly definitely has not been here for a couple of days. Look in the closet. Are Molly's clothes still in there?"

"Her clothes, what little she has, seem to be here."

"Where is Molly?" I pondered out loud. "She must have left, but here's her purse and her coat."

"Maybe she changed pocketbooks before she left. I do that all the time," Bess answered thoughtfully.

"Her little change purse and a comb are in the pocketbook. I don't know; she could have changed purses. It's possible, I guess. Keep looking. Check all the pockets in Sam's clothes, and I'll check Molly's clothes. You never know, there might be some kind of note or something stuck down in one."

"Nothing but a chewing gum wrapper in Sam's pants," Bess replied, after she had turned the last pocket inside out. Oh, here's a handkerchief that's been wadded up. Yuk!"

"Nothing in Molly's dresses, either. Bess, check out the bathroom."

Bess walked to the bathroom door and looked in. "The potted plant on the windowsill is wilted and almost dead. The trash can is overflowing. The toilet tissue roll is empty, and there's a dirty glass by the sink. Two toothbrushes are in the jar, and the toothpowder is on the shelf."

"Molly's gone, and I'm sure she left in a big hurry." I almost surprised myself with my next statement. "Could she have been forcibly taken out?"

Bess gasped. "You really don't think something terrible has happened to Molly?"

"I don't know. All we really know is she's not here, and she hasn't been here for a couple of days."

We continued plundering, opening and going through drawers and cabinets. I turned the contents of a trash can unto the floor and quickly noticed a wadded up receipt for a tire repair at Floyd's Station on Monday. I thoughtfully read it to Bess. "'Tire repair and patch. Two dollars received.' Bess, it should be fairly simple to check this out with Elmo. It could have some bearing on our investigation." I stuck the receipt in my pocket. "Bess, pick up all the trash, and I'll stick these dirty clothes back in the hamper. Let's get outta here while the getting's good."

"That's what I've been waiting to hear! I'm right behind you!"

CHAPTER FOURTEEN

We quickly scoped out the street from behind the living room curtain. Noticing no living creatures about except an old tabby cat sunning on Mrs. Ricketson's front porch, we quickly sneaked out the front door and hurried back down the sidewalk toward Bess's house. "Bess, I'm determined to get to the bottom of all this."

"I am too, Bee. I'm more than a little concerned about Molly. You don't really think something terrible has happened to her, do you?"

"I don't know what to think. We can only pray that the child is all right. Why don't we ride over by the schoolhouse and see if Sam's car's still in the parking lot before we head over to Floyd's to talk to Elmo about Sam's tire. Maybe, by chance, Molly has the car."

"Good idea."

As we turned the corner in the car, a real investigative thought kicked into my brain. "Let's ride around town a little before heading over to the school. That way, if anybody's watching us, it'll confuse them. We don't want nosy people getting any ideas about what we're up to."

"Okay, I only hope I've got enough gas. Maybe Elmo won't realize we're drilling him for answers about Sam's tires if my gas supply is really low."

It took two whole minutes to tour town. We rode by the courthouse, the library, and past the funeral home. Mr. Lawson had the hearse, with the rear doors wide open, backed up to the front door of the funeral home as if he had been unloading something.

"Who died?" I asked Bess, as we rode by.

"Beats me. I haven't heard a thing."

After a quick detour by Thelma's Cut and Curl and back around by Jake's Hardware, we made a quick run by The Jeffersontown First Baptist Church and the cemetery, cruised Broad Street, and watching closely for pedestrians, turned at the post office. *I really didn't know if Bess was attempting to avoid one particular pedestrian, or aiming for him. Thank heavens; Earnest Lee was nowhere to be seen. I thought it was probably my civic duty to warn that poor man that Bess might be gunning for him before he really gets hurt.* We had hit the high spots and now headed for the school. Sam's car was parked right in front, along with all the teachers' cars.

"There's Sam's car," Bess excitedly pointed in that direction. "Now what do we do?"

"Wait just a minute, Bess," I said, as I glanced in my side view mirror after we rode by. "Hey, Sam just left the building and is walking toward his car! Let's follow him! We might find something out. You never know."

"I just told you I was low on gas. We can't go far."

"Don't worry about your gas, Bess." I glanced over at the instrument panel. "Your gauge shows you've got a little. We've probably got enough to go to Atlanta and back."

"You're out of your mind."

"I know I was exaggerating a little. But don't worry, we'll get some soon." We pulled over to the side of the street and watched Sam crank up and head out. He drove right past us without even glancing our way and soon turned onto River Road, a winding, narrow, dirt road that connects to Route 3 after it crosses over the river about two miles out from town. We pulled out after Sam was a safe distance ahead and rode past the butchering plant and a few houses and barns sprinkled alongside of the road, following behind in the dust of Sam's car. Sam slowed his car as he neared the wood-framed bridge that stretches across the flowing waters of the river, and suddenly stopped in the middle of the bridge. Bess quickly slammed on the brake to keep from getting within his sight.

"Pull over there in the bushes, out of sight," I quickly instructed Bess.

"What's Sam doing, stopping right on top of the bridge? Doesn't he know that's dangerous? Somebody might come barreling down the road from the other direction and cream him," Bess admonished, as she maneuvered the car off the road and into the undergrowth beside the road. "I hope we don't get stuck in these bushes, and my car better not get scratched. We don't have enough money in the business treasury for a paint job on my car."

"Quit worrying about everything, for Pete's sake. Now, let's get out and sneak up closer to the bridge so we can see what Sam's up to. Open your door gently, and don't close it. We've got to be really quiet."

With knees creaking, backs bent, and heads down, we sneaked through the thick bushes to get a clearer view of Sam. From our lookout position behind a fallen tree, we could tell Sam had gotten out of the car and was standing by the wooden railing of the bridge, smoking a cigarette. Appearing haggard, as if he hadn't slept for a while, Sam remained there, motionless, except for the movement of his hands as he smoked, staring into the dark water, seemingly deep in thought. After a moment, he threw his cigarette into the river and walked over to the trunk of the car. He reached into his pants pocket for the keys and opened the trunk. He struggled to lift a large, cumbersome, tubular object, wrapped in canvas, out of the trunk and carried it over to the side of the bridge. Maneuvering it slowly over the railing, he dropped it into the moving waters of the river. We heard a loud *splash* as the heavy force hit the water. I could hear and feel Bess's gasp when her hot breath hit my neck, as Sam stood there looking down. He remained still, immersed in the sudden silence, seemingly spellbound by the living force of the river.

We didn't dare move. My imagination went into total overdrive, as I'm sure did Bess's. Bess soon began to shift from one foot to another. She gasped, grabbed me for support, and I swayed as I attempted to hold the both of us up as a little black snake crawled out of the brush about four feet away. It must have thought the coast was clear, as it slowly left a winding trail directly in front of us and moved toward a large flat rock. I hurriedly placed my hand over Bess's open mouth, since I was certain she was on the verge of screaming bloody murder. Somehow she held it in. Frozen in position, but posed to move if need be, we watched the little snake crawl on, as if he wasn't interested in us at all.

Our focus immediately returned to the bridge. Sam was still motionless, gazing down into the deep water, but he soon reached down and relieved himself into the river. Bess swooned and grasped me even tighter. He zipped his pants back up, walked around to the trunk, slammed it closed, and drove off. Thank heavens! He didn't turn the car around but continued on toward Route 3 and then probably back into town. We watched as the last of the dust floated down to blanket the sandy road, and then we hurried toward the bridge, only to find the waters flowing swiftly on with the object of Sam's errand gone from our sight and probably several hundred yards downstream.

"Holy Moly, Bess. Do you think a body was in that rolled up canvas?

"You mean 'Holy Molly,' don't you?"

"And she's probably singing with the angels in heaven by now," I sadly added.

I reached over to steady myself with the rail as Bess collapsed and slid down into a sitting position. "Are you all right? You're not going to pass out, are you? " I asked anxiously, as I patted her on the face. "Bess, talk!"

"Quit, Bee. I'm all right, just a little faintified."

"Bess, could that really have been Molly?"

"Oh, it was Molly all right," Bess quickly answered, as she was regaining her composure. "That husband of hers is a bona fide murderer! Now, before the evidence is too far gone, don't you think we need to inform Sheriff Ledbetter about what we've just seen?"

"Maybe if we can get to the sheriff station fast enough, he can get to the body before it gets too far downstream." Then after a second thought, I cautiously added, "You don't suppose he wouldn't believe us, do you? He might say Sam was just dumping garbage or something."

"Bee, we've just left the man's house. He doesn't throw garbage or anything else away. The house was a mess. Have you already forgotten?"

Regaining my self-assurance, I replied, "We do have a civic duty to tell Sheriff Ledbetter exactly what we've just witnessed."

"We most assuredly do!" Bess answered confidently, as we hurried back toward the car in a panic.

"Let's get outta here," I said, as I slammed my door.

* * *

Bess quickly looked in the rearview mirror to check her lipstick and pat her hair. *Habits are so hard to break.* She nervously attempted to turn the ignition. Nothing happened. She stomped the foot feed several times and tried again. Nothing happened again. "What's wrong with this car?" I asked, as Bess anxiously tried a third time.

"I'm probably out of gas. I told you I was low, but no-o, you said, 'You've got plenty'."

"What else can happen to us? We need to be at the sheriff's office right now."

"And we need to be checking up on old Melvin about now too. He's probably out of Lucky Strikes again and has paint smeared all over the floor."

"Don't worry about Melvin, for Pete's sake. Let him get his own cigarettes. Well, Bess, I guess we don't have much of a choice. Let's walk. Get your keys and pocketbook, lock the door, and let's go."

"Bee, I told you we were almost out of gas, but, no-o, you didn't believe me. I guess you believe me now. I don't know how I let you talk me into getting into these situations," Bess argued as we opened the car doors and attempted to step through high overgrown grass and weeds.

I didn't answer. I knew she was right.

Down the dusty road, over the bridge, and on and on we trudged. "I'm probably ruining another pair of shoes, and these cost more than those green ones. Put me down for seven ninety-nine this time."

"Listen, Bess, don't ever mention those green shoes again. Somebody might hear you."

"Well, I don't see a living soul around here to hear, unless you consider that old crow over there in the sky, or that squirrel that just ran across the road in front of us."

"I'm just saying…"

"Oh, all right. I get your message." *Bess was getting pretty ornery by now.*

"You need to start wearing sensible shoes now, anyway. You're about to become a farm woman, and a top-notch detective woman on top of that."

"Just because I'm moving to the farm doesn't mean I have to dress dowdy. I do have my standards, you know."

"I guess I forgot."

"I'm thirsty," Bess whined as we walked on. Suddenly a motor noise filled the silence of the countryside. We stopped and listened as the sound came closer and closer. As luck would have it, Earl Williford, a crusty old bachelor who lives a piece down the road, off on an old logging trail, came barreling down the road toward us in his old beat-up pickup truck. Earl, whose hair is never combed or cut properly, and with a mustache that seems to be perpetually stained with tobacco juice, was the victim of a robbery last year when his run-down home was ransacked and robbed.

"Stop him," Bess anxiously said, and grabbed my hand to pull me out of the middle of the dusty road. "We can catch a ride to Floyd's with him."

Earl had already spotted us and was pulling over to the side of the road. He leaned his head out of the truck window and spat. With a jaw still brimming with chewing tobacco, he hollered, "What in blue blazes you two a'doin' out walkin' on this here deserted road? You not a'walkin' fer your health, I know not."

"Oh, Earl, we're so glad to see you," I called back, as we hurried toward the truck—but not too close. Dammit Junior, Earl's new bulldog, with a mouth big enough to neatly fit one of our heads inside, was barking and drooling all at the same time. His big neck and head were hanging over the side of the back of the truck, and I suspected he was ready to pounce on us at any minute.

"Shet yor mouth, dog," Earl hollered. "I done told you about all that barkin'. I'm gonna leave you to the house next time if'n you don't quiet down."

Dammit Junior lowered his head and whined.

"He's a mite young yet, ladies, and hasn't learnt no manners. I don't think he'll bite you, jest scare you a bit. He's a good watch dog, though. He ain't as good as ole Dammit was, but he's a good bit o'company to me. You know, I'm by myself."

"Er, yes, we knew, Earl," I replied. "I'm glad you found a replacement for Dammit." Earl's dog, Dammit, was killed by the robber and left out in the yard for the buzzards "to make a meal off of," Sheriff Ledbetter had said.

"Earl, we seem to have given out of gas down the road," Bess explained, not taking a step closer to the truck. "Is there any way you could take us to Floyd's to get a can of gas and bring us back to the car?" Then with her head tilted down and sounding a little too sugary to my notion, she added, "I know it'd be a bit of trouble, but we surely would appreciate it."

Earl, evidently picking up on that sweet expression of Bess's, replied, "I can do better than that, ladies. I got a can a'gas in the back of the pickup. H'it's your'n if'n you want it."

"Oh, yes, we want it," I immediately answered, with hope in my voice. *Maybe too much.*

"Well, get in, then. I'll ride you to yor car. Where in blazes is it?"

"Just on the other side of the bridge, in the bushes," Bess answered, as we started around the back of the pickup.

"What y'all doing in the bushes?" Earl asked.

"Oh, we were just admiring nature and decided to pull over," Bess answered, as if that was a good enough explanation. Bess grabbed the door handle and motioned for me to get in.

"After you," I replied. Bess gave me a funny look but slid in anyway. With Bess right beside Earl, she was a better target for his roving hand than she realized. *She just didn't know about that hand YET.* I would have suggested we ride in the back, but with a choice between Earl's romantic advances and Dammit Junior's big, slobbering mouth, I felt we would be better off with Earl. *What a choice, but at least we weren't walking!*

Earl reached down and roughly started changing gears. His big gnarled hand accidently, but maybe on purpose, brushed the side of Bess's leg. She didn't flinch or move a muscle. Earl turned the truck around, and we rode back over the bridge and to the car. A perfect gentleman couldn't have been nicer. *What a surprise! He must be buttering us up for something.* He poured the gasoline into the tank from the can and remarked, "That'll get you to town. Now go on straight to Floyd's."

"Oh, we absolutely will. What do we owe you, Earl?" I asked, as he screwed the top back onto the can.

"Not a thang. Just remember me sometimes around supper time. I heard tell you was moving back to the farm, Ms. Bess. That'll be a double dose of goodness." *I told you he was buttering us up for something!*

"Well, uh, thank you again, Earl. We'll plan something sometimes," Bess replied, with a little less sweetness in her tone.

We followed Earl's truck back over the bridge and down the road until he turned onto the tree-lined trail toward his house. "I see why you wanted me to sit beside Earl now. He accidently touched my leg when he was changing gears. I absolutely froze!" *Did she really think I hadn't noticed.*

"I'm sure it was just a mishap, Bess. I suppose we'll have to entertain Earl some night soon."

"Ugh, we might as well ask Old Man Peterson and Foy Jackson as well. We can get all our entertainment obligations over in one fell swoop. We'll put our body armor on and fight them all off at one time."

I laughed out loud at the thought of us entertaining all the old goats in the neighborhood. What a night that would be! And as much as Bess liked to protest, she liked having a man to admire her and give her a little attention. *The pickin's aren't much around here, but like Mama used to say, "An old fence post is better than no fence post at all."*

I just wasn't looking to hold up my fence right now.

CHAPTER FIFTEEN

We decided to follow Earl's advice and fill our tank with gasoline before we looked up our illustrious sheriff. Sheriff Ledbetter had actually become our comrade and confidant over the last year, and as bad as I hate to admit it, he'd gotten a tad smarter. He'd come around to our way of thinking several times since we had butted heads in our initial investigation regarding Preacher Henry and his so-called sister. *Oh, that's another story.*

"Why do you think the hearse was parked out in front of the funeral home earlier today unless Mr. Lawson was unloading a body?" Bess asked me, as she applied rouge while driving along. "He usually keeps that thing in the back shed, covered with a big ole bedspread to keep the dust off. I haven't heard about any deaths in the community...except perhaps poor Molly's, I'm afraid." She closed her rouge case and reached in her pocketbook for a tissue.

Attempting to brace myself with my feet and legs against any sudden crashes, I pleaded, "Bess, please keep your eyes on the road. We're likely to have a wreck if you don't start watching the road a little more carefully, and then we'll both join Molly in the great beyond. That's about the only thing we haven't experienced today."

"I have this car completely under my control. You have gotten so skittish lately. I'm beginning to think you might need to get on some kind of nerve medication."

"If I keep riding with you, I might have to. Just please pay attention to the road."

"I'm watching, I'm watching!"

Waiting as Bess calmed down a bit, I chatted on. "You know, I did hear Thelma say Shirley's Aunt Dora is very close to death's door. She might have decided to go ahead and throw in the towel. That dear old soul's had a hard life. She's one of those people who has been old and decrepit as far back as I can remember. I can't ever recall her without a cane and hearing horn. And how she's put up with Shirley all these years is absolutely beyond me." Shirley, Jeffersontown's aging librarian, has continued to live in her family's ancestral home her entire life without the benefit of husband or beau. She mourns her solitary life but has yet to find an eligible suitor who would put up with her abrasive personality or her relentless smoking. *I pity the one that ever does.*

"We really ought to find out about Aunt Dora in case we need to start cooking for the 'setting up.' Shirley might have family from out of town coming in to feed, and you know as well as I do, she can't cook beans without them scorching. We can't let our social obligations go just because we're on an important case."

"We'll have to ask Elmo when we get to the station. Maybe he'll know something. I sure do hope he's gonna be talkative today. We've got to get more information about Sam's tire repair. That could be very important evidence."

"My hair and makeup are so badly in need of repair," Bess mused, as she checked herself in the rearview mirror again and adjusted her earbobs. "I hate to see anybody the way I look." *I guess I could fuss and fume until the cows come home, and nothing I say would ever register.*

"You look fine. Now, pull into the station, and remember, let me…"

"Do most of the talkin'. I know."

Bess pulled the car into the grimy little station, careful not to hit any of the containers of oily rags or worn-out machinery parts that were cluttering up the place. "Let's get on out of the car so we can talk," I said, as a gangly young man, dressed in a grease-smeared mechanic's uniform, walked out of the building toward us.

"Howdy. Watch where you step. There's grease and oil everywhere. I ain't had time to clean up the place today. Been too busy pumping gas and waiting on customers. Everybody wants their fan belts checked or their radiators filled with water. All that extra service takes time. I ain't complain', though. That's what I'm here fer."

"We're in need of gasoline," I said to the young man, as we opened our car doors. "Where's Elmo? He usually waits on us."

"He's took the day off. I'm helpin' him out now. What'll it be, regular or high-test?"

"Regular, and fill my tank completely up, please," Bess answered. "And check my oil."

"Oh, I will, and I'll clean your windshield too. You two ladies, just step aside. It won't take me but a jiff."

Careful not to step in any of the numerous pools of oil or grease, we walked over to stand next to a rack of used tires. "You don't happen to know what Elmo's doing today?" I asked.

"No'um, I don't really know what he's doing. He just said he'd be back later on this afternoon. As pretty as the weather is, I'd bet he went a'fishin'. That's his hobby, if'n you didn't know. Yes ma'am, he loves to fish. Generally goes to the river, I think. He's liable to bring home a string of red bellies."

"Well, that's nice," Bess answered. It seemed as if Elmo had a talkative new assistant. Now if he only had the information we needed.

"How long have you been helping out down here? Er, I'm sorry, I didn't catch your name."

"Donnelle. My name's Donnelle. My daddy's name is Donald, and my mama's name is Nell. So they named me..."

"Donnelle. That's nice, Donnelle. I don't believe I know your parents. Are they from around here?" asked Bess.

"No'um. Elmo is my mama's second cousin, once removed. Most of my people are from Savannah." Donnelle started the pump. "I've been told I was some kin to Floyd, too. You know Floyd, who used to own the station here, until he was killed a year or so ago. That was so-o heart rendering. Mama really ain't over it yet. She takes everything so hard. She cried a week when our milk cow died from old age. Oh, to answer your question, I almost forgot. I been here about two weeks now, give or take a day or so. I'm staying at the boardinghouse for right now. Maybe later on I'll find something a little more permanent. I ain't really crazy about Miss Airy's boardinghouse. She cooks good, but half the time we ain't got hot water."

Donnelle was very chatty. I wondered if he knew anything about Sam's tire repair. "Donnelle, do you do tire repairs by yourself?"

"Oh, yessum. I do 'bout everything 'round here." Donnelle proudly puffed out his chest. "I can even work on your engine or your brakes. There ain't much I can't do."

"You didn't happen to work on Sam Turner's car a few days ago. His wife, Molly, mentioned that he had a little work done here, and he was well pleased with the service."

"Yessum, I shore did. Now there's one you can't tell nothin' to. I don't care how educated you are, sometimes you need to listen to somebody who knows more than you do about your vehicle. He's as stubborn as the day is long, too. Oops, I need to shut my mouth. Elmo told me not to talk about the customers, and here I go, yakkin' away."

"I need to pay more attention to my tires than I do," Bess replied. I could see she had an ulterior motive, so I just listened. "How far can one go on a bad tire?"

"Well ma'am, it's all according to how bad they are. Now you take Mr. Sam Turner. Elmo had told him and told him his tires needed attention, but he wouldn't pay Elmo no mind. What he really needs is a whole new set, but that'll never happen."

"You don't say, Donnelle. That is very interesting. You really are knowledgeable about cars and tires and such. Sam should have listened to you. Now, Donnelle, when did Sam bring his car in for a tire repair? I'll bet he waited too long. He didn't have a blowout on the road or anything, did he?" Bess was on a roll.

"Oh, no ma'am. Nothing like that." Donnelle stopped the pump and hung the nozzle back up. "He brung his car in—let me think, I believe it was early Monday morning—and had to leave it. That front left tire was so far gone you could 'bout see clear to the inside air. I have my doubts it'd made it back to his house. He don't even keep a spare. An educated man like that, and he don't know nothin' about a tire. He left here walkin'. Anyway, we patched the worser tire up, and he picked the car up just this morning. He's riding on a lick and a promise right now. I warned him about going out of town on them sorry patched up thangs. He don't listen, though."

"Well, that certainly has taught me a lesson, Donnelle. I'm definitely going to watch my tires more closely from now on. You are so knowledgeable about tires and all. You've been very helpful, young man," Bess added. *She knows how to flatter a man.*

Donnelle beamed with pride. "Oh, and let me tell you about Old Man Peterson's tires. They's 'bout as bad. We've told him and told…"

"Oh, yes, I'm sure you have. People need to listen to you a little closer. Let me pay for my gasoline now. How much?"

"That'll be two thirty-seven. I've been so busy talking, I haven't cleaned the windshield or checked the oil. It'll take just a minute."

"Do hurry, Donnelle. We've got an appointment to keep," I replied, as all the new information began to crowd my thoughts.

"And that hearse is another story. Mr. Lawson is so-o tight. He's done let the fan belt dry rot in that thing. I had to put a new one on earlier today. Belt cost him a dollar and a half." Then Donnelle proudly added, "Labor was fifty-five cents."

"You know, we noticed the hearse backed up to the front door of the funeral home earlier today, and we were wondering if Mr. Lawson was unloading a body," I replied.

"Oh, no ma'am, he weren't. Mr. Lawson left here a little while ago. He was going back to the funeral home to give the hearse a good cleaning. In my opinion, you can't keep a hearse too clean. He was probably getting all those portable chairs out. He ought not to haul that kind of stuff around in that vehicle. That's what he's got a pickup truck for. You know a hearse's kind'a holy, in a way. Can't tell him nothin', though..."

We had heard enough. "Well, thanks, Donnelle. We really need to be going," Bess said as she paid him. We climbed back in the car, much wiser than when we had driven in. Bess drove off, scraping the car's gears again and checking her hairdo at the same time. I suppose she had become so accustomed to the racket under her hood, she didn't even notice it any more.

As Bess continued to shift gears, I held on and said, "Bess, I think we've found a real honey hole for information. We can bring my car in next time we need some gas or info. Oh, and thank goodness, Aunt Dora must still have a little breath in her worn-out old body. We don't have time to worry about cooking right now."

"Thank heavens!" All gassed up and full of information, we set out toward the sheriff's office. "Bee, I believe we can take Sam's name off our list of suspects in Dixie's murder. He couldn't have gotten over to Burt County without his car, and I just can't believe the man would borrow a car to go and...you know...murder somebody."

"It does seem doubtful. But listen, Bess, let's don't check him completely off the list. He might not have done Dixie in, but he didn't have to travel very far to murder his own wife. I suppose he did have to wait until today to get rid of her body since he didn't have a car to haul her off in." Shaking my head sadly, I sighed, and said, "I just can't believe poor Molly is dead. I feel responsible in a way. We should have done something sooner, for goodness sake. She was so young. She didn't deserve to die at the hands of her own husband."

"I know. But what are we going to tell the sheriff? Bee, we really don't have any concrete evidence about Molly's disappearance or murder yet. Maybe we need to wait for Molly to be missing a little longer. Sheriff Ledbetter's not going to attempt to drag that river with the information we have, anyway. With that fast current, Molly's body's already been washed way downstream, but I know it's down there somewhere, stuck to a limb or wedged under a rock."

"I guess you're right. Let's wait to see the sheriff until we know a little more."

Bess made a U-turn right in the middle of the road and headed back toward Route 3 and home. I braced myself again and lectured Bess. "Bess, I've told you and_told you to quit making those turns like that. You are absolutely determined to get yourself arrested for disorderly driving."

"Not one soul, other than you, saw me. I know how to drive this car. Now, it's way past time to see what kind of mess Melvin's made."

"Okay, but Bess, even though we think Sam is probably innocent of Dixie's murder, we need to continue our investigation. We know more than the law since we were the first to witness the murder scene, and besides that, we have the ledger. That ledger is absolutely the key. Just think how our cap will be feathered when we crack the case. Everybody in two or three counties will want us to work on all their investigations. We'll be famous!"

"We'll be famous all right when that sheriff over in Burt County finds out that it was my green shoe Biscuit was chewing on. We could become the murder suspects; after all, we were at the crime scene. I'm sure that mailman or that young woman who saw us walking down the street noticed I was barefooted. That little boy noticed right off."

"That could be a problem. We probably need to disguise ourselves when we go back to Burt County."

"Well, it'll have to wait until tomorrow. I'm absolutely exhausted. I just want to go home and soak my feet."

"Well, get yourself prepared, because first thing in the morning, we are back on the case. And wear sensible shoes tomorrow."

"Oh, I will, and I do hope Melvin's made progress today."

Suddenly thinking about home, sweet home, I jokingly replied, "You reckon Vonion's still speaking to us? I imagine he's been fuming all day long about us leaving him alone with 'burtsitis,' 'aurther-ritis,' or one of those other 'ritis' brothers that he says keeps him company most of the time. Bless his ole heart!"

CHAPTER SIXTEEN

The ledger had to be the key, I thought to myself as I lay in the bed soaking in the stillness and quietness of the night. I was allowing the murder investigation to consume my thoughts, but that's what a good detective does. I would bet money something had spun out of control with one of those gentlemen callers of Dixie's, and a struggle took place. Dixie, just as Molly, had died at the hands of an abusive killer, someone probably stronger and bigger, with anger fueling him into a rage of passion.

Dixie's blackmailing scheme had come to life, and someone had wanted it stopped. If not Sam, who? Maybe somebody who wanted sexual favors...no, that could be bought and paid for with money. It had to be somebody who desperately wanted something that Dixie wasn't willing to give. Whatever it was, it had cost Dixie her most precious possession, her own life. Even an unworthy young woman such as Dixie didn't deserve to die at the hands of a vicious murderer.

My mind wondered...*What would Will really think if he knew about my new endeavor?* He never would have dreamed how involved I had become in the world of murder and mayhem. The price of cotton and corn or how much rain had fallen had consumed his life, many times overriding everything else. Never even knowing any difference, I had always taken a backseat to his vocation of farming the land, never really demanded much of his attention. What was the difference? Now, at long last, I had a vocation, maybe not as conventional as his, but none the less, a reason to get out of the bed in the morning other than to wish Vonion good morning or quiz him about whether he had reached far enough into the hens' nest for all the eggs. My life was taking on new meaning and I was feeling alive again.

Margaret had her own life, and I had one too. Even if Margaret married Walter (which was my heartfelt desire), I knew in my heart that their union would never include me. What was left of my life was to be lived on the outside of their tiny circle, hopefully a circle that included children. That was the way it should be. *I had to constantly remind myself of that.*

My thoughts lingered as I lay there as new and strange ideas passed about in my head. I was living in two worlds now. Really, I believe every man lives in two, maybe even three, worlds. The world of the here and now: the farm, Margaret, social obligations, trying to meet all my financial needs. And then there's this new world looming ahead: excitement, a challenge, and fewer boundaries. And of course, always the past. Everyone lives with memories. I knew I was the culmination of all my years, some spent in childhood and others as an adult, but always following the guidance of Mama and Daddy, and then of Will. Now I was beginning to experience something else, a sort of freedom, but it, too, had limitations. That's what life is all about—adjusting to your limits and still living to your full potential. Thank You, God, for giving me this time to ponder about things. Thank You, God, for helping me realize how fortunate I am to have all my memories and also to be able to look ahead to make new ones. Thank You again, Lord. *There, I had said my prayer and didn't even realize it.*

Secretly I was glad to have Bess tag along. What good was having so much fun if there was no one to share it with? If she could just control her driving a little better. I smiled as I snuggled a little farther down under the covers.

The investigative business paid about as well as my last business venture of running a boardinghouse, but even so, I knew I was totally hooked. Actually, I had lost money with each undertaking, but everything has a cost. A visual picture of Will giving me a quiet nod to go ahead with life was the last thing I remembered that night as I drifted off.

I thought I must be dreaming about being in the middle of an orchestra—a very loud orchestra. One sound after another drifted through my consciousness—a loose shutter banging against the house, telling me that the wind must have gotten up during the night; crows cawing; Hortence mooing; Vonion hitting the side of the bucket with a stick, feeding the greedy, squealing hogs; Melvin, Bess's painter, who must have arrived before daylight. I could hear banging ladders and then him belting out his own rendition of "I've got a Home in Glory Land." His voice sounded a lot like a youthful Foy Jackson. Foy, in years gone by, was one you could always count on to sing a special on homecoming day or a solo for a funeral. Foy thought he should have been singing on *The Grand Ole Opry* stage, but he had really outstepped his vocal ability just singing in our little Baptist church. I listened from my bed as Melvin suddenly stopped his singing in the middle of his spiritual refrain to let out a few choice curse words as he banged the ladder against the floor. All two hundred and seventy-five pounds of him must have been hopping around, causing the whole house to shake, as he cursed that confounded blankety-blank ladder that had just landed on his big toe. I smiled a little in spite of the tragedy.

The morning sunlight had slipped into the house as I slept. Mercy, I felt as if I had just closed my eyes to go to sleep as I pulled the warm covers over my head. Ignoring all the commotion, I closed my eyes again, considering whether I was ready to meet the demands of the new day.

That's when I heard another masculine voice. "Hey, Melvin, quit that hopping around. Make yourself useful and come in here and hold this here measuring tape."

I really must be dreaming now. Who on earth belonged to that voice? It sounded as if it was coming from another room in the house, one closer to my bedroom. I lay completely still, daring not to move, as I listened intently to the strange, new voice. Somebody other than Melvin was in my house, and that voice absolutely did not belong to Vonion, I was sure of that. I slowly pushed the covers back and put my feet on the little throw rug I kept by my bed. Grabbing my robe, I cautiously tiptoed across the bedroom floor, where I detected heavy steps moving around right outside the bedroom door.

"I'm a'coming. Just hold yor horses. How do you think I can get anything done if'n you keep bothering me? I ain't even wet my bresh yet." Then more steps. "Now, Lambert, where you want me to put the tape?"

"Aw, shut yor fussin' and hold it right here," the strange voice said.

Melvin...Lambert? Who is Lambert? I stood by the door another minute before I gained enough courage to ease it open. I hesitantly walked out and followed the voices into my guest room, the room Bess was to occupy. There stood Melvin, with one hand scratching his backside and the other hand holding one end of a measuring tape. Another Melvin was holding the other end. Each glared at the other with aggravating expressions, but one Melvin still had a look of throbbing pain in his eyes. *Melvin and another Melvin? Did my eyes deceive me? Was I seeing double this morning?* I knew I needed to see an eye doctor, but this was ridiculous. I cleared my throat as an introduction and sternly asked, "May I ask what you, or you, are doing in my house?" I pointed at each one as I spoke. Two men, identical down to the color of their red handkerchiefs hanging out of their faded overalls, stood in front of me. Two large bellies, two shaggy beards, two caps with turned up bills covering the same uneven haircuts. Two Melvins? Double trouble!

That morning I was to learn that there was a significant difference between Melvin and Melvin, oops, I mean between Melvin and Lambert, Melvin's identical twin brother. Melvin only had one front tooth missing. Lambert had two front teeth missing and a small wart on his right ear. *As if one Melvin wasn't enough!*

"Oh, Ms. Bee, we was trying not to disturb you. But as long as you're up, I'd like to introduce you to Lambert, my twin brother. Ms. Bess didn't tell you Lambert was gonna do the carpenter work on the new bathroom?" Lambert nodded. *I guess it was Lambert. It could have easily been another Melvin.*

"Pleased to meet you, ma'am." Lambert, *I think,* tipped his cap. "We'll try to be a little quieter from now on, especially in the mornings, but carpenter work can be a little on the noisy side."

I nodded as I pulled my robe a little tighter around myself and then ran my fingers through my unruly hair.

"Now where was you thinking about putting the new toilet?" Lambert asked. "I don't like to face'um toward the east. I'm just superstitious about that. How about this here outside wall? Make the plumbing a whole lot easier."

I stood there, hardly awake, but so angry now I could have chewed a nail in two. I turned around and muttered, "I'm sorry, but you'll have to ask Bess those world-shaking questions. I'll get her on the telephone."

I walked to the hall and reached for the telephone. Nellie finally answered. "Nellie, good morning."

"Morning, but I can't say it's a good morning. My cat drug in a dead rat sometimes during the night, and I've got a splitting headache. I haven't had time to make my coffee yet, and my supper dishes are still in the sink from last night. Do you think you could make this call a little later?" Nellie, with the telephone switchboard right in the living room of her own home, always complained it was confining, but at least she could go about the telephone operator business and keep house at the same time.

"No. I'm sorry I can't. I need to speak to Bess right now."

"You know good and well she's not up yet. She probably won't answer. Now take my advice and call later."

"Listen, Nellie, I'm sorry you've got a dead rat in your house, and I'm sorry you've got a headache and dirty dishes, but ring Bess. If she doesn't answer immediately, don't hang up. I don't care if the telephone has to ring a hundred times, don't hang up. She's there, and I know it."

"I can't imagine what's so important that you have to call at the crack of dawn, but if you say so..."

"I do say so."

I counted the rings. Thirty-nine. Bess finally answered as if she was in another world.

"Hello. I know this is Bee. What do you want?"

"Get over here right now. Your carpenter, Lambert, is here and is waiting for you to give him instructions. Remember you are paying him by the hour. Every minute you waste getting here is gonna cost you money, money, money."

"Tell him to sharpen his saw blade or something. I'll get over there as fast as I can." Bam—the telephone went dead. I went to make coffee, telling myself that this situation would soon pass.

* * *

Bess arrived a few minutes later with a scowl on her face. No makeup had touched her face, and no comb had run through her hair. It was a scary sight. I guess if she was going to move in, I'd better get used to seeing her natural before she gets all dolled up for the day. She walked straight into her new boudoir. *That's what she calls it.* Lambert was sitting on the bed, smoking a cigarette *(I'll bet it was a Lucky Strike)* and reading a week-old newspaper.

"Let's get to work, Lambert. I can't pay you to sit around all day. Now, I've got a drawing of what I want. And we don't smoke in the house. Melvin didn't tell you?"

I stood in the door with my coffee cup in my hand as Lambert put out his cigarette between his finger and his thumb and abruptly jumped to attention as if an army sergeant had walked in. *Little did the poor man know, but an army sergeant would be tame next to sister Bess. He'd find out in due time.*

"Now, Lambert, I want a very professional job done here, no shoddy work. I've got this drawing, and I want you to go strictly by it. I want good lighting and good water pressure. I need a big soaking tub on the inside wall and the toilet on this wall. I want a large mirror over the counter, a large basin, a closet with shelves in this corner with a full length mirror on the door. The new wall will go about here and the door over there. Do you think you can get all that in this space? I'm thinking about pink floral wallpaper and a pink linoleum floor." Bess never stopped to catch her breath as she waved her arms in the directions of where the new wall and door and everything else should be located.

"Mrs. Johnson, just step aside. This will be a piece of cake for me."

CHAPTER SEVENTEEN

C ome on, Bess, and let's eat. I've made us a little breakfast. We've got so much to do today, and we're burning daylight."

"Burning daylight? The sun has hardly made an appearance," Bess answered in that annoying, exasperated tone of hers. "Mercy, let me at least get myself a little presentable. I've brought a few things along with me from home to leave in your bathroom for emergencies—a comb and a little makeup."

"Go ahead, but hurry every chance you get. You never know, we might have the sheriff knocking at our door anytime, asking us about that green shoe of yours. I don't know why you don't wear common everyday walking shoes like everybody else."

"Listen, Bee, if you're gonna start the day complaining about my wardrobe again, I'm going back home and go back to bed."

"I'm sorry. I promised myself that I would not criticize your shoes and clothing anymore. But hurry."

"Okay, okay." Bess scurried toward the bathroom, and I went to get the ledger.

Looking a little less frayed, but still sleepy, Bess soon walked into the kitchen as I poured myself another cup of coffee. "Want coffee? It'll help wake you up."

"That sounds good. You do make good coffee, Bee."

"Thank you very much. Let's eat and then get down to business."

"Do you think we need to see the sheriff about Sam Turner now? You know we've got to face the fact that Molly's probably dead, sooner or later."

"Later," I answered, matter-of-factly. "We absolutely cannot draw attention to ourselves in any way right now. Molly's more than likely dead, and nothing we do will bring her back. We know what we saw, and that's not going to change. Sam hasn't left town so we can keep an eye on him. Maybe he'll make a mistake, and his guilt will be revealed without any help from us."

"I guess you're right. Let's wait it out."

"Now let's get back to our other investigation." We slid our empty breakfast plates across the table, and I reached for the ledger and a pad of paper. "Okay, Obe Jordan—let's focus on him first. His first visit was in February of forty-three, and his last visit was in June of this year. "It looks as if ole Obe was a regular of Dixie's for almost four years. His first visits were sporadic, but for the last year, very regular, according to these notations." We checked off his visits and listed the times and dates on the notepad. "He came over to Dixie's house mostly in the afternoons. Do you think that means anything, Bess?"

"It means he couldn't wait until night to jump out of his britches, I guess. Now how are we going to find out anything about ole Obe?" asked Bess, as she leaned over the table with a coffee cup in one hand and the other hand in front of a yawn. "I haven't been up this early since the last time you woke me up before dawn. How do you ever get used to rising this early?"

"I don't know, but you'll get used to it soon too. Vonion doesn't allow anybody to laze around here in the mornings. Out here your day starts when you hear the stick hitting the side of the bucket."

"Stick hitting a bucket?"

"You'll find out soon enough."

We heard the screen door scrape, and Vonion appeared in the kitchen doorway with a bucketful of warm milk in one hand and a basket of eggs in the other. I closed the ledger and casually put my coffee cup on top.

"I's know y'alls will be glad to know, I's found some outside help to pick up pecans. Ms. Waters has done volunteered all her young'uns to help after school. I's thought that might relieve y'all's minds a little 'bout leaving me in a pinch with that important case y'all's working on. They's gonna start this afternoon. Roscoe promised he'd help too, as much as he can. I's don't know how the boy gonna work it into his busy sche-dul-e. He got courtin' heavy on his mind."

"Vonion, I didn't know Roscoe had a girl. I'm so glad. He needs a little female companionship," Bess replied.

"I's just hopes it companionship all the boy want. He at a dangerous age, and Boss Patterson's oldest daughter mighty appealin', from what I's seen of her lately. Jest pray fer the best."

"That's what we'll do. How's Ora Lee this morning? She up and about yet?" I asked, as Vonion started straining the milk.

"She up, but I's doubt she about. Takes a hour or so fer her to start movin' around good. She be crying the blues 'cause she know she can't bend over to help with the pecans this year. I's thought 'bout puttin' a milkin' stool out under the trees fer her to set on whiles we work. She can order the chil'ren about that way. She do love to boss, and she good at it too. Why, yestidy she make me sweep the entire yard...just like hit need it. That be 'bout as useless as tits on a boar hog...sweepin' dirt...oh, 'scuse me ladies. I's shouldn't have said that. Hit just slipped out." Vonion tipped his cap and shyly added, "Can't tell that woman notin' after she set her mind to somethin'."

"The way you go on, Vonion." Bess smiled and took another sip of her coffee. Vonion poured the milk into several clean quart jars and placed them on the shelf of the refrigerator.

As he rinsed and rung the straining cloth, he boasted, "Ora Lee said she gonna make bread puddin' this mornin' fer Ms. Waters' chil'ren, and that milk'll wash it down right nicely."

It always amazed me how thoughtful Vonion and Ora Lee were. They had taught me many a lesson about sharing our bounty over the years. He had a heart of gold under that ole thick, leathery skin.

"Does y'alls think you's might stay outta trouble one day? I's knows you ain't got that ledger book out fer notin'. Don't call me 'bout no detective work today, either. I's got my work to do right here that ain't getting done with me worrying 'bout what you two is up to." We smiled sweetly and nodded toward Vonion as he left muttering something about them darn painters smelling up the whole place, and that strong odor probably gonna pol-lute Hortence's milk.

As soon as I was sure Vonion was out of hearing range, I said to Bess, "I know how to find ole Obe. Let's call over to the courthouse in Burt County and ask if Obe Jordan has any land recorded in those deed books. We can get his address from those public records. It'll be easy. The hard part is getting by nosy Nellie. Maybe you should make the call, Bess. You're firmer with her than I tend to be. When she asks why you're making a call over to Burt County, why don't you tell her you're looking up a man about buying some Rhode Island Red pullets? I'll clean the kitchen while you make the call."

Bess soon bustled back into the kitchen as I was rinsing the milk bucket. "I've got the address," she excitedly boasted, as she waved a slip of paper. "After I told Nellie the call was about chickens, I think she lost interest. The people in the tax office readily gave me the address. It was so easy. Bee, we're really getting the hang of this detective work."

"I think we are too," I answered smugly. "We might have to go up on our fees in the future. Anyway, where does old Obe live?"

"Fifty-two acres of land and a homestead—that's what the tax people call his house—is located twelve miles west of Waynesville on Verdette Road. I've got a map in my car, Bess. I think we can find that road without going all the way into Waynesville. That would save us a lot of time and gas."

"Get the map, and I'll finish getting ready for the day. I know you need to give Lambert and Melvin more directions, so get on with it. We're still burning daylight."

* * *

The temperature had dropped during the night, leaving a nip in the clear, clean morning air. Leaves, beginning to turn from their faded summer greens to shades of burnt orange, browns, and deep purples, were a beautiful contrast to the cloudy morning sky. "A good day for a drive through the countryside," I said, as we headed out. And today I was driving my car. I offered to drive, knowing full well Bess was willing, but we needed to take turns with the expenses. *And I really didn't feel inclined to risk getting another crick in my neck today from all Bess's sudden stops and turns.*

Bess arched her head from one side to another as I cautiously maneuvered the car around Melvin's old pickup truck and Lambert's large panel truck, both parked catawampus about the yard. "Aggravating men! I'm going to speak to the brothers about where they park those trucks when we get home. They think they can just leave those hunks of junk anywhere they've got a mind to. They are so inconsiderate."

I nodded and agreed with Bess as I pulled the car out into the highway, smoothly shifted gears, and headed toward town. "Bess, have you noticed I've lost a little weight lately? I'm not sure, but it seems this dress is a little looser than it used to be. I think I'm going to start a diet and really get serious about losing these extra pounds. After all, we need to stay fit now that we're really in business."

"I haven't noticed, Bee, but all the walking we've been doing is good for us. I know one thing, I'd rather walk for my health than because we're out of gas. Anyway, keep up the good work, and soon you'll be fit as a fiddle. I'll teach you to eat healthier when I move in. See, this move is going to be good for everybody."

"Thanks, Bess. I'd really like that." *And I think I really meant it.*

Excited and uneasy about our mission, we motored through town and on out the highway toward the county line without much conversation. *I was beginning to feel a little apprehensive in the unusual quiet of the car.* Maybe we had bitten off more than we could chew. This Obe Jordan could turn out to be a maniac. If he had killed Dixie, he probably wouldn't think twice about murdering two old ladies he didn't even know. He could have us six feet underground by nightfall.

Evidently Bess was thinking along the same lines. "You don't think we'll be in danger, do you, Bee? Maybe we ought to go straight to the sheriff of Burt County with all the information we have. I really don't think they'll think we're involved if we come forward now."

"Bess, don't get cold feet now. Every time we get close to apprehending a criminal, you get all upset. Now, I'm a little nervous too, but let's keep our wits about us, and we'll be okay."

"You know if we get murdered, you'll never see your grandchildren, and I'll never see mine again. I'll never get to show off my new beige coat that I've been putting off wearing until the weather turned a little cooler. Bee, I don't think I told you about it, but it has a mink collar. Let's go back; I want to live to wear it."

"For goodness sake, Bess, don't get all melodramatic. You'll get to wear that coat, sooner or later. Now keep your mind on business. " A road sign soon popped up as we passed a curve in the road. *You are now entering Burt County, Pit Bulldog Capital of the World.* "Okay, now we're in Burt County. Do you know where Verdette Road is? You've got the map."

Bess glanced down at the map as if it were a difficult puzzle with small pieces. "I think we go a little farther. We should see the road on our right. Maybe we missed it. Hey, maybe that's a sign from God we need to go back home and start minding our own business."

"Bess, please don't chicken out now!"

"Okay, okay. You drive, and I'll watch for the road."

I drove...and I drove..."Bess, where is the road?" I annoyingly asked. "You've let us miss it? You said it wasn't but a little ways past the county line, and we've gone at least two miles since you said we were almost to it."

Bess sheepishly answered, "You must have missed it." (Notice she said I missed it, not her.) "Turn round and let's go back. This map must be wrong."

"That map isn't wrong," I sternly replied. "Pay attention now and holler if you see anything, even if it's a pig path." I turned the car around and slowly drove back a mile or so, peering from one side of the road to the other. "Hey, Bess, there's a house over there. Let's stop and see if somebody's home. We can ask directions."

I pulled into the driveway of a nice little farmhouse with an attractive manicured yard. We immediately noticed a young woman hanging diapers to dry on a clothesline that was strung between a tree and a metal pole. She looked to be about Margaret's age, obviously with a baby to care for. She spotted us and trotted over to the car.

Not bothering to get out of the car, we introduced ourselves and asked if she could assist us in finding Verdette Road. "We were thinking it was around here somewhere, but we seem to have missed it," I said.

"Oh, it's back that way about half a mile from here," she replied, as she waved her arm in the direction we had just come from. "It's just a little dirt county road that's not even marked. It winds back through the woods a piece and then cuts back toward Verdette. Verdette is just a little hole in the road, no bigger than a country store and a couple of houses. You'll see several other dirt roads back in there, but Verdette Road will eventually take you right into Waynesville."

"You wouldn't possibly know Obe Jordan, would you? I believe he lives on Verdette Road," I asked, eager to get a little more information.

"I do know him, but I haven't seen him in years. We went to school together, that is until he dropped out. That Jordan family lives way back in those woods. I'm sure you'll find him if you stay on Verdette Road."

We thanked the pretty young lady and drove back several hundred yards until we found the road. "This must be it," I hesitantly told Bess, as I turned down the narrow, ditch-lined, dirt road. "I don't know how we missed it."

We had ridden a mile or so into nowhere when Bess squeamishly complained, "I don't feel good about this road. We haven't passed a house or anything since we turned. We don't have a clue what we're getting into. Maybe we should turn around and go straight home. I'm not feeling well, anyway."

"Hey, look up ahead, Bess. There's a crossroad. The lady said we'd pass by a road or two. Maybe we're getting closer to Obe Jordan's. What's wrong with you, anyway?"

"Bee, that coffee went right through me. I'm getting very uncomfortable." Bess shifted in her seat.

"I'll stop anytime. I don't think you'll have to worry about being seen by anybody back here in these woods."

"I'll hold it a little longer. You know how I feel about going alongside the road."

"Suit yourself," I answered, as I drove on, beginning to feel slightly more nervous about our situation. Bess was fretfully fingering the map and fidgeting in her seat.

The woods on either side of the road were enveloping us deeper and deeper into foreboding shadows as we rode farther and farther into unknown territory. Adding to our anxiety, pebbles, completely covering the narrow, rutted road, continuously hit the underside of the car, causing a thudding, ominous, dinging noise. My apprehension about our situation was intensifying with every minute.

"Look ahead," Bess said, with a little more optimism in her voice, as if she were finally seeing a mirage in the desert. "That looks like a sawmill up there."

"I believe you are right," I slowly answered, as I slowed the car and stretched my neck to look ahead. We soon entered a little clearing where the morning sun had filtered softly through the dense woods. I stopped the car in the middle of the rutted road.

Bess grabbed the door handle to get out. "I can't wait a minute longer. See that pile of logs over there? I'm going behind it. Be on the lookout for me."

Bess took out across the sawmill yard before I could answer. I was left sitting in the car with the motor running, my foot on the clutch, watching her run and dance at the same time across the wood yard and around to the far side of a large pile of logs.

Suddenly, out of nowhere, I heard a knock on the car window right at my head. I jumped straight up and let out a screech that must have scared the old man peering in the window. He awkwardly stepped backwards and fell over his own two feet. Quickly opening the car door to help the old geezer, my foot slipped off the clutch, causing the car to start rolling forward. As I attempted to grab the door handle, I tumbled out the door with my dress tail flying. I soon fell right over the old man, and we rolled, side by side, both eating dirt and dust, until we eventually landed in one large lump. Dazed and disoriented, he attempted to get up but stumbled and fell squarely right back on top of me.

Bess, rounding the pile of logs just as we were performing the tumbling act, obviously thought I was being assaulted by the old man and came running to my assistance. She tackled him just like a linebacker on a football team and landed right on top of the pileup. Bess grabbed the old geezer by the hair on his head and hollered, "You'll never get away. I'll beat you to a pulp if you lay another hand on my sister!"

I awkwardly struggled out from under the pack. Attempting to get my dress down below my hips, I clumsily tried to sit, as the old man, realizing he was outnumbered, hollered for mercy. Bess still had him by the hair when he howled, "I don't want to hurt you! Turn me loose! Who do you think I am, anyway?"

Bess, straddling the old man and holding onto his hair with the strength of a lioness, announced, "Bee, we've got our man!"

"Bess, turn that man loose. He was attempting to help me when I fell out of the car on top of him."

Bess released her grip but continued to sit on the man, looking more perplexed than ever. I slowly stood, regained my balance, and reached over to pull Bess up. The old man rolled over and was soon on his knees. "Lady, you need to try out for the New York Giants with that powerful tackle."

"Mr. uh, I'm sorry, we didn't catch the name. My sister must have thought you were assaulting me. Please, forgive us?"

With a face full of dirt and a ripped dress, a dazed Bess cautiously stood. "Oh, I'm terribly sorry. I misunderstood. I guess I overreacted."

"I can see how you would. I'm sorry if I startled you ladies." As if he still wasn't sure just what he had experienced, he quickly explained, "We don't have many visitors back here. I meant no harm."

"That's quite all right. Are you hurt?" I asked.

"No, I'm okay, I think."

"How about you, Bess? Are you hurt?"

"I'll be sore tomorrow, but nothing seems to be out of place. I guess I'm okay, if you don't count my stockings being ruined and the dirt stains all over my dress."

"We've all had a nasty fall. Thank heavens, your car stopped before going into the ditch. By the way, I'm Henry Lee, foreman of this lumberyard."

"Thank you for all your help. I believe we owe you an explanation. I'm Bee Martin, and this is my sister, Mrs. Bess Johnson. We're out here looking for someone. You don't happen to know Obe Jordan? We understand he lives back in here somewhere."

"You lookin' fer Obe Jr. or Obe Sr.? They's two of um."

"Oh, ah, I guess Obe Sr.

"I'm sorry, but you've missed Obe Sr. by about three years. He went on to meet his maker after a bout with pneumonia. Caught cold, and before you knew it, it had turned into pneumonia. Didn't have good doctorin'. After he took to his bed, he didn't last long. You'll find Obe Jr.'s house down the road about two and a half miles. You can't miss it. It's the first house past the creek bed. I'd be happy to escort you ladies there. There ain't no harm in him, though."

"Thank you, but since we've made it this far, I guess we can make it a little farther down the road. We're sorry for the whole misunderstanding," Bess answered.

As we left the bewildered old man in the dust of the car, Bess teased me as she checked her hairdo in the rearview mirror. "Bee, that old man was giving you the eye. I believe he could fall head over heels for you if you gave him half a chance."

"Bess, he did fall head over heels for me. Have you forgotten so soon?"

Bess suppressed an eye roll.   I changed from first gear, into second gear, and gradually into third, as we traveled closer and closer toward the unsuspecting target of our investigation.

"Put me down for another thirty-nine cents. Another pair of my hose are completely ruined."

I'll bet you know who said that.

CHAPTER EIGHTEEN

Obe Jr.'s house had obviously seen much better days. It sat back from the road on a patch of barren earth. Although the small house was shaded from the sun by a massive oak tree, the once brown, painted exterior was faded to the color of wet sand. The weather was very mild today, but a thin chain of smoke was steadily rising from the crumbling brick chimney. An old pickup truck, parked to the side of the house amidst several boards and large brick blocks, immediately caught my attention.

The play area for the children was under the stately oak tree, which canopied the front yard and house. A rope swing, hung from one of the graceful lower limbs, idly swayed in the morning breeze, as two little girls sat on the ground, playing with cans and spoons. They jumped up to run behind the tree to hide when they saw us drive into the yard but were soon peering from around the huge tree trunk to watch us as we opened our car doors. The bigger girl bravely called out, "Ma, somebody here!"

For fear of scaring the children, Bess and I waited by the car for the screen door of the house to open before going any farther into the untidy yard. A young woman with a sad expression on her plain face opened the door to the porch and welcomed us. "Morning, ladies. Is you lost?"

Not wanting to raise our voices to be heard, we walked a little closer and gave the little girls friendly smiles as they curiously peeped around the tree at us. "We're looking for Obe Jordan. Does this happen to be his residence?" I asked.

"Hit be his house, but he ain't able to do much visitin'. He's laid up in the house with a crushed leg. Truck over there fell on it whilst he were working under it. Can I help you ladies? I'm his wife mate."

"Is there any way we can talk briefly with Obe? We've come a ways to get here, and it's important that we speak directly with him. Tell him we've come from Dixie."

"This here is Dixie Land. You know another Dixie?"

"You might say that. He'll know what I mean," I answered.

"Wait out here, and I'll tell Obe you're here."

"Oh, ma'am, if he's not able to get up, we'll go to him," Bess answered, knowing full well he wouldn't want his wife to hear our conversation.

The troubled young woman turned to go back into the house as the little girls became braver and came out from behind the tree. They stared directly at us. "You sure are pretty little girls," I called to them in my friendliest voice. "What were you playing?"

They stood like little tin soldiers and didn't answer. Bess reached into her big purse, brought out two Milky Way bars, and held them up. "If your mama doesn't care, you can have these candy bars. Go ask her if it's all right."

Faster than you could blink, the little girls scooted through the screen door and were out again. "Ma said it be okay."

"Come get them, then," Bess answered. "I've been waiting to give them to some pretty little girls."

The girls, both dressed in drab dresses and oversized faded sweaters, ran over, grabbed the candy bars, and ran back behind the tree. We could hear them giggling and squealing as they tore into the candy wrappers.

Obe's wife soon came back to the door. "Obe said he'll come out to the yard to talk. Just give him a minute or two. He's propped up in bed 'cause of his leg. He ain't been able to work lately at the sawmill. Y'all ain't bill collectors, is you?"

"Oh, no ma'am, we're not. This is just a friendly call. We'll wait out here."

The woman called to the girls to come into the house. They went running toward the door, each with a little happy face covered with chocolate and big smiles. "Tell the ladies thank you for the candy," she instructed, as they reached the porch.

They both stopped and turned, and in low, shy voices, in unison they said, "Thank you, ladies," and then skedaddled through the door into the darkness of the house. The woman gave us an inquiring glance and turned to go back into the house, letting the screen door slam behind her. From inside the house, we could hear the low mumbling of a masculine voice as the children ran around in the house, giggling.

"Let me do most of the talking," I whispered to Bess.

"I don't know why you keep telling me that," Bess replied in her aggravated tone.

Presently the screen door opened again, and Obe Jordan hobbled out, leaning on a homemade crutch. He was a muscular, good-looking young man, dressed in well-worn work pants over a union suit. A pained, puzzled expression covered his face as well as the shadow of a several-day's old beard. His eyes were dull, and his feet were bare. He motioned for us to walk back toward my car, and he limped a few feet behind us.

"Now ladies, I don't need no more trouble. You can see I got more'n I can handle right here. I'm laid up, ain't able to work, got children to feed, and a grumbling, complaining wife. Now whatever it is you got to say, get on with it, and leave. I ain't got no money fer nobody."

"What about Dixie? She says you owe her plenty. We're here to collect. You think you got problems now, wait until we give this note from Dixie to your wife." I pulled out a folded scrap of paper and waved it in front of Obe's face. "You owe Dixie, and she's ready for you to pay. She says she's waited long enough. Either pay up now, or she'll be back this afternoon to see your wife with the ledger."

"That ledger don't prove nothin'. I told you, I ain't got no money. I been in that bed for days now. My wife's had to wait on me hand and foot since that truck over there fell on top of my leg. This is the first time I've been up walkin' around, 'cept to the pot, in more'un ten days." Then, as if he was almost pleading, he added, "You tell Dixie she'll either have to wait for her tarnished blackmailing money or do without. I just ain't got it."

My heart jumped with grief and regret for this man and his family. Bess broke her silence, and asked, "Did you see a doctor after the accident?"

"The doctor come out and said my leg weren't broke, but hit's busted up pretty bad. He give me some medicine—what good it do, I don't know—and told me to stay off'a it. He didn't have to tell me that; the pain tells me.

Hit's gettin' better, but I still got to keep it propped up." He quickly glanced toward the house. "I ain't got no excuse fer seeing Dixie, 'ceptin' I'm a man, but she's done turned greedy and evil. I ain't got no more to say 'cept I'm ashamed of myself, and I'm through with her." He lowered his head and hobbled back toward the house. After a few awkward steps, he stopped, turned back toward us, and said, "And you can tell her fer me." He had said his piece. He turned and limped back into the dark house.

We didn't move, but stood frozen to the spot. We had learned the truth. Obe's manly desires were his downfall. He was stealing from his family's welfare for his own guilty pleasures, but Obe was no killer. He wasn't even aware Dixie was dead.

"Let's leave it with him. He needs to worry and fume about what Dixie's next move will be until he's learned his lesson," I sadly told Bess, as I turned to leave.

"Just a minute, Bee. I want to speak to Mrs. Jordan. It won't take but a minute."

Bess walked back toward the house, knocked, and waited until Mrs. Jordan came back to the door. I watched as Bess reached into her purse as she softly said something to the woman and then pressed a green bill into her hand. She gave the woman a reassuring smile before turning to walk back toward me.

"Bess, what did you give Mrs. Jordan?" I asked, as I turned the car around.

"Just a little something to tide them over until Obe's able to get back to work. I told her we had come out to give them their refund from the tax office at the courthouse. She gave me a knowing look, but took the money. Now that Dixie's out of the picture, maybe Obe'll keep his needs at home, and be thankful for what he has right here."

"Vonion would be proud of you, Bess. Let's check Obe off the list."

"That's two out of seven. Let's go home. Melvin and Lambert are probably out of smokes again."

"Probably."

CHAPTER NINETEEN

Bess was right. We had not laid our purses down on the hall table before Melvin dropped his brush in the paint can and pitifully asked Bess if she would make a fast run to the store for smokes. Bess surprised everybody by reaching into her purse and bringing out a brand new package of Lucky Strikes.

"Now smoke, and get back to work. You know those things aren't good for you. I'd try to quit if I were you."

"Yessum. My wife keeps telling me the same thing. She dips, so she ain't really got no room to talk. By the way, Lambert said he wants to talk to you as soon as possible. I think he's got a situation in there. Don't be too concerned, though. Lambert can fix anything."

"Ump! Lambert will have to wait a few minutes. I need to hurry home and get out of this torn, stained dress. Bee, do you have any Ben-Gay? My elbow is killing me. I must have twisted it a bit back there while I was risking my life saving your life."

ANN COBB

"As I recall, my life didn't need saving, but it does make a body feel real warm to know her sister would risk her own life trying to protect her. Thank you, Bess." Melvin stared at us with his mouth wide open and with a questioning expression. "Melvin, it wasn't anything. I was involved in a little incident and Bess came to the rescue. I would have done the same thing for her."

Bess sarcastically replied, "I have my doubts you'd have been able to react as fast as I did. We've got to get you in shape with an exercise regimen."

"I'll think about it later," I answered. "Remember Bess, time is money, and if I were you, I'd see what Lambert wants before traipsing off just to change clothes. He's probably in there sitting on the bed reading the newspaper, waiting on you for some executive decision. I'll find the Ben-Gay."

From the kitchen I could hear Bess's voice coming from her bedroom as it climbed higher and higher in an attempt to deal with Lambert's catastrophe. It seems he had misjudged the space for the bathtub; therefore, the closet would have to be a smidgeon smaller. Bess was enlightening a baffled Lambert that he should have allowed a few more inches before studding up the wall. Lambert explained that he put the wall exactly where Bess told him, not an inch over or under.

"I want the closet the exact size I originally told you, and the bathtub still has to go right here. I'm sure you can do it."

"But..."

"No buts about it. Just do it. I'm paying you to think and measure before you nail or saw. Now move the wall over; that's the only thing you can do." Knowing this was to be a long and arduous task for Lambert, I shook my head and put up a little prayer for the man. Leaving the

Ben-Gay on the table where Bess would easily find it, I walked out to the pecan orchard where Vonion had an army of children scampering around, each with a small lard bucket.

Laughter prevailed as the children crawled around picking up the nuts just like it was an Easter egg hunt. Ora Lee sat majestically in the center of the throng of children with a large croaker sack, already half full of nuts, encouraging the children. Since my dress was already stained and dirty from my wrestling match earlier in the day, I found a spot on the ground amidst the children and began filling my lap with nuts.

Bess's promise to help with the nut gathering must have weighed on her conscience that afternoon, also. She soon joined the workforce, explaining that strenuous exercise was the only way to calm her frayed nerves after her confrontation with Lambert. Still dressed in her soiled dress and torn stockings, she fit right in with the rest of us as we scrambled about in the orchard filling buckets with the bounty that only God can provide. To my total delight, Bess's presence under the heavy tree limbs that afternoon demonstrated to me she was definitely becoming a part of the team. And for some strange and odd reason, that gave me a warm feeling, a feeling of comfort and unity. Were Bess and I entering into another level of sisterhood, with common goals and a need for security? I just wonder about that...

Soon after the tired, but happy, children left to go home for their suppers and beds, Vonion tied the ends of the sacks together and drug the heavy bags off toward the barn. Explaining her need for a hot, soothing bath, Bess, too, left for home. Truck doors slamming and then a rumbling noise alerted me that Melvin and Lambert were loaded and leaving, also. They had made another day.

* * *

A gentle breeze washed the air as the sun began to set. The gaiety of the children, along with the backbreaking labor, had helped to clear my mind, but I was still feeling perplexed and confused. My thoughts went back to the ledger as I hesitated before going into the house, and decided to sit on the porch a spell to ponder. My feelings and emotions brought me right back into reality. Dixie was dead. Sam Turner could not have made it to Burt County in the time frame as her death. His car, his only means of transportation, was in the shop, waiting for much-needed tire repairs. Obe Jordan was laid up with a bad leg. He certainly would not have been able to struggle with a youthful Dixie. There were five other names listed in the ledger. All we had to do was find the person who had the opportunity to kill Dixie and had much to lose if she continued with her threatening blackmailing scheme.

Molly's disappearance and likely death were more disturbing to me than ever. Why would Sam want to kill his wife? She was certainly no threat to him. I'm sure there was nothing she wouldn't have forgiven him of. She had expressed to Bess and me that she knew something was terribly wrong, but she never said anything about leaving Sam. In fact, she said she had nowhere to go. Bess and I should probably make another trip back to Sam and Molly's house. I'm sure we had missed something of importance in our haste to leave yesterday. Maybe I should go alone next time. I'd have to think about that.

With the gentle rocking of my chair, back and forth, I became drowsy. My head was nodding and my eyelids had just about covered my tired eyes when I detected a rattle in the distance. Glancing up, I saw a faded blue pickup truck pulling into the lane up at the highway. Of all times for a visitor, this was not it. I was dirty, tired, hungry, and pretending to be hospitable would be more than a challenge for me right now. I had a fleeting idea that maybe I'd go in, close the door, and pretend I wasn't even at home. Before I could manage to move, the old truck rolled into the yard. It looked and sounded as if it could probably belong to one of Vonion's old cronies, so maybe there really wouldn't be any need for me to hurry in; it'd just pass right on by. My lopsided logic didn't prevail. The truck rolled right to my door and quickly stopped with a jerk and a loud popping noise. It was far too late to get into the house unnoticed.

At the short distance, with the late afternoon sun behind low thick clouds, I couldn't immediately identify my visitor. It wasn't until he was on the bottom step to the porch that I realized that I had seen this man earlier in the day. Why, could it be Henry Lee? And why did his name seem so familiar to me? Did I know another Henry Lee? I didn't recollect knowing any Lees. The only Lee family I could recall had moved away years ago, before I graduated from high school. They had a daughter a grade or two behind me. I remembered her so well because she had been cursed with flaming red hair that frizzed so badly she would always cover it with a cap the day the photographer came to school to snap our school photographs.

I eased out of my chair, walked to the screen door, and stopped. Mr. Lee probably didn't notice, but I reached out and grabbed the door handle to secure the door closed.

Mr. Lee stopped on the top step, removed his weather-beaten cap from his head and stuck it under his arm. Speaking through the screen, he said, "Evening, Mrs. Martin. Hope I didn't scare you none. I'm not going to take up much of your time, just want to speak briefly and privately. Don't bother to ask me in. This ain't no social call."

"Evening, Mr. Lee. I'm surprised to see you again." I stood my ground and didn't remove my hand from the door handle. "You've come a ways. This must be important." I could feel the tension mount between us as he cleared his throat to speak.

"Mrs. uh, Martin, I got something to tell ya' and then I'm gonna be leaving. Soon as y'all left the sawmill today, a friend of mine stopped by and told me about Dixie being murdered and all. It wasn't until I talked to Obe Jr. a little later, and he filled me in on your mission that I put the pieces together. I'm sure you've figured out by now that that's my name in that ledger book, too. Now I don't know what you're up to, but something's fishy. Dixie is murdered, and then you come looking up Obe Jr. to pressure him into paying up to a dead woman. Makes no sense at all. Either you're taking up her blackmailing scam, or you're investigating her murder. I thought I'd save you the trouble of coming back to the woods. I ain't killed nobody, and I ain't got no money to be paying no blackmailer. I ain't involved in nothing, 'cept using bad judgment when it comes to bad women. I got a good wife, and I intend to keep her. Do you hear what I'm sayin' to you?"

I suddenly heard the distinct sound of a familiar, nearby whippoorwill call. "Wait a minute. You're Mr. Henry Lee...Spears? Your name is...Henry Lee Spears? You said your name was Henry Lee. I thought your last name was Lee."

"Well, I guess I could've stayed home, but you would've figured it out sooner or later, I'm sure. Now you know, I'm the Henry Lee Spears in the ledger, and I ain't proud of it."

My heart raced and my mind began spinning. Quickly regaining my composure, I answered, "Yes, you've saved me some time, all right. Your name is in the ledger, quite a few times, in fact, and I do have questions for you." *Goodness, what an oversight! My detective skills weren't as sharp as I thought.*

"Mr. Spears, where were you last Monday evening and last Tuesday morning? Be careful and don't lie. The ledger is evidence that you were a regular customer of Dixie's, and notes found in her house lead me to believe you were being blackmailed by her. Am I correct?"

"You ain't far wrong. I never would 'a kilt nobody over money, though, and I got an alibi fer my time. You can check it out too. We left Monday morning to get to North Carolina with a load of oak lumber we had just milled. I got to the flooring factory with the order about seven p.m. If you'll open the door, I'll give you the receipt with the time of arrival written on it, along with another receipt for a night's stay at The Lazy Days Inn, where we always stay, right down the road from the factory. I couldn't of been in two places at one time. Silas Jernigan went along with me. You can check that out, too, if you put in a call to the motel. I expect you found his name in the ledger book along with mine and Obe's."

With new thoughts whirling, and trying not to miss a single clue, I listened as this pitiful old man admitted to his reprehensible behavior in his desperate attempt to explain his recent whereabouts. "Now that you've confided in me, Mr. Spears, may I confide in you?"

"I guess you can. I ain't really got much choice in the matter."

"Please come on in." The whippoorwill sounded very near as I pushed the door out. Henry Lee hesitated a bit but stepped in. I didn't ask him to sit. The porch had grown dimmer as the sun had completely disappeared, but I didn't reach for the light string. I knew the added light would just add to Henry Lee's discomfort and embarrassment about the whole situation. I was quite sure he wasn't interested in prolonging his visit any longer than necessary, so I asked to see the factory receipt for the lumber and the motel receipt. He reached into his frayed jacket pocket and handed me the crumpled pieces of paper.

Since the darkness prevented me from reading them right then, I asked, "Will you trust me to keep these a few days?" Knowing full well they were very important pieces of evidence, I quickly added, "You can trust me, Mr. Spears. I'll make sure to keep them in a safe place. My interests in your despicable actions only include finding a murderer, not invading your privacy."

"I guess you can keep them. Tell me, Mrs. Martin— what's your interest in Dixie's death? She ain't no kin to you, is she?"

"No kin. I'm investigating for a friend. I'm sure these receipts will completely exonerate you in the investigation."

"Don't misplace them. I'll be back to get them if'n I need them."

"While we're being so honest with each other, will you fill me in a bit about some of Dixie's dealings? Do you know if she had many clients?"

"I ain't too sure of that. We didn't run into each other over there, if you know what I mean. I know about Obe and Silas. Since we worked together, we talked some, you know, 'bout it. She always was keeping accounts in that big old book of hers, though. You know, I ain't really been seeing her too long."

"May I ask then, how did you find out about her services?"

"Well, it ain't a pretty story. I used to go next door, until I seen Dixie lollygagging about in the yard, sort'a advertising, you know. She'd be out there tanning and relaxin'. She got my attention pretty quickly and invited me in fer iced tea one day. I got iced tea...and more."

"You mean to say the woman next door, the one with the dog named Biscuit, is a...you know, a working woman too? I've met her. She's a little old to..." As soon as I said it, I thought better. Embarrassed, I repeated myself. "She's a little bit older, isn't she?"

"She's a good bit older, and she's done let herself go. I mean, she's done got heavy. Anyway, there ain't much else fer me to tell ya'."

"One more thing. Did the woman next door know you and your friends were seeing Dixie?" *I thought I was beginning to sound like a real detective.*

"Oh, yea, and she was furious 'bout it too. I 'spect her business is off some, with Dixie promoting herself right next door. But, it's a free country after all, ain't it."

"Other than Biscuit's owner, what name does the woman next door go by? If you don't mind me knowing, that is. I'm sure her privacy is very important to her."

"All I know is Tempest. I 'spect that's not really her given name, but that's what she told us to call her. Please keep all this confidential. My wife would murder me if'n she knew 'bout all this."

"You can count on me, Henry Lee. You've been a big help."

Obviously dejected and discouraged, and praying that his name in the ledger would never come to light, Henry Lee turned, opened the screen door, and slowly walked down the steps back to his truck.

Trembling, I plopped back down in the rocker. As I watched the truck return to the highway, I quietly said, "Vonion, you can come out now."

Vonion stepped out from around the house. "You's know I was here all along?"

"Vonion, you know I heard your whippoorwill call. It gave me all the confidence in the world, knowing you were just a few steps away."

"Can't never let my guard down. You's need constant patrolling."

I knew I'd have a hard time sleeping that night. I'd have to wait until morning to tell Bess all the new developments. Too many listening ears on the telephone. Two more names checked off the list at one time!

CHAPTER TWENTY

The horrible paint odor and that same old lonely feeling greeted me as I walked back into the house. As the door closed behind, I thought I had left the outside world behind. But not for long! The telephone began to ring. Two rings— one long, one short. That's me. My mood quickly changed as I remembered another connection to the world was sitting right there on the table, just waiting for me. What a blessing! Hurrying down the hall, I reached for the telephone. "Bee Martin speaking."

"Mama, where have you been all day? You're never at home anymore. I've been trying to get you on the telephone since school let out this afternoon."

"Margaret, I've been out and about all day. Bess came over, and we did a few errands together, and then we helped Vonion pick up pecans. I just came in." I slowly sat down, ready for the long lecture. "I'm sorry you've had trouble reaching me. Do you have something exciting to tell me?"

"No, nothing exciting. I just can't understand how you can be gone from home so much. I get worried about you."

"Margaret, I'm not going to sit in the house waiting for the telephone to ring. I have work to do and a life, you know, like you do. Now, let's don't fuss. Tell me about your day."

"Oh, it was a little sad. I told you earlier about Dixie. You know, the secretary at school. You remember, I told you she was murdered. Anyway, the sheriff came by the school today and questioned the teachers about her. From what I've heard, they haven't found one clue, except if you consider that green shoe the dog from next door was chewing on. We're all a little skittish right now, wondering if that murderer is still roaming around town. I'm not too concerned, though. With the judge and Eli right next door, I feel very safe."

"Oh, dear! Just be careful, and don't go out at night by yourself until the murderer is found. Maybe you could get one of your fellow teachers to stay with you temporarily."

"There's absolutely no need for that. Mama, I...um...really haven't been perfectly honest. Rest your mind, we think Dixie was murdered because of her 'other profession.' Since her murder, news about her personal life has come to light. I hate to speak badly of the dead, but Dixie was a paid prostitute. I'm sure it was a crime of passion, so don't worry about me."

"Oh, dear me. How sad. I just can't imagine..."

"Mama, this world is not like it used to be. Things like that don't surprise me anymore. You're stuck out there on the farm, isolated from the 'real world.' You'd be surprised to know what really goes on out there."

"You're right, dear. I'm sure I'd be very surprised. Margaret, did you have any knowledge about Dixie's other life? I mean, did you ever notice any clues about how she spent her time away from school?"

"Other than the way she ran after every man that wore pants, or parted his hair on the left...or the right, for that matter, but that really isn't any indication of her other profession."

"What about the way she dressed or looked?"

"Mama, she dressed nicely; most of her clothes were fairly tailored. She wore a little makeup, always pale pink lipstick, and always kept her hair in a nice soft pageboy. She looked just about like everybody else."

"Was she pretty?"

"No, not what you'd call really pretty, but not plain, either...attractive. She loved the attention of a man, and she had a flirty way about her. I tried to ignore her as much as possible."

"Any other developments regarding the murder?"

"Well, the buzz around school is that one of her clients probably became jealous and things must have gotten totally out of control. We don't really know. All we can do is speculate. We're all still in shock about the news."

"I'm sorry, dear. But, oh, to change the subject. Are you coming home this weekend? I'm dying for you to see the changes to the house. It's really coming together. I think you'll like the new paint color, and Melvin and Lambert are really making headway now."

"I wish I could, but there's a field trip to the state park over in the next county for the fifth and sixth graders, and they've asked me to chaperone. Walter's going along too. He's such a good sport. He asked me out for the day and agreed to help me chaperone after I explained to him that I was already committed to school activities. Wasn't that nice of him?"

"Why, yes, it is." Visions of yellow bridesmaids' dresses fluttered into my thoughts. "That's very nice. I hope the weather's good. I'll be thinking about you two."

"Mama, I've got to go now. My hair needs washing, and I want it to dry before bedtime. Tell everyone 'hello' and I love you."

"I love you too. Good night, dear." I slowly laid the telephone receiver down.

In the dim light, I began to stare, without really focusing, at the framed camellia watercolor that hung over Mama's pedal sewing machine on the opposite wall. A single, twenty-five watt bulb in the lamp on the hall table provided the solitary illumination for the entire house, and the constant hum of the refrigerator's motor from the kitchen was the only sound invading the quiet stillness of the night. I sat, as in a spell, fingering my wedding band on my third finger of my left hand.

My mind began to wonder. What really were the necessary tools in solving a crime? Did I possess any of them? Intelligence, deductive thinking, wit—that's what it takes to solve a mystery and, *Bless Pat*, I believe I had it all! Without an ounce of humility, I reasoned with myself. My teachers had always sent home good reports of my work at the end of the terms at school. Reading other people's minds was a characteristic I had always possessed. Bess could never pull anything over my eyes, and I could read Vonion like an open book. Margaret said I knew when she was going to be naughty before she even misbehaved. Judging when it was a good time to ask Will about a new purchase or to tell him when something was broken or needed his attention had always been a cinch for me.

But keeping my good wits about me was a constant struggle. Most of the time, I reacted to problems and difficulties with a pretty level head, except when it came to Bess's driving or to Sheriff Ledbetter's investigative inabilities. He was improving, though, mostly because Bess and I were constant reminders to him that he was, more than likely, shirking his duties. Where there's a will, there's a way, I thought, as I continued to give myself a pep talk. A little something to eat, a good night's sleep, and tomorrow, I'd be sharp as a tack, ready to dig out the ledger again and continue to use all my deductive skills.

Oh! Another necessary tool I almost forgot—and most importantly—the facts! I needed all the facts. Tomorrow was another day to think about our strategy in solving this murder. I was narrowing the field of prospective suspects when suddenly, another unlikely culprit popped into my mind. Someone with motive and opportunity! I'd have to sleep on that, but between the awful turpentine smell and all the new developments floating around in my head, I knew I'd probably have trouble closing my eyes, much less sleeping a wink.

* * *

Friday morning started out with a bang. And I do mean a bang. Melvin dragging ladders and Lambert's constant nailing and sawing. Progress, progress. It was really beginning to sink into my head that permanent changes were taking place, and now there was absolutely no turning back. I avoided the commotion in the house and worked around in the kitchen until I noticed Vonion crawling around under the pecan trees. Without even a peep into the ledger, I decided to give all my attention that morning to our overwhelming task at hand, gathering all the nuts on the ground.

Without much in the way of conversation, Vonion and I worked side by side most of the morning. He said Ora Lee wasn't feeling herself today, and he had left her watchin' the redbirds. After a quick lunch and a quick check in with Melvin and Lambert, I resumed my position under the trees, a lowly second in demand. Mrs.Waters' children arrived to help in the middle of the afternoon, so with not much regret, I gave up my rank for the day and returned to the house. Thoughts of the ledger were drawing me. Without Bess (she obviously had better things to do today) I pulled the big gray book out and made a quick check of it. With great delight and personal satisfaction, I checked off Sam Turner, Obe Jordan, Henry Lee Spears, and Silas Jernigan. I had completely eliminated each one. But now, I felt there was another name that should be added to the list of suspects. I inserted a small slip of paper into the folds of the ledger. I had written the name "Tempest" in big letters across the top of the paper. A major possibility! And with a big motive! JEALOUSY!

* * *

Skimming the names and dates, I decided to focus my attention on E.N. Frost next. I knew many of the old Frost family lived around and about the New Hope Methodist Church community. The church was situated a good ways from Jeffersontown, closer to the Burt County line. We had passed the little frame church, along with the ancient cemetery, when Bess and I made our pilgrimage yesterday. I wondered...Hester Beck, an old acquaintance of mine. It seemed as if she had been a Frost before she married Prentiss Beck. But I hadn't thought of her in years. If I remembered correctly, she and Prentiss lived somewhere around that church. The telephone book? Maybe their number was listed in my telephone book. I could call Hester about...oh, I don't know. What do you say to somebody you haven't seen in years? I guess I could say that I had heard E.N. Frost had some chickens for sale, and I was interested in buying some. What a pack of lies. Could I pull it off? You betcha I could! I went for the telephone book. Now where was Prentiss Beck? He had to be somewhere in the book of names and numbers. No Prentiss Beck and no Frosts were listed. There had to be one or two Frosts with a telephone. I knew they were slightly backward, woodsy people, but surely one or two had a telephone. I know! Nellie!

I picked up the receiver. Nellie answered as if she were in a hurry. "What number do you need, Bee? I need to get to my stove. My collards are gonna boil over any minute." *Nellie must have heard my excuses too many times. She's using them now.*

"Nellie, would you mind looking to see if there is an E.N. Frost listed anywhere in any of those telephone books you keep around there. I think he might live over near Burt County. I need his number if you can put your finger on it. And if you can't find it, I need Prentiss Beck's. You remember Hester Frost, don't you? Well, as I recall, she married a Prentiss Beck."

"I remember her. You and Bess certainly have been interested in folks over around Burt County lately. Y'all still lookin' for chickens?"

"That's right," I answered, with a sigh of relief. *Another fib!* "We're looking for some Rhode Island Reds to raise. We heard E.N. Frost had some, but we don't know how to get in touch with him. Thought Hester might know how to reach him."

"I doubt it. She's a little touched in the head now, from what I hear. E.N. Frost—that name does seem a mite familiar. Seems like I've heard of him, but I don't see a number for him here in any of these books. Oh, here's

Prentiss Beck's number in the book. Do you want me to dial it for you? I warn you, Hester might not make good sense."

"Dial her up, Nellie."

"I will, I will, but I want to tell you. I saw Vonion in the hardware store yesterday and asked him what kind of chickens you and Bess were looking for. He acted as if it was news to him that y'all were lookin' for any kind of chickens at all. He told me I must have overheard something wrong, and you didn't know one chicken from another. Bee, you and Bess need to think up a better excuse than chickens for calling all these people out of the county."

Exasperated that I even needed an excuse at all, I replied, "Dial her up, Nellie, and don't expect to get any eggs when we have an overflow." *That ought to teach her to not be so bossy… and nosy.*

CHAPTER TWENTY-ONE

"E. N. Frost, Hester," I yelled into the receiver. "Do you know him? I heard he was raising Rhode Island Red pullets, and I'd like to buy some. E.N. Frost, Hester."

"Who is Ena Frost? I never heard of her. Does she live up the road, or down the road?"

"E.N. Frost. It's a man, Hester. Do you happen to know him?" I had just about lost all my patience. Nellie had told me Hester was senile, and now I knew she wasn't far from wrong. *Dear Lord, give me patience.* "Weren't you a Frost before you and Prentiss married?"

"Who got married?" Hester yelled in a quizzical voice.

"Nobody got married," I exasperatedly yelled back into the receiver. Now knowing Hester was deaf as a signpost as well as "touched in the head," I was beginning to feel defeated. "Hester," I shouted into the receiver, "do you know E.N. Frost? Just answer one question. DO - YOU - KNOW - E.N. - FROST?"

"Frost, no, I don't know if we're gonna have any frost today, but it might rain. I think it rained yesterday…or either the day before. It rained one day."

Nellie was right. I was getting absolutely nowhere with Hester. Hester wasn't capable of giving me any information, but I'd give it one more try. "Hester, is your husband there? Prentiss, is he anywhere around?" I bellowed.

"Prentiss, are you here?" Hester hollered, as if she was in a total fog.

Maybe Prentiss was there and could help me, but Hester certainly couldn't. I could hear the telephone drop and clang about. And then a masculine voice came over the line.

"Can I help you?"

"Is that you, Prentiss?" I asked. *Maybe I was getting somewhere now.*

"This is Prentiss Beck. Who is this?"

"Prentiss, this is Bee Martin, from over near Jeffersontown. I hope I'm not disturbing y'all today. I was asking Hester about E.N. Frost. I'm interested in buying some chickens—Rhode Island Reds. I heard that E.N. Frost had some. Do you know him, by any chance?"

"E.N. ain't never had no chickens to sell. Where the devil did you hear that from? That man didn't even know where eggs came from. I 'spect you got the wrong E.N. Frost."

"Er, maybe I did, but uh, Prentiss, do you happen to know an E.N. Frost? Does he live near you?"

"The one I used to know lived about a'hunderd yards down the lane from Hester and me. I think hit'd be fair to say he lives in hell now. Died recently, and good riddance to him. We're all a good bit better off now without that womanizing, whore-hopping, no-good, son of a gun a 'worrying us. He should have been shot dead years ago. He was undoubtedly the sorriest, low-down, rotten, worthless scumbag that ever walked the face of the Earth, and those were some of his good qualities."

"Oh, well, err—I'm not sure that's the same E.N. Frost I'm looking for. But you say the E.N. Frost you knew was a womanizer and didn't raise chickens? Is he the only E.N. Frost you know?"

"Onliest one around these parts, I reckon. He ain't never raised no chickens, though. Onliest thing he knew about chickens was how to eat them after they was fried."

"How is it that you know so much about the man, Prentiss? You say he lived down the lane from you and Hester, but now he's dead. The E.N. Frost I'm lookin' for is alive. At least, I believe he is. He was a month ago, anyway." (According to the ledger, he was very much alive thirty days ago.)

"He was Hester's onliest brother. We never liked to claim him, though. And oh, he was goin' strong thirty days ago. Died three weeks ago today from a massive heart attack. Probably from visiting one of those whores he frequented and exercised with too much. We ain't gonna miss him, and I doubt anybody else will, excepting that whore he was paying good money to. Good riddance to him is what I say."

"Err, Prentiss excuse me for being so nosy, but did he have any children, maybe a son with the same name?"

"None that I know about. He could've had some yard children, though. He practiced fer children more than any man I ever knew. E.N. didn't have no legal chil'ren, though."

"So there's no other E.N. Frost around in these parts?"

"Naw, none around here. But Bee, if it's Rhode Island Red chickens you's a'wantin', I got some. How many you's lookin' fer? I 'spect we could get rid of a few. Ain't never sold any, but they's a first fer everything."

"Well, err, Prentiss, let me get back to you about that. I'm not sure just how many chickens we really need. Now that I've got your telephone number, I can check back with you. Please tell Hester I said good-bye. It was good to talk to her."

"You want to tell her yourself? She's a'standin' right here beside me, and she loves talking over the telephone."

Hurriedly, and almost frantically, I shouted, "Oh, no! No thank you, Prentiss. Don't bother her. You can tell her bye for me. Y'all come over to see me sometimes. Bye now, and thanks for all the information."

Of all of the most unlikely things I had ever heard. E.N. Frost, the sorry rascal, was stone cold graveyard dead! Died from a heart attack. I could definitely check him off the list for good. It sounded as if he got his just desserts. And poor Hester! But what I should say is poor Prentiss.

I had so much new information to tell Bess, she'd never believe it all. Where was she anyway? I should have heard from her today. She was probably cleaning closets or weeding her flower bed, without one thought about the investigation.

My mind was flooded with information. Five suspects had all been cleared. Each one had good alibis. E.N. Frost had the best alibi of all. The list of suspects was getting much shorter. There was only one name left for us to investigate in the ledger now, with the exception of the judge, and I was leaving him for last. Surely to goodness, the judge didn't have anything to do with a murder. It was bad enough, him just visiting over at Dixie's, but to think he could be responsible for the murder? I'd never forgive myself if anything happened to Margaret, over there living practically under the same roof as that whore-hopping man.

UPPS, I didn't really say that.

* * *

My thoughts were interrupted by a loud thud. I heard Lambert holler from the bedroom, "Hey, Melvin, get in here and give me a hand. I need help getting this confounded bathtub in the right position."

Melvin hollered back, "Hold yor horses. Be there in a minute. I've got to get down from this dang blasted ladder."

Maybe I could help. The situation seemed to be pretty dire as I walked to the new bathroom door and looked over Lambert's shoulder into the big gaping hole in the floor where plumbing pipes were sticking up from under the house. The bathtub's position was several inches from where, it seemed to me, it should have been. "Lambert, is the tub in the wrong place or are the pipes in the wrong place? I don't see how they're ever going to connect. I don't know anything about plumbing, obviously, but something seems a little out of whack."

"Never you worry, little lady. I've got everything under my control. Soon as Melvin gets in here, we'll wiggle this tub over a hair and bend the pipes over a tinch, and everything will fit perfectly. " Sweat was pouring out of his red, unshaven face and head like a mountain waterfall.

Bess, overhearing the conversation, called out as she appeared from nowhere. "I hope you know what you're talkin' about, Lambert, but I'm not fully convinced." She scurried across the room to peer over my shoulder into the large hole in the floor. "And have you got the hot water and the cold water connected properly under the house? Those pipes don't look like they're positioned just right to me. You might need to double-check their positioning."

"It's about time you got here, Bess. Where'd you come from? We didn't hear you drive up."

"From the door over there. You know you never think to close one. Lambert, do you know what you're doing?"

Lambert looked up at Bess and irritably answered, "Ms. Bess, I've told you, and I've told you not to judge my work until it's finished. These pipes will carry you all the hot water and cold water you can use in a lifetime. Just give me time to connect everything up. Ain't but three things a plumber needs to know about anyway."

"And what on earth would that be?" Bess asked, in her most critical voice, with her hands on her hips.

"Hot on the left, cold on the right, and number two don't run uphill. You got any more questions?"

A stunned Bess stood frozen, but began turning every color of the rainbow. Ignoring us completely, Lambert hollered again, "Melvin, where the heck are you? Git in here!" It was quite evident Lambert was very agitated.

A mortified Bess, attempting to regain her composure, lowered her head in embarrassment. "You asked for that, Bess," I said, as I walked to the porch. Speechless for once in her life, Bess followed close behind.

"Bess, we need to talk. Where have you been?" I asked, as we sat down in the rockers on the porch.

"I told you the other day I had to get my hair retouched today. How do you like it? Did you forget?"

"I like it, and I guess I forgot."

Bess's eyes got bigger and bigger, and she rocked faster and faster as I told her all the new developments. Almost out of breath from all the explaining, I added, "And Bess, by the way, Nellie's on to us about buying chickens. She had the audacity to tell me today that if we were going to continue making all these long-distance calls all over the place, we were going to have to put in a business telephone line, and you know they cost more per month than a regular telephone."

"We need to straighten her out, Bee. We can use that telephone for anything we want to. I happen to know she has overstepped her boundaries this time."

"I think you are absolutely right. But Bess, I've been thinking. Maybe we do need to buy some Rhode Island Red pullets. That would shut her mouth. And besides, we'd have more eggs to give away."

"Now you're talkin' just like Hester Frost Beck!" Bess answered with a laugh.

I smiled, and admitted, "I guess you're right. We don't really need any more chickens. We need to get back to the investigation, anyway. We're really narrowing our list of suspects down."

"Maybe it's time for us to talk to Sheriff Ledbetter, Bee. I wouldn't be surprised if he didn't drive up anytime with warrants for our arrests. You reckon none of those people who saw us walking down that street the other day reported anything? We know that young lady out with her children and the mailman saw us, as well as that little boy. I can't believe nobody has said a thing yet."

"Bess, let's just lie low for now and not say a word to the sheriff. We've got to keep investigating until we've got our man. If we have to go back over into Burt County, we can always disguise ourselves. You haven't seen Sam Turner around town anywhere by any chance, have you? We've got to keep an eye on him. He could be planning to escape right under our noses."

"As a matter of fact, I saw him just today. He was coming out of Shorty's barber shop as I was driving through town this morning. Maybe we should come forward now with our information about Molly's disappearance before he escapes."

"No, not yet. A good detective knows when the time is right to reveal her information. It's not quite that time yet. Sam's still acting normal, and anyway, I don't think he's a flight risk. Now let's get the ledger back out."

"Okay, but first I want to look around the house. Is Melvin about through painting the front room?"

"The dining room and the front room are both finished, and I think he's finished with the ceiling in the hall. I guess he'll start painting the walls in there next. Everything is looking so fresh and clean. I really like the color you picked out. I don't know why I've resisted painting this long."

"I'm glad you like the color. Now you get the ledger, and I'll inspect Melvin's paint job... And, Bee, by the way, I've got a whole pocketbook full of Lucky Strikes."

CHAPTER TWENTY-TWO

W ho's the next suspect, Bee? Get the book out. We're really on a roll now."

"You mean *I'm* on a roll, don't you? I haven't noticed you being on the job for the last few hours. I wouldn't go so far as to say we're *both* on a roll."

"We're a team. Remember, both of us don't have to be working together *all* the time. You hold up your end, and I'll hold up my end. Besides, I've got new information."

"You do?"

"Yes, I do. I've been at Thelma's today, remember."

"Well, that says it all. What is it?"

"Okay." Bess took a deep breath. "Thelma asked if I had seen Molly around town lately. You know I really think she was just trying to make a little conversation while she pin curled me. Anyway, she mentioned that Mrs. Ricketson had been in the shop a couple of days before to get that mousey thin hair of hers washed. I don't know why she can't do it herself at home."

"Stay on the subject, Bess."

"I will if you'll quit interrupting me. Now where was I? Oh yes, just before she leaned back in the chair she told Thelma that she had not seen Molly around for some time and thought Sam and Molly might possibly have separated. She mentioned to Thelma she knew they were having marital problems because she had heard the two of them yelling and carrying on several times in the past few weeks. Thelma made a real point of telling me that Mrs. Ricketson told her she hadn't seen a soul over there in the past week or so except Sam and...you and me."

"Oh dear."

"I told you that nosy old busybody saw us. She was spying on us through her front window, behind those ratty old curtains. Nobody has a bit of privacy in this town!"

"We've got to be a lot more careful next time we break in somewhere. Maybe we should always go at night or wear disguises from now on."

"Next time we break in?" Bess indignantly replied. "I didn't know there was going to be a next time."

"Bess, there's always a next time. Remember our motto: 'We go where you can't.' Now let's get back to business. Zeniss Coleman—ever heard of him?"

"Never heard of anybody named Zeniss. It's really a peculiar name."

"I have. Don't you remember that crazy old man that toted a sack stuffed with smelly garbage and old tin cans he had picked up off the road when we were growing up? He lived over on Ice Plant Hill. Don't you remember him, Bess? His first name was Zeniss, but I'm not sure about his last name. He raised goats in the field beside his shack. He even had a goat with two heads."

"The man had two heads?"

"No, Bess. I'm beginning to believe you need a hearing horn like Hester."

"I do not. You just need to pronounce your words a little more precisely. I can hear what other people say all the time."

"He had a goat with two heads. He named him Thisum and Thatum, same as Old Man Peterson's mules."

"Now I know you're teasing me, Bee."

"Just the part about the names, but he really did have a two-headed goat. It died soon after it was born, but don't you remember? Daddy took us over to see the poor creature right before it died."

"Oh, yea, now I remember. Old Zeniss must have gotten restless because I remember he started traveling up and down Highway 1 with his goats pulling a cart. You know what! I remember that old man had a son by some woman who moved away with the child. Do you think there could be a connection to the Zeniss we're looking for?"

"It could be. After all, there aren't many Zeniss's running around in the world," I replied.

"Who do you know who would know anything about that woman? Bee, it'd have to be somebody really old since all that happened a long time ago. Hey, how about Shirley's Aunt Dora? She remembers way back when. But if we're gonna question her, we better hurry before she checks out for good."

"She is the oldest living person around here, if you don't count Mr. Hodges, and he doesn't even know he's in the world anymore. It's sad how people's minds go before their bodies do. We've got to watch out for that, Bess."

"Well, we are both getting a little forgetful. Do you know we completely forgot about the missionary meeting last Monday at Nina Mae's? I've told you, we've got to watch that. Bee, we can't let our social obligations go. You know that's how we keep up with all the news around town."

"That, along with Nellie's network," I laughingly added.

We decided we'd wait until morning to attempt prying information about Zeniss from Shirley's Aunt Dora. We knew we'd have trouble just carrying on a conversation with Aunt Dora, but to actually get vital information from her would be a real challenge.

We soon noticed Melvin and Lambert standing around on the porch, waiting for Bess to bring them their weekly paychecks. We scurried out just in time to witness Melvin flip his cigarette butt onto the porch floor. When Bess gave him a harsh look, he quickly and ashamedly reached over to retrieve the butt as if he were a child caught with his hand in a candy jar. Lambert hastily cleared his throat before he addressed a formidable Bess, and Melvin nonchalantly dropped the cold cigarette butt into his overalls pocket. "Sorry, ladies, but you won't have the pleasure of our company 'til Monday morning next week. We always take weekends off. We usually go to the river fishin' on Saturdays—anything to keep from hanging around the house with our old ladies. And Sunday is a day of rest."

Melvin grinned at Bess as he sheepishly added, "Yep, that's right. My old lady can find a million things fer me to do if I'm not a'workin'. It's best for me to just hightail it out early in the morning before she has time to think about what needs doing around the place. You know how it is?"

"My old lady is worser," Lambert quickly added. "She'll wake me while's I'm sleeping to get me to fix anything. I swear, just last week I had to get up from my warm bed right after I got really comfortable to change a lightbulb in the bathroom. She said she couldn't see her way around in there after dark, and she might have an emergency during the night. I ain't figured out yet why she didn't think to remind me 'bout that lightbulb before I went to bed. Women! Can't live with'em and can't live without'em."

Bess and I pretended to act interested in each man's pitiful sagas, but I tell you, my sympathies went straight out to those tortured women. Melvin and Lambert eventually gave out of personal grievances and moseyed out to their trucks as if they hated to head home to demanding wardens. After a laugh and a word or two out in the yard, they drove off.

Thankfully, activities around the farm were beginning to wane down for the day. I knew Vonion had loaded the children in the back of his pickup truck earlier that afternoon and carried them to Floyd's Station for candy and a soda, a treat from me for all their hard work. He'd then settle up with Mrs. Waters when he dropped the children off for the afternoon. Peacefulness settled around me a few minutes later as I stood on the porch waving to Bess as she drove up the lane behind the settled dust of Lambert's old panel truck and Melvin's pickup truck.

Time alone at last!

* * *

Instead of ladders and paint buckets banging around inside of the house, Vonion, hitting the side of a bucket with the stick, woke me the next morning from out in the barnyard. He had told me earlier in the week he intended to cut firewood on Saturday while he had Roscoe to help. Roscoe usually had Saturdays off. They were probably trying to get an early start. Thankfully, Vonion was still able to cut wood, but I didn't like him in the woods by himself. It was far too dangerous. In the past, he had chopped down a tree with a hornets' nest attached to one of the dead limbs. The hornets swarmed, and he was bitten five times. Another time a limb from a felled tree rolled over his leg, mercifully, only bruising it.

Getting over to Aunt Dora's early that morning was totally out of the question. We knew Aunt Dora slept late in the mornings, and there would be no way to question her until at least eleven or twelve. We decided to have an early lunch at Bess's and then go over to Aunt Dora's little framed house on Chinaberry Street, pretending this was strictly a friendly neighborly visit. Knowing Aunt Dora loved sweets, Bess made tea cakes earlier that morning to entice her. We knew if we could get her eating and enjoying the conversation, she was more likely to talk freely about the past.

"It's Bess Johnson and Bee Martin, Aunt Dora," Bess called from the porch, as Aunt Dora slowly turned the doorknob. Aunt Dora was deaf as a fence post, and we were aware we'd have to yell the whole time we attempted to have a conversation with her.

"We've come for a visit," I yelled, as she slowly opened the door and ushered us into the dimly lit front room. "How are you today?"

"What's that you say?" Aunt Dora answered, as if she were in a fog. *This was going to be hard.*

"I said how are you? You're looking good."

"I doubt that," she answered. "I haven't put my teeth in yet." She rested her walking cane against the faded settee, reached into her apron pocket, pulled her false teeth out, and clamped them into position in her mouth. "There, that's better," she replied as she wiggled her jaw. "You'll have to excuse me. Those dentist teeth scratch my gums, and I only wear them when I'm around people. Now, can I get you ladies anything? Maybe a Coca-Cola." Everybody in town knew that Aunt Dora loved her Coca-Colas. She bought them by the case and drank at least a case every week.

"Oh, no, we just had lunch," Bess replied. "My, the weather is certainly mild today. Have you sat on the porch today? It's really nice out today."

"No, not today, but maybe later, "Aunt Dora replied, with her ear horn pressed against her head.

"Your house looks nice," I said, as I noticed a fine layer of dust over the wood floors and dark furniture. After easing myself onto the settee, I dared not move around too much for fear of dust billowing up all about me.

"The house is a dusty mess," answered Aunt Dora. "I don't even pretend to keep house anymore. Just do a little cookin' now and then. I send my clothes out to be washed. I'm just makin' time till it's all over."

"Aunt Dora, you're doing great for somebody as old as you are, and you know it."

"Most people my age are dead, and my friends are all dead. According to Mama's Bible, come November third, I'll turn ninety-one. Don't know if I'll make it 'til then, and don't really know if I even want to."

"That's nonsense. You know you do," I replied. "You'll make a hundred, I 'spect.

"I don't know. I don't have anything to look forward to anymore, except heaven. Nothing ever happens around here."

Bess offered Aunt Dora the cookies. "Aunt Dora," Bess yelled, "have you ever heard of anybody named Zeniss? We thought since you have lived here in Jeffersontown for so many years, you might recall somebody with that name."

"Well, you know my mind is still sharp. Let me think. Zeniss. That is a strange name." Aunt Dora stared off in space as if she was giving it a great deal of thought. "Oh, my yes, I believe I do recall someone by that name. He lived here years and years ago, until he started walkin' the roads with a goat cart. Zeniss. Oh, what was his last name?" Aunt Dora gave Bess a puzzled look. "Y'all are workin' on a case, aren't you? You want me to help with a case!"

"Aunt Dora, we are looking into something, but we really can't talk about it yet. Do you remember Zeniss and anything else about him? Please tell us; it's vitally important," I pleaded loudly.

"Well then, in that case, I reckon I remember a little something. Zeniss kept goats about his place until he took to wandering the roads. I always thought the poor old fool might have been traveling around looking for his son. You see, a young woman came to town and lived in that shack with him for a time. She helped out in a few houses around town while she was here, including mine, cleaning and washin'. He eventually got her in a womanly way, and she gave birth to a boy child. Old Zeniss never would work none, so I suppose she figured she'd be better off to leave and go back to her family with the child. She never did come back. I believe she came from—let me see—where did she come from?" Bess and I were leaning forward by now, breathlessly waiting for her to remember.

Aunt Dora thoughtfully continued, this time with her mouth full of cookie, "They had a barbecue business, as I recall. That's probably how she met Zeniss. He probably sold goats to some of her people, you know, for barbecuing. That's right; they had a barbecuing business over in Burt County. You know, I haven't thought about that girl for years. I just wonder what happened to her. I don't know what possessed that girl to stay with the likes of Zeniss in the first place. He must have had something in his britches that didn't show." We smirked, and Aunt Dora giggled.

"Aunt Dora, you say her family came from Burt County, and they had a barbecuing business. Try to remember, what was her name? It's really important," I pleaded, trying to prod her little.

Then as if a notion suddenly hit her, she brightly replied, "Y'all *are* on a case. I'd bet money you are! I believe I could remember what her name was and where the barbecuing place was if you'd let me go with you to find it. We could buy Coca-Colas and have a nice ride through the countryside. I'd pay for the drinks."

"Aunt Dora, are you sure you could remember where the barbecue place was and the woman's name, or are you just saying all this to get us to take you for a ride? We'll be glad to ride you around sometimes; we just don't have the time for a joyride today."

"Oh, I know where it was all right. We used to go over there to get barbecue for the Fourth of July. And just to show that I'm serious and remember a few things, her name was Minnie something. I just can't think of her last name right off. I believe I could think better if I was riding through the countryside with a Coca-Cola. Yes, that's right; she was a Minnie something from Burt County."

I looked at Bess, and Bess smiled back at me. Aunt Dora knew her name all right, and she had outsmarted both of us.

"Are you sure you can show us where the barbecue place is?" I asked.

"I shore can, and I will!" exclaimed Mrs. Dora, as she impatiently beat her cane on the floor. "I'm in on the case with you, whatever it is! This is the most exciting thing that's happened to me since I was outside pruning my rose bushes when Old Man Hodges streaked right by the house on his way to the barber shop."

CHAPTER TWENTY-THREE

A re you comfortable now, Aunt Dora?" I asked, as we positioned her old, brittle body in the backseat of Bess's car.

"I'm fine and dandy. You know I haven't ridden in an automobile in over a year. The last time I took a ride, Shirley and I were calling on the new pastor. You remember Preacher Henry, don't you?" Aunt Dora brightly added, as she wrapped her shawl a little tighter around her chest. "And this is such a fine car."

"Thank you, Aunt Dora," replied Bess, as she hurried to get in. "It's old now. I've been thinking about getting a new one, but after discovering their cost, I've pretty well changed my mind."

"Why, this one is just fine, it seems to me. There's so much room back here. It's just like riding in Shirley's daddy's, you know, my late brother's, Cadillac. Now that was one of the first and the finest car around at the time. You know my family was noted for buying nice things, mostly unnecessary things. That's why we don't have two cents to rub together today. They squandered it all. You remember my brother; he spent every nickel he could get his greedy hands on."

We were finally all loaded up and ready to go. Testing Aunt Dora's directional skills right off the bat, I looked back at Aunt Dora from the front seat and asked, "Now, Aunt Dora, which way is it to Burt County from here?" Aunt Dora was happily perched in the backseat amongst all her paraphernalia, as excited as a child going to the circus for the first time. She had her spectacles, her cane, her hearing horn, her dentist teeth, a seat cushion from one of her porch rockers under her to help with the bumps along the way, a canvas traveling bag with headache powders and ointments, a blanket for her lap, a hot water bottle, an extra apron, her shiny, patent leather pocketbook, and a Coca-Cola. Bess and I had waited impatiently on the porch while she gathered everything for the trip. When she finally walked out to the porch to go, she looked as if she was going on an "around the world" excursion with all her gear. She was even wearing a traveling duster over a different dress. She had rolled on a good pair of stockings too, saying the pair she had been wearing was a little picked, and she wanted to look her best. Her thin grey hair was twisted under a black felt hat, and fresh face powder and a touch of rouge were smeared across her smiling, excited face. Bess and I were a little concerned about her taking the trip, but she was certainly prepared for any emergency.

I asked if she needed for us to swing by the library to tell Shirley she was going for a ride with us, but she indignantly replied that Shirley was not her boss, and she didn't have to answer to Shirley for one thing. I just hoped Shirley wouldn't come looking for Aunt Dora while we were gone. I'm sure she would have an all-points bulletin out for her before we returned. Thinking we might be making a mistake by not leaving a note about Aunt Dora's whereabouts, I excused myself back into the house, explaining I needed to use the facilities, and left a note on the hall table. *I could have just as easily written it on the dusty surface of the table.*

We were all ready to go at last and back in the car, when Aunt Dora said she might need to use the facilities in the house also, just one more time before we left. With much ado from everyone, we proceeded to get her into the house and then back out. Finally we were all set...again...and I asked Aunt Dora the same question. "Which way is it to Burt County, Aunt Dora?"

I knew we were in deep trouble when she sat up, peered out of the car window, and very self-assuredly answered, "Why, it's just around the corner. You know where the old hollow mulberry tree fell beside the road and the honeysuckle is blooming all the way down the fence row. That's where you turn off. " Bess gave me that knowing look again, and we drove off with our eager passenger in tow.

Bess pulled out on Route 2, and we rode along peacefully and quietly for a while. Bess and I knew the road to Waynesville fairly well, and we knew we were almost to the county line. I glanced back at Aunt Dora as she held tightly to the armrest as if she might fall out at any time, and asked, "Now we're about to enter Burt County. Do you remember how we get to the barbecuing place? Do we go all the way into Waynesville, or do we make a turn before we get there?"

"Oh, we make a turn or two. First we need to get to Verdette. The place isn't far from there. Daddy always watered the horses in Verdette. You know back then, this was an all day trip. Daddy would always stop and buy a penny's worth of peppermint candy for us in Verdette. It's not far now."

"We're almost to the county line, Aunt Dora. What do we do now?" asked Bess, this time only as a test.

"We turn to the right at the first road. Am I going to have to tell you girls every turn?" We knew the road to Verdette only too well, recalling our recent venture over into this backwoodsy part of the world. Motoring on, I began to have that same uneasy feeling I had felt several days before, the day of the wrestling match. Glancing back again, Aunt Dora still seemed undaunted and delighted, with a look of wonderment on her old, wrinkled face. Whatever the result of this trip, Bess and I had certainly done a good deed, just getting Aunt Dora out into the world again.

"Now keep to this road, and I 'spect we'll come to a cross in the road fairly soon. Don't turn, just keep on goin'. I don't really know how far Verdette is, but there's no turn until we get there. I swear, this road doesn't seem to have changed in all these years. I remember honeysuckle growing all over these woods; it's just not blooming this time of the year. Keep going, girls, we'll be there when we get there. Let's get another Coca-Cola in Verdette."

"We don't need to be drinking too much, Aunt Dora. You know it goes right through you. You know you've already drunk one," I cautioned.

"And I'm gonna drink another one when we get to Verdette. Y'all promised we'd get one, and I want a Johnny Cake with mine too. Keep on goin'."

We stayed on the road, never turning, past the sawmill—*thank heavens we didn't see anybody around*—and on down the road toward Obe Jordan's house. Bess exclaimed, "Those little girls are out playing again today. Let's stop and give them another Milky Way bar. I don't think their mother would mind." After our unscheduled stop, we motored on, hoping we were almost to our destination. Verdette appeared about a mile down the dusty, deserted road, just as Aunt Dora told us it would.

"Aunt Dora, I believe we are in the middle of Verdette right now," I said, as we rode up to the country store with a wide, unpainted front porch and one gas pump. A lopsided, rusty Coca-Cola sign reminded Aunt Dora we were to be treated with a Coca-Cola.

"I'll get the drinks," I said, after Bess pulled over into the shade of a giant oak tree. "Anybody want something else?"

"I'll take a drink and my Johnny Cakes; add a little cheese too," Aunt Bess said, as she dug into her pocketbook for some change. "Y'all get anything you want," she added, as she handed me a folded dollar bill. "It's my treat. I've been saving this dollar for this day for a long time."

"Just a Coca-Cola for me," said Bess. "I'll wait out here with Aunt Dora." I knew Bess wanted to come into the store with me, but she knew better than to leave Aunt Dora by herself.

The interior of the country store was dark, with only one lightbulb hanging from a long cord in the ceiling of the narrow room. Rows of canned goods, flour, meal, lard, and other pantry items were on deep shelves anchored together down the middle of the back of the room. Stacks of washtubs and galvanized buckets, brooms, a rack of starches and laundry powders, and other household items were lined around the exterior walls. I walked over to one of the three glass counters just inside the front door. I immediately noticed an elderly man, wearing a dingy white apron over his overalls, sitting on a stack of chicken feed. After I cleared my throat to alert him that a customer was in the store, he reluctantly stuck his head up from a magazine with a pretty girl in a daring swimming suit posed on the front cover. I nodded to him and asked if he had Johnny Cakes.

"Over in the food section," he said, as he nodded toward another glass counter with a drink box beside it. He eased up and hid his magazine under a rack of automobile hoses and belts. The food section, I discovered, contained an assortment of candy bars, large jars of crackers and cookies, crocks of pickled eggs and pigs' feet, and a big wheel of cheese.

"I'll take six Johnny Cakes and three wedges of cheese, please."

"Yes, ma'am. I'll get right on it. Do you need gas for your car? We got it all right here. No need to go anywhere else."

"Just some drinks from the box. I hope they're cold," I answered, as I reached into the box for the drinks. I waited as the man automatically wrapped the crackers and cheese in wax paper as if he had done it time and time again for many years. "Just charge me for the bottles; we'll be taking them with us," I said, as I popped the caps off the bottles with the little metal opener hanging from a string. "Sir, you don't happen to know where a barbecuing place is around here, do you? I heard there might be one back in here somewhere."

"Oh, no ma'am. Ain't no barbecuing place around back in these woods. My daddy used to barbecue years and years ago, though. Best barbecue around. People came from all over to get his barbecue. His place was up the road a piece toward Waynesville. That was a long time ago. Nothing like that around anymore. I imagine you'd have to go clear into Waynesville for barbecue now."

"Your daddy, I don't suppose he would be around, would he?"

"No ma'am. He's been gone a good many years now. We quit all that barbecuing years and years ago. Daddy was a master at it, though. His barbecue goat was the best. I can just taste it now."

"Are there any Colemans around in these parts? I'm looking for a Zeniss Coleman."

"There are some Colemans around here. Zeniss is my aunt's boy. If you're looking for Zeniss, you'll have to go slam into Waynesville. Zeniss is presently residing in the county jail."

Startled at the reply, I said, "Jail?"

"We're all pretty shook up by it. Zeniss got into a little trouble he couldn't get himself out of. It's a bad situation. You see, Zeniss is a good boy, just a little touched in the head. My aunt did the best she could do with him, but since she died, he ain't had no real guidance."

"Dear me. Your aunt's son is Zeniss? Was she a Coleman?"

"She was a Coleman, same as my mama. You're getting a little personal now, ma'am. We don't talk much about it, but Minnie left home and came back with a boy child, Zeniss. It happened so long ago. Anyway, the boy never could learn right. She mostly let him have his way about everything. She took care of him until a few years ago when she died. He stays by himself in her old house now and lives on what she left him. Ain't much money left, and he squanders it on...you know, stuff he ought not to do. He's finally landed in jail."

"Is he there for drinking...or what?" I shyly asked.

"They claim he beat up some woman a week or so ago. He's really very gentle. He must have gotten riled up over something. You know men can get into bad situations with a bad woman. That's about all I know. The sheriff is keeping everything pretty hush-hush. I need to go see him at the jailhouse, just haven't had the time."

My mind was spinning. Could Zeniss Coleman be the killer we were looking for? "Sir..."

"Listen lady, that's about all I know. I don't like to talk about kin."

"Well, err, thank you for everything," I thoughtfully replied, as I walked out with more than just my purchases— more information. *Just how far was it to that county jail?*

Bess and I couldn't dare walk into that jailhouse building for fear of being recognized, but what if Aunt Dora was to...

CHAPTER TWENTY-FOUR

"A unt Dora, how do you feel about stepping into the sheriff's office in Waynesville and asking to speak to one of the inmates?" I yelled, as I got back into the car. "Bess and I could put you off at the front door and wait around the corner for you to come out. As soon as you come out, we'd drive over and pick you up."

"Really! You want me to spy for you," Aunt Dora exclaimed, as she reached for her drink and crackers. "I can hardly wait! All you have to do is tell me what you want me to find out, and I'll be Johnny-on-the-spot. Just fill me in on all the details. I knew you were on an important case the minute you walked into my house this morning. I just knew it! I could have helped y'all on that case about Ida Wallace throwing her garbage by the road, but y'all figured it out before I could get in on the investigation. Shirley told me about it later on. Ida's been throwing her garbage all over the place for years, and now, because of your help, the sheriff finally nabbed that old biddy." Aunt Dora became so excited she could hardly restrain herself as we sat in the car under the oak tree, enjoying our snack. I (loudly) filled Aunt Dora and Bess in on all the latest details. "Let's get this show on the road," she hollered, as we wadded the wax paper, and Bess gathered the bottles.

"Now, Aunt Dora, you know what to say," I hollered, as we traveled over the red clay road toward the county seat. "Tell the jailer you want to know what the charges are against Zeniss Coleman. If he won't tell you, bring out the pad and pencil I just handed you and tell him you're with the press from a big newspaper in Atlanta, and the people of Georgia have a right to know exactly what's going on in this podunk town. I'll bet he'll jump then. Get all the information you can on Dixie's murder...and anything to do with Zeniss. Now, do you think you're up to it?"

"You bet I am! I'm good at prying information out of people. Why, I've pried more gossip than you can imagine out of Shirley about everybody around town all these years. Why do you think I've put up with her so long?" Aunt Dora proudly declared. "I knew all about you gallivanting around with that fertilizer salesman last year, Bess. You're a whole lot better off without that two-timing scallywag." *Aunt Dora knew more about what was going on than we did, and she rarely left home. Maybe we had found another honey hole for information.*

"You do know what's going on, Aunt Dora, and just to think you don't even have a telephone. If you had Nellie to talk to every day on the telephone, you'd never miss out on another thing," I hollered.

"I have been thinking about getting one of those newfangled talking machines. About how much do you pay to get one? If it's more than a dollar fifty a month, I can't afford it. You know my budget's pretty tight now that I'm making payments on an icebox to Sears and Roebuck. My payment is four dollars a month, and I've got twelve more payments. They don't know it, but they'll never get it all. I won't live that long. I didn't think I really needed one, but Shirley insisted. I do like my Coca-Colas cold. Before I got one, I had to keep them in the well out back."

"You really can't afford one," Bess interjected thankfully. She knew nobody could yell loud enough over the telephone for Aunt Dora to hear.

"We're almost to the jailhouse. Are you ready?" I hollered from the front seat.

Aunt Dora replied, "Girls, I was born ready." Aunt Dora was certainly up to the challenge, we thought, as we watched her determinedly waddle down the street with her cane and black patent leather pocketbook in tow toward the old gray house with the big metal sign in front that read "Sheriff's Office and Jail." She glanced back toward us and appeared to be very confident just before we watched her pull the heavy front door open and disappear into the house. With sighs of relief from both of us, Bess backed the car down the street, and we began our vigil.

We waited...and we waited. No Aunt Dora! We waited some more...no Aunt Dora!

"You don't suppose she got in there and had a heart attack?" I nervously asked Bess.

"Well, we haven't seen an ambulance pull up. If she had a heart attack, surely somebody in there would have called an ambulance by now. And, thank heavens, we haven't seen any sign of a hearse! But I can't imagine what's going on in there. A little questioning shouldn't take...what, has it been an hour since Aunt Dora went in?"

"It's been a little more than an hour," I answered, as I glanced at my watch. "If she doesn't come out soon, I guess one of us will have to go in after her. How long does it take to question somebody, anyway?"

"Hey, look! Somebody's coming out! I'll bet that's the sheriff. You know he looks kind of familiar. Maybe it's the way he walks."

"He looks like Sheriff Ledbetter, and it's not just the uniform. They favor a good bit!"

"They both have a big belly and a huge mustache," Bess replied with a chuckle. "I wonder if they have the same low I.Q." *We were later to learn that they were first cousins. Their mamas were sisters.*

"He couldn't be as clueless as Sheriff Ledbetter!" I replied. "An accident of nature couldn't strike so close two times in a row. And he must have been in a fight recently. Look at that big goose egg on his forehead and that Band-Aid stuck across his nose."

"Oh, I need to use the bathroom, Bee. If Aunt Dora doesn't come out soon, I've got to find one. I could go to the courthouse across the street, but I'm afraid some busybody over there would recognize me. I'm sure that milkman or that young mother has described us to the sheriff by now. There's probably a wanted poster for us hanging on the wall over there somewhere."

Bess had begun wiggling and squirming so badly by then she was making the whole car shake. "Hold on a little longer, Bess," I nervously replied. "She's got to come out soon."

"Well, she better, or it's gonna be too late."

"We're going to have to go in after her," Bess finally said. An anxious expression covered her face, and she was beginning to turn several shades of green. "I'm going in anyway, right now before I bust."

"Listen, Bess, run into that office building over there." I pointed toward a small brick building next to the jailhouse. "They won't care."

Before the words left my lips, Bess had flung open the car door and was trotting frantically across the well-manicured lawn like a flash. As I sat in the car, contemplating our next move, an idea suddenly burst into my mind. I hastily put on Aunt Dora's duster and black felt hat. By the time a relieved Bess walked out of the office building, I had changed my whole appearance. Aunt Dora's dark red lipstick and rouge were smeared across my face, and I had donned her spectacles across the lower part of my nose. Luckily, deep in Aunt Dora's traveling bag, I had found black hose and a pair of size nine black oxfords. They were a little big, but by squeezing my toes, I figured they'd temporarily stay on.

"I'm going in after Aunt Dora. She's had time to read the whole Bible, forward and backwards, since she went in there."

"You're absolutely crazy. You can't go marching in there dressed like a...I don't know what you look like."

"Hey, this is a great disguise. Nobody will ever recognize me in this getup. You stay out here and be ready for a fast getaway."

I was out of the car and prancing down the street before you could spell your name. Determined to find Aunt Dora and get her out of there, I hiked up my sagging stockings, adjusted my spectacles, gathered all my courage, and opened the same heavy door Aunt Dora had disappeared through over an hour ago.

"You must be the old lady's niece," a fat deputy, sitting behind a scarred metal desk, remarked between bites from a ham sandwich. "We gave her one telephone call, and after she made it, she said you'd be here to spring her soon. Lady, that's her words, not *mine*."

"Oh, err, yes." *Wonder who she called? I didn't know Aunt Dora even knew how to use a telephone.*

"If you'll wait a minute, I'll get her for you. I hope you don't let her out of the house too often," he said with a smirk. "She's really an old sports model." The deputy laid his sandwich down on his dingy handkerchief and slowly heaved his considerable weight to his feet. I stood just inside the front door, nodded without speaking, and waited. He ambled toward the back of the room, removed a set of keys off a big nail, unlocked a heavy metal door, and disappeared, leaving me alone and wondering what kind of story Dora had concocted, and what the heck was she doing behind a locked door. I nervously glanced around. That's when I noticed a half-eaten green shoe, with a large tag attached, on top of a metal filing cabinet in the corner of the official-looking room. *Holy Moly! Bess's shoe!* I quickly grabbed it and stuck it into Aunt Dora's traveling bag.

The metal door soon opened again, and Aunt Dora, with her cane, smiling just like the cat that ate a canary, triumphantly walked out with the bewildered-looking deputy following behind. As soon as the deputy closed the door, Aunt Dora indignantly remarked directly to the deputy, "I'll take my pocketbook now, if you don't mind. I'm sure you've snooped all through it. Every bit of my three dollars and fifty cents better be in there, or I'll know who snitched it."

"Just a minute, lady. Nobody's been through your purse, but somebody's got to pay some bail money. Nobody gets a free ride around this jailhouse. That'll be two dollars." He held his huge hand out.

"Give the man my bail, niece, and let's hightail it outta here."

I reached into Aunt Dora's large traveling bag and retrieved my purse. Quickly finding two one dollar bills, I curiously, but silently, offered them over to the deputy. He hastily scratched out a receipt from a pad lying on his desk and handed it over to me. If I hadn't seen it with my own two eyes, I would never have believed what happened next. Aunt Dora revved back, and with all the strength in her ninety-year-old body, she swung her cane over the deputy's head and began beating him with the strength of a woman half her age. Not once, but twice, she struck him, triumphantly shouting, "That'll teach you for locking up a defenseless old woman! Your mama would be purely ashamed of you!" Seeing the situation was totally out of control, I unsuccessfully attempted to pull Aunt Dora's cane away from her.

"Oh, no, nobody's gonna take a helpless old woman's cane." She held on tight, adjusted her teeth with a grimace, and without the help of the cane— or me— marched toward the front door. "Let's get outta here, niece, before I do something I'm really ashamed of!"

The deputy hollered after her, "I ought to throw you into solitary!"

I gave the deputy a helpless, distressed glance, and followed behind the "helpless old woman."

As soon as we closed the door, Aunt Dora whispered, "Don't worry about a thing, Bee. I'll pay you the two dollars back. They put me in the same cell with Zeniss Coleman, and he gave me the whole lowdown."

"In the same cell as Zeniss Coleman!" Unbelieving, I repeated, "They put you in a jail cell with Zeniss Coleman?"

"You betcha! And it wasn't by accident. I had to break the law to get in there. I'll explain the whole thing in the car. Let's get outta here!"

Expecting the deputy to come running out after us, we hurried as fast as a ninety-year-old can hurry, toward the car. Bess had seen us as we closed the jailhouse door, and the car suddenly lurched forward, soon jerking to a stop right in front of us. I reached to open the back door and shoved Aunt Dora in, as she protested that she could get in under her own steam. I quickly ran around the car and jumped in the front seat as Bess revved the car again, and with another sudden jerk, she threw the car into first, and off we went at least a city block in first gear, causing the car to backfire and make a horrific grinding noise that prompted a pack of dogs off in the distance to start howling. I looked back into the backseat as Aunt Dora rolled down the window and stuck her head out, giving a heroic yell, "Off we go into the wild blue yonder! Hallelujah!!!" Bess flung the gear into second, floored the gas, and with another screech and grind, threw the gear into third. We were off! The dogs were still howling as we roared away.

Aunt Dora jumped and Aunt Dora bounced as we rode along. It took five or six miles for Aunt Dora to calm down enough to tell us what had actually happened back at the jailhouse. She confessed she hit the sheriff over the head with her cane a couple of times when he realized she wasn't a reporter. He wouldn't volunteer any information about Zeniss or Dixie's murder so, knowing the only way she was going to be able to get any facts or to interview Zeniss, she'd have to get herself thrown into the pokey. *That was her slang word for jail.* Back in the cell, Zeniss soon filled her in on all the facts. He admitted he wasn't proud of it, but he was a regular of Dixie's and had visited her the weekend before her murder. When Dixie tried to blackmail him for more money, he confessed he got a little out of hand with her and hit her a time or two. Dixie called the sheriff from next door after he left, and he was soon picked up. That was the end of the story. He told Aunt Dora he hadn't been able to make bail and was rotting in jail. Aunt Dora said he was so nice and polite to her that she thought she'd try to get together some money and send Shirley over to bail him out in a day or two.

We informed Aunt Dora that she'd have to stand before the judge on court day and pay another fine for all her unlawful actions, or they'd throw her back in jail. She triumphantly responded, "That'll never happen. Look at that receipt the deputy gave us. I gave them my late Aunt Prudence Jenkins's name and address for mine, and she's been dead close to forty years now. They'll never come close to finding her or me!"

We were finally able to get Aunt Dora back through her front door that night. Her last words to us were, "How about it, girls? Would y'all be willing to give Shirley a ride back over to Burt County next week to bail Zeniss out? I could ride along, too, and wait in the car. I'd treat everybody to another Coca-Cola."

* * *

Sadly, Aunt Dora died in her sleep that night, probably after having the biggest time of her life. Bess and I thought Shirley would probably accuse us of causing Aunt Dora's heart attack sooner or later, but Aunt Dora must have torn up the note explaining her absence before she died. Shirley never knew about our romp through the country, nor did she ever know of Aunt Dora's detainment in the county jail the afternoon before her death, and we certainly never told anyone! I did notice a day or two later at her viewing, Mr. Lawson had put those dentist teeth that pinched Aunt Dora's gums into her mouth but had not been able to remove that devious smile from Aunt Dora's face.

Oh, and by the way, Sheriff Oscar Fay Cornfoot never did find Prudence Jenkins when she missed her court date...and he never discovered what became of a certain green shoe. Those facts would remain mysteries!

CHAPTER TWENTY-FIVE

I just can't for the life of me believe Judge Harmon could have anything to do with a murder. There's just no way!" I thought to myself, as I finally sat down on the porch to rest a bit. And poor Molly was still in my thoughts. Where was she now, if she wasn't at the bottom of the river? Sam was still around town; I had seen him today, going about life as if nothing was wrong.

It was late Tuesday afternoon of the following week. Bess and I had spent the last few days helping Shirley attend to all the funeral arrangements for Aunt Dora. It had been the least we could do. The constant hammering and swearing of the Norton brothers had become part of everyday life, and I hardly even noticed it anymore. The front rooms of the house really looked charming. Melvin had finished all the painting and had successfully stripped and varnished the floors in the front room, dining room, and hall. We were coming and going through the back of the house now until the floors were good and dry. It was a nuisance, but with the fresh appearance of everything, it was really worth it. Melvin had begun painting Bess's boudoir, and Lambert had finally positioned the tub where it needed to be, with hot and cold running water too, I might add. He was busy adding shelves to the bathroom closet now, and all was going pretty much as scheduled.

Bess said she was exhausted. She had been a real lifesaver for Shirley. Why, Bess had taken over the kitchen at Shirley's and attended to every need as people flooded in to sit up with Shirley during her time of grief. *I'm not real sure Shirley was grieving; she was acting more relieved than anything.* Bess, Mildred, and I had headed back over to Shirley's right after the funeral to help with serving. A few straggling cousins had come in right before the service and had not had time to do any visiting with Shirley or the rest of the family, so all the food had to be drug out one more time and then a final cleanup. With Shirley's house back into order, I had headed home and was finally resting on the porch. What a relief!

The investigation had come to a total standstill the last few days. At least the sheriff from Burt County hadn't showed up to arrest us. I was planning to completely reorganize my thoughts now and focus on Judge Harmon. Could the judge really have anything to do with Dixie's death? I didn't know, but I was bound and determined to find out. With Sam Turner, Obe Jordan, Henry Lee Speirs, Silas Jernigan, E. N. Frost, and Zeniss Coleman all out of the way, only one name in the ledger was left to be investigated.

A trip back to Burt County had to be planned. That next door neighbor of Dixie's might be able to tell us something about Judge Harmon's comings and goings. Maybe we should speak to her before muddying up the waters by talking directly with the judge. Yes, the more I thought about it, that was a good idea. Tomorrow, a trip to see her was in order. Please, dear Lord, I prayed, help us get past Biscuit.

We definitely needed to go in my car this time. Bess's car might be too easily identified. We had ridden in Bess's car last week on our trip to the jailhouse, and we had been in Vonion's old pickup truck on our first trip over to Burt County. We definitely couldn't use it. Vonion wouldn't allow us to drive it, anyway. He always said it took a special touch to drive his truck, and I positively knew I definitely didn't have the touch. I'd tell Bess to wear her pedal pushers tomorrow, and I'd wear mine. Some dangly earbobs and chunky bracelets, along with lots of makeup and black hair dye would complete our disguises. We'd look like a couple of modern day women, not two dowdy old widow women. *Bess would not like that description.* Hopefully, nobody would recognize us over in Burt County in our new getups. Yep, my mind was definitely made up.

Applying black hair color was probably out of our expertise, so a trip to Thelma's was on my list of things to do. I'd have to think up some good explanation to tell Thelma why we wanted our hair colored, but I'd think about that later, and I'd also wait until morning to fill Bess in on our new adventure. I knew she'd be less than thrilled about the trip, but hopefully, she'd be willing. The truth was out there, and we were going to find it, if it killed us trying.

Oops, surely our efforts hadn't killed Aunt Dora. Had it?

* * *

"I'm not going anywhere in pedal pushers, and I'm not dying my hair, so you might as well get over it. You've gone too far this time...pretending to be flappers or whatever you want to call it. This idea is totally ridiculous."

I had hurried over to Bess's house early the next morning, hoping to catch her in a good mood. I soon found out that was way too much to ask for. She was sitting at her kitchen table, in a daze, as she sipped her coffee. "And anyway, Thelma won't take us this early. For heaven's sake, it's only eight o'clock in the morning. I happen to know she doesn't take customers until nine, and I'm not dying my hair for anybody, except maybe Clark Gable."

"Yes, you are," I emphatically answered. "You don't want to get arrested, do you? If we get identified as those ladies who were leaving Dixie's house after she was killed, who knows, we could even get arrested for murder. Now, let's hurry, and let's get over to Thelma's before any old busybodies show up. Now come on." I almost lifted Bess out of her chair and pushed her right out the door. We didn't have a minute to waste. I threw open the car door and heaved her into the seat.

Thelma was standing at the door of her little shop in the back room of her house as we rode up, waving to her children as they walked across the street on their way to school. As soon as I saw her, I stuck my arm out the window of the car and frantically waved. "Thelma, we've got to get our hair done right now. It's a hair emergency! Turn the water on, and I'll get sleepyhead in there in a flash."

Thelma yelled back, "I haven't even had my second cup of coffee yet. You know I don't do hair before I've had all my caffeine. What's your rush, anyway?" Thelma wrapped her bathrobe a little closer around herself as she pulled a package of cigarettes out of her pocket.

I had to think of something in a hurry. "Bess's late mother-in-law's highfalutin' cousin called during the night and wants us to hurry to Savannah for a big funeral," I called from the car, as I jerked the door open and ran around the car to pull Bess out. "One of their other cousins is supposed to be buried today in one of those big-city cemeteries, and they've requested that Bess say the closing prayer at the funeral. None of those rich city people have seen us lately, and we certainly don't want those hotsy-totsy people thinking of us as country people who don't know a thing about style or how to fix up. We've got to leave this morning, so we don't have a minute to waste."

Thelma gave me a knowing glance and lit her cigarette. "Do you really think I believe that? I was born at night, but not last night. You two are up to something, but I'm scared to ask the real truth."

"Listen, Thelma, it's the truth. We want our hair dyed jet black, both of us. Do you think you can do it or not? We don't have time to stand around all day. We can always go over to Trudy's Hair Palace if you're not up to it. Trudy's wanted our business for a good while anyway." I knew if I told Thelma we were thinking of moving our business to the Palace, she'd definitely cave in.

"Oh, okay, I'll do it. Both of you get in here. Now who's first?"

Bess and I both answered at the same time, "She is."

"Okay, Ms. Bee, sit down and put your head back. Y'all want Raven Black or Midnight Black?"

"Whichever one is quicker," I hastily answered, as I sat down. "Bess, you be ready to sit down as soon as Thelma is through with me. Maybe you can fix us all a cup of coffee while you wait. Now Thelma, get going, and do it right this time."

A little later, as Thelma towel dried my hair, she looked over at Bess. "Ms. Bess, are you sure you want your hair dyed too?" Thelma had already squirted some black goo all over my head, and now she was rubbing it into my hair. I was sitting in front of the mirror but had not dared to open my eyes to look at the results.

"Not if it's gonna look like that, I don't," I heard Bess answer. "Can you make me a blond instead? I think I'd look better as a blond, anyway." I opened my eyes as Thelma started combing my jet black hair.

"Hey, that looks pretty good," I said enthusiastically as I studied the results. "I like it. Bess, are you sure you don't want to have black hair? You're too old for blond hair. Black hair looks more natural."

"Yea, your hair looks natural all right—about as natural as Hortence giving chocolate milk. Thelma, I'm not so sure about all this. Maybe you should just give me a wash and curl."

"No, absolutely not. Bess, do you want to be a blond, or do you want black hair? Make up your mind, and make it up now!" I interjected, before Bess had time to back out.

"Heaven's, you are so-o bossy. Make it blond, Thelma, and try to make it look a little more natural. I don't want those people at the funeral to think we're a couple of country hicks who dunked their heads into a can of black tar."

"Thelma, you did a great job on my hair. It looks real good." Thelma was taking the pin curls out and combing in the waves while Bess slept under the hairdryer. "You don't happen to have any dangly earbobs, do you? I feel kind of frisky today. Maybe Bess and I both could borrow a pair or two."

"Now I know for sure y'all aren't going to any ole funeral. Dyed hair and dangly earbobs? Y'all are going on a manhunt. Lordy, Ms. Bee, I never figured you'd be after another man."

"Thelma, think what you want. Just let us borrow those earbobs. And if you've got some bright-colored bracelets, we could use them too."

Bess's hair looked really nice, I thought, as Thelma combed it into a modern wavy bob. Thank heavens we were out of Thelma's Cut and Curl before any of her regular busybody customers came in that morning. We simply didn't have time to make up any more fibs.

Over at Bess's house, we completed our new look. After donning our pedal pushers and all that junky jewelry Thelma had loaned us, we layered on the makeup. As we stood, side by side, in front of the mirror in Bess's back bedroom to admire ourselves, Bess complained, "Bee, we've gone to all this trouble to disguise ourselves, and you've still got on those old brown house shoes. Try on these nice red heels of mine. You've needed to upgrade your shoes for a while anyway and now's the time."

Knowing better than to argue with Bess, especially when she's right, I slipped on the shoes. "You know, Bess, I hardly recognize us. We really do look different. Maybe we should have made this transformation years ago," I admitted, as I gave us one last glance in the mirror. "Grab your big ole pocketbook, Bess, and let's go. Oh...Are you armed with all the Milky Way bars you think we'll need? Biscuit might be extra hungry this morning."

"I've got a whole new six-pack. Now let's get to that funeral you were talking about. I just hope it's not our funeral. I'm not ready to die today. Everybody says that blondes have more fun, and I want to enjoy life as a blonde for a little while.

CHAPTER TWENTY-SIX

I hope nobody we know sees us in these getups. I can hear Mildred and the rest of the girls gossiping about us," Bess said. She had just added a little more red lipstick to her already blood-red lips, as I cautiously drove along the road toward Burt County. I wasn't really paying much attention to what she was saying.

"What'd you say, Bess?"

"I said," and she raised her voice, "I hope nobody we know sees us today. I've never worn a pair of pants out the back door, much less on a road trip."

"You know everybody'd probably be jealous. It's kinda freeing not having a dress tail to worry about. I really believe it's gonna catch on—wearing pants, I mean. I like it, but I guess we do look sort of cheap in a way, with all this makeup lathered on our faces and our hair dyed." I took my eyes off the road and quickly checked my "Midnight Black" hairdo in the rearview mirror. "We've got to pray nobody over in Burt County recognizes us. At least we know Biscuit can't talk. Oh, and listen Bess. When we get to that woman's house, will you please let me do most of the talking?"

"Bee, if you tell me that again, I'm going to stay home next time we have to interrogate somebody, and then you can do *all* the talking. For Pete's sake, you'd think I didn't have a grain of sense."

"I'm sorry. I know I can be a little overbearing sometimes when it comes to our investigations, but I do mean well. Do you think we should drive right up to the front of the house, or do you think we need to walk over from someplace else?"

"Let's park in the same spot Vonion parked the truck the other day and walk over again. That way, hopefully, nobody will notice the car or get our license plate number. You do remember how to get there, don't you?"

"Oh, yes, I remember all right. It's easy—just one street over from Margaret's. Oh, speaking of Margaret, she'd be furious with us if she knew what we were up to. We've got to hope and pray she never finds out." Bess nodded in agreement as she patted her hair.

We pulled into the vacant lot where Vonion parked the day we made our initial investigation, and I switched the car motor off. "Oka-ay, we're here," I announced, as if I was a tour director on a big bus. "Make sure you bring your pocketbook, and it better be loaded with ammunition." I opened the car door, said a little prayer, and waited as Bess walked around the car.

"Ammunition?" she inquisitively repeated. "What on earth are you talking about? You know you talk in circles about half the time."

"Milky Ways, Bess. Milky Ways."

"Oh, that kind of ammunition. You know I always have my ammunition. "

Trying to appear casual, but with real determination, our mission began as we started our walk down the same sidewalk as the last time we had graced the neighborhood with our presence. Bess soon reached into her big pocketbook and brought out a package of Juicy Fruit chewing gum. "Here. Start smacking. That's what modern women do."

"Good thinking," I said, as I folded a strip of the sugary gum into my mouth. "This gum is another good touch to add to our disguises." *It calmed my nerves a bit too.*

"Not much has changed around here," Bess said, as we trudged along, toting our purses and smacking our gum. "Not one soul has cleaned a flower bed or washed a single window."

"A lot has changed around here in the last couple of weeks. I know this looks like a nice, quiet little neighborhood, but looks can be very deceiving. A murder took place here."

Bess suddenly stopped, grabbed my arm, and glared straight ahead. Pointing her finger toward the end of the street, she whispered, "There's that mean ole dog, Bee. He's prowling around that house again like he's a guard at Fort Knox. He looks just as ferocious and hungry today as he did the last time we were over here."

"Listen, Bess, instead of acting all nervous and afraid of him, get out the Milky Way bars, and I'll hold one out for him to eat. Maybe he'll come right up to me for the candy, and we can pet him. We've got to show him we're not frightened."

"Are you serious? Bee, that dog is not friendly; he *is* ferocious. He'll probably bite our hand off, but if you want to get dog bit, you go ahead, and I'll watch while you pet Biscuit. If he doesn't eat you up, I'll follow you into the yard."

With all the courage I could muster, I slowly walked toward the yard with Bess lagging at least twenty feet behind. Biscuit soon noticed me and began to growl. Terrified, I kept on walking and waved the candy bar in the air. Biscuit lowered his big head and growled again. I said a quick prayer and kept on going. As soon as I was close enough to reach out and touch him, I held the candy bar out a little farther and dropped it right into his huge, drooling mouth, where every one of his razor-sharp teeth were shining. As he chewed and slobbered, I cautiously reached over and gently petted his basketball-sized head. "Good boy, good Biscuit. You want another one? Bess, come on over, and hand me another candy bar."

Bess, trembling all the way, bravely inched her way toward me as Biscuit continued to slobber and chew. I dropped another candy bar into his big, eager mouth, and we watched as he smacked and finally swallowed his second treat. I kept petting him and talking to him as he chomped and crunched one candy bar after another, as I kept dropping them into his mouth. When I held out candy bar number five, he grabbed for it, and then, as if he had enough, let it fall to the ground, and he slowly dropped right on top of the gooey candy and rolled over, looking nauseated and sick. "Good boy, good dog," I gently said, and motioned for a cowering Bess to come on.

We slowly tripped right past a queasy Biscuit and headed toward the little front porch of the house next door to Dixie's. I hastily knocked, and we nervously waited. I could hear a radio or a record player somewhere inside the house playing my favorite song. The haunting melody of "I'll be Seeing You" floated out into the air, calming us a bit. I knocked again, and soon we detected the sound of footsteps inside the house. The front door opened, and the same overweight woman, with the same old bathrobe pulled around her large buxom body, peered across the threshold at us.

"Who's there?" she asked straightaway, as if she didn't see us standing right outside the door.

I immediately noticed two scratch marks across the woman's wide, unattractive face. The marks were healing, but still quite visible, and ran about one inch apart, from under her left eye all the way across her jaw to the corner of her fat lips. Some people might think the scratch marks were made from a cat attack, but I deduced they came from another person's fingernails. Surely her attacker had caught her off guard, with results of the altercation very visibly left behind.

Quickly coming back to reality, I said, "Uh, ma'am, excuse our rudeness, but we weren't sure if the house next door was the one for rent. My girlfriend and I are looking for—I think the address is 24 Fourth Avenue. We were told that house was available for rent."

"That's 24 Fourth Avenue next door, but I didn't know it was for rent. You might not know, but somebody got themselves killed over there recently, and I'm not real sure if the sheriff has allowed anybody to go back into the house since then. You might need to check with Judge Harmon about that. I believe he owns the place. He owns at least half the other houses around here."

"Oh, dear. We were hoping we could go in and take a quick tour of the house. Oh, err, may I introduce us to you. I'm Trudy, and this here is Debbie. We're from, err, out of town and just looking around for a suitable house to move into. Would you mind if we sat on your porch a minute to rest? We've been walking a while, and we're really tired."

"Oh, uh, I guess so. I'm glad to meet you. I'm Tempest Lamoure. You can come on into the house if you don't mind the mess. Come on into the living room, and I'll get y'all some cool water."

"Oh, thank you very much," I swooned, unable to believe our luck. "We sure could use a little something cool to drink." I grabbed Bess, aka Debbie, by the arm and pushed her forward. "Come on, Debbie."

We followed the slovenly women into the cluttered front room of her tiny bungalow. She politely asked us to be seated and excused herself to get the water. We gingerly sat down on a very lumpy settee, covered with a deep red fabric that reminded me of a bed sheet. *WE WERE IN! Now to get as much information out of this woman as possible.* I looked over at Bess and gave her a reassuring nod, and then a grin. I whispered, "Did you notice the scratch marks across Tempest's face?" She knowingly and silently nodded back.

I knew Bess and I could talk the ears off of a dog, and now we had the opportunity to try out all our newly developed detective skills. Just as soon as Tempest walked back into the living room with our drinks, Bess jumped up as if she were in pain and hastily asked, "I hope I'm not imposing too much, but is there any way I could use your facilities? It's been a long morning, and I don't think I can wait another minute longer."

Tempest quickly handed me my drink and gave Bess, I mean Debbie, directions to the bathroom down a narrow hallway. Tempest soon returned to the front room and shifted a few papers and circulars off the overstuffed chair in the corner of the room onto the floor and heavily plopped down.

"Nice day, isn't it?" I said, trying to make conversation. "It's so nice of you to let us rest in here a few minutes. We've walked our legs off trying to find a place to live that's decent. You've got a nice place here. I just love your color scheme."

"Oh, this place is a real dump. It's all I can afford right now, though. It's hard being a single girl out in this world today, but I hope things are going to pick up real soon now."

A few minutes later, after our conversation was beginning to lag, Bess walked back into the room, gave me a strange glance, and sat down beside me on the settee. Reaching for her glass of water from the coffee table, she casually remarked to Tempest that she just loved her red color scheme. I immediately could tell she was up to something, so I ate my very own words and let Bess "do most of the talkin'."

"You said a murder recently took place next door?" Bess asked. "Who was murdered, and how on earth did it happen?"

"My neighbor was murdered a few days ago by an intruder, but that's about all I know about it. The sheriff questioned me afterwards, but I told him I didn't see anything unusual that day. I did notice a young woman that I had never seen before go into the house earlier in the afternoon, but she was gone when I went over to talk to Dixie about three o'clock in the afternoon. But I told the sheriff all about it." She paused, and then added, "I never did particularly like Dixie. Oh, uh, Dixie was my neighbor's name."

"Goodness, you must have been horrified when you learned Dixie had been murdered," I replied. "Did the sheriff give you any indication how she was murdered or who did it? You know, you could have been in danger yourself. Maybe that young woman you saw had something to do with the murder."

"I don't see how. I saw Dixie very much alive after that woman left. I guess we won't ever know what really happened, but I did hear that Dixie died from a lick with a blunt object to her forehead."

"You don't say," I answered. "Does the sheriff have any more clues that you know of?"

"I doubt the sheriff has found out another thing. You know, we've got a real dumbass sheriff in this county. He doesn't know his butt from a big hole in the ground."

"Sounds like a sheriff we know," I added.

"You girls probably wouldn't want to live in that house now that you know what happened over there. It might be haunted. You never know."

"And you don't have any idea who that young woman is?" Bess asked, getting back to the subject.

"I had never seen her before, but I suspect she's some young wife checking up on her husband's activities. You see, uh, I want to put this delicately, but, err, Dixie was known to entertain men all hours of the day and night."

Bess threw her hand to her mouth in make-believe shock. "You don't mean Dixie was a...you know...a lady of the evening, or should I say, a lady of the evening and the daytime?"

"I ain't saying nothing about that," Tempest replied, as if Bess had accused *her* of something.

After a small pause in the conversation, Bess hesitantly spoke up. "Tempest, I've got to come clean with you. Trudy and I aren't really as naive as you might think. We, err, are trying to set up a little business over in this neck of the woods, uh, of a similar nature. We were just checking out things to see if there were good pickin's around here, if you know what I mean." Bess clicked her lips and eyed Tempest out of the corner of her eye. "Are the pickin's good around here? Is there enough business for everybody? We don't want to horn in on anybody else's space, but we were told this territory is wide open. We could all go together in a little commercial venture and divide the profits—you know, corner the market, so to speak."

Tempest didn't answer right off, and I sat straight up, dumbfounded and totally confused. Bess was really on a roll now, I discovered, when she asked Tempest how much we could get paid per hour. I silently cringed.

"Listen, girls, there's hardly enough business around here for me, much less two more girls. Now that Dixie's totally out of the picture, I might get a few of my old clients back, but probably not all of them. I think you two need to investigate another area to set up your operation. I don't need any more competition."

Shocked and mortified at the direction of the conversation, I stood up and quickly announced, "Well, we certainly appreciate the water, but we need to be on our way. Thank you…"

Bess suddenly horned in. "Listen, Tempest, I hope you don't think we're being too nosy, but Trudy and I are really interested in going into a little business enterprise right here. We were just wondering if there are enough men to go around for everybody. That's all we wanted to know."

"Now you are getting nosy! And don't get any ideas about setting up business around here. I've got this corner of town all to myself now, and I don't want any competition. I was doing just fine right by myself until Miss Sweet Pants Dixie showed up and started all that advertising. Every time one of my good customers came over, she'd be out in the yard with her little swimsuit on, gardening, or maybe out at the clothesline hanging out her lacy underwear. It's a wonder I had one good customer left. Good riddance to her is what I say! Listen, I don't want any trouble. I told the sheriff over here that Dixie and I had a tussle earlier in the day, but when I left her house, she was a little banged up but very much alive, and that was all there was to it."

Bess, *or should I say Debbie again*, quickly stood up and pointed her finger right at Tempest. "Listen, sister, we don't know anything about that situation, but we can work anywhere we want to, and furthermore, there's nothing you can do about it. I hope, for your sake, you didn't kill Dixie just to get rid of her. I've got a good mind to go see that sheriff over here and tell him Dixie was taking your clients and let him figure out the rest!" Bess sounded triumphant. *She was terrific!*

"Y'all are so stupid. Sheriff Oscar Fay Cornfoot of Burt County *is one* of my clients, and he is very loyal to me. He considers this to be his honey hole," Tempest smugly replied. Then with renewed fire in her eyes, she yelled, "Now you get out of here before I show you just how dangerous it'd be for anybody to set up business around here." Tempest began to grit her teeth directly at Bess and then balled up her fists as if she was about to let'm fly. Bess's elbows went up in defense, and I quickly grabbed her by the collar and declared, "We really do need to be going now." I rapidly started for the door, pulling Bess with me. "It's been real nice…" Before I could finish my sentence, I pushed Bess out the door, and I was right behind.

Tempest followed us to the door and hollered at Biscuit, "Sic'um, boy. Go get'um, boy."

We ran right past Biscuit as he raised his big head off the ground just long enough to give a long, pitiful moan. Bess threw her last candy bar at Biscuit, and he miserably looked at it as it landed in the dirt by his head.

* * *

We hastily headed back toward the car. As we passed the house where the small boy lived who had seen us on our previous trip, we noticed him playing with a squirt gun out in the yard. He aimed his water gun at us and called, "Hey, lady, are your feet any better?" He hit his moving targets, but we kept on going right through the drizzle of water and didn't bother to answer.

"Bess, have you lost your mind or something? I've never been so embarrassed in my entire life," I exclaimed, with my limited breath, after I slammed my car door. "You could have gotten us killed back there."

"I took a chance and it paid off. My trip to the bathroom was really enlightening, Bee," Bess excitedly answered. "Tempest's color scheme throughout the whole house is red, and you wouldn't believe the way she decorates. Red heart-shaped pillows, red curtains and bedspread, red silky sheets, red towels, red underwear, red nighties, and red everything else. She's got a closet full of whips and belts, and all kinds of tools of the trade. She's been around the block and back a few times, I'd say. I know we're on to something."

"You didn't go through the woman's drawers for heaven's sake?"

"Oh, yes I did! I'm getting better and better at this detective business, Bee."

"Maybe you are right. We are on to something; I just don't know what it is."

"Don't you see, Bee? Tempest had a good thing going until Dixie showed up. Young, pretty Dixie stole a lot of Tempest's customers. Tempest is really getting old and out of shape now, so it's hard for her to keep her customers interested. But now, with Dixie totally out of the picture again, she'll get some of her old clientele coming back full time. She's a fighter and a survivor."

"I think you're absolutely right. We can't strike Tempest off the list just yet. Where there's heat, there's always fire. We've got three suspects now: Tempest, Judge Harmon, and the young woman Tempest saw go in and out of the house. How much do you want to bet that young girl was Molly? I'd bet she's alive! Remember that pink sweater we saw in the kitchen? That had to be Molly's sweater. I remember she had a pink sweater on the day she came out to the house to ask for our assistance. She must have accidently left it in Dixie's kitchen. And if I'm right, Molly's still alive. Thank goodness! We've got to get over to nosy Mrs. Ricketson's this afternoon and find out when's the last time she spied on Molly. I don't know if we're getting any closer to solving this thing or not, but at least we aren't stuck at home listening to Melvin and Lambert swear and grumble."

"Yeah, and we're not in jail with Zeniss yet either, but give it a little more time. Bee, we've got to get out of here. If that little boy recognized us, who else could?"

More unanswered questions. Was Molly alive? Was she the young woman who was seen going into Dixie's house? How did Molly, if it was Molly, get to Waynesville? What or who did Sam Turner throw over the bridge? My head was swimming as I pulled the car back onto the highway, heading for home. "Let's get home and wash this color out of our hair."

"I'm not washing mine. I like mine. I think I'm going to stay a blond," Bess answered, as she glanced at herself in the rearview mirror. "I've wanted to wash all the grey outta my hair for a long time. Do you think I look younger, Bee?"

"I don't know if you look younger, but you sure do look available."

Bess readily replied, as she ran her fingers through her hair, "Really!"

"Mercy!" *I told you, Bess, aka Debbie, didn't have men totally out of her mind!*

CHAPTER TWENTY-SEVEN

We planned on meeting back at Bess's house about four o'clock that afternoon. I needed plenty of time to wash all the black goo out of my hair and get myself looking presentable again. Getting back into the house without anybody spotting me would be a challenge, but I figured I could park at my back door and sneak in without anybody noticing me. As soon as I drove up, I could hear Lambert hollering to Melvin to get his fat rear end into the new bathroom and hold the dang ladder before it collapsed right out from underneath him. I carefully and quietly headed for my bedroom and thankfully closed the door. Thank goodness, nobody noticed me, especially Vonion. I'd hate to have to explain to him the change in my appearance. I quickly changed into an old housedress, and checking the hallway to make sure the coast was clear, headed for the bathroom and closed the door. One shampoo after another, and I knew I was doomed. My hair wasn't completely black now but had turned a dark reddish color. There was absolutely no solution to the problem except to accept the truth. My hair would have to grow out, and the color would just have to wear out. A quick pin curl was in order.

As I waited for my hair to dry, I decided to check in with Lambert and Melvin. I found Lambert standing in front of the new mirrored medicine cabinet, picking at his teeth, with a grin across his unshaven face. He had just finished wiring the new bathroom light fixture, and low and behold, I switched it on, and it actually worked. "Looks pretty good, wouldn't you say, Ms. Bee?"

"What, the bathroom or you? I'd say you both need a little more work. When is Melvin planning to start painting in here?"

"Tomorrow morning, bright and early. I'm gonna put in the new light fixture in Ms. Bess's bedroom and then move on to the kitchen. Ms. Bess ordered me to install new cabinets in there. Where do you want me to throw that old wood-cooking stove when I drag it out? Want me to chunk it in the woods out behind the house?"

"If you so much as touch that stove, I will personally kill you, that is, right after I kill my sister. Hold up on any kitchen remodel until you hear directly from me. The very idea, ditching Mama's stove, of all things; I'd rather throw out the electric stove."

"Ms. Bess did mention you might be a little annoyed about the stove. Oh, and what about your refrigerator? If you don't want it, me and my wife would sure appreciate it. Ms. Bess said she had a new one on order from the Sears and Roebuck catalog."

"Lambert, you won't be getting *that* refrigerator, and don't put *one* finger on it. In fact, don't even go into the kitchen until I have a talk with Miss Moneybags! Mercy me!"

"Ms. Moneybags, err, excuse me, Ms. Bess wants new shutters made for the house too, so I guess I'll start building on them tomorrow. When y'all get your dispute settled about the kitchen, let me know. You know I can't just whip up those cabinets overnight."

"Just work on the shutters, and I'll let you know about the kitchen."

Now that my blood pressure was really up, I thought I might as well check in with Melvin. He was cleaning his brushes with turpentine when I found him sitting on a paint can under the oak tree. "What you think, Ms. Bee? Did you see that shine I put on those old floors? You gonna have to wait a few more days before you can walk on them, though."

"They look great. You've done a wonderful job. I'm tempted to talk to you about doing the bedroom floors too."

"You're too late. Ms. Bess already has. I'm gonna start painting Ms. Bess's bedroom and bathroom tomorrow. Work's going good, and I hope you're satisfied."

"Oh, I am." And I was secretly glad to see all the changes to the old place. "Listen, Melvin, I've got to get back into the house. I'll see you later."

My dark red hair was about dry by then. After a sad attempt to comb my old hairdo back in, I changed my dress, grabbed my purse, and headed out the back door. Trying desperately to avoid Vonion since I knew it was about time for him to start feeding up for the afternoon, I quickly cranked the car and aimed it up the lane.

Molly's nosy neighbor, Mrs. Ricketson, knows more about what went on outside her windows than anybody else in town. *Except maybe dearly departed Aunt Dora and, of course, Nellie.* If Molly had left home on her own accord or if she had been thrown out or even carried out, she had more than likely witnessed it. Bess and I planned to drop in and interrogate Mrs. Ricketson without her suspecting a thing. All we had to do was bring up the subject of Molly and Sam, and she could probably fill us in on everything that had happened across the street since Molly and Sam first moved in.

I tapped on Bess's back door but didn't wait to be invited in. "Are you ready to drill Mrs. Ricketson?" Bess was busy sweeping her kitchen floor.

"As soon as I get through with this floor. Don't step in my trash."

"Listen Bess, you can clean all night long if you want to, but right now we've got to get over to Mrs. Ricketson's and cross-examine her. Maybe she can remember the last time she spied on Molly. Now, put that broom down and let's go."

"Okay, but I really need to mop too. Ever since we started this detective business, my house and yard have suffered terribly. I haven't ironed my sheets or dusted this house in days. My flower beds need weeding, and my silver needs polishing. I've got to get this house in shipshape condition for Jean and Freddy. I want them to maintain the house as good as they find it when they move in, and I've been letting too many things slide lately."

"This house is spotless, Bess. You've got to lighten up a little. Our case is more important right now than this house being clean as a whistle. Now let's go. Oh, we need to have a discussion about *my* kitchen first chance we get."

Bess frowned and started to say something, but I put my hand up and said, "Not now. We can kick that can around later. First things first."

Bess had changed her clothes and washed off all the dark makeup, but her hair was still that nice ash blond color Thelma had put in that morning. I was beginning to like it, but I wasn't about to let on to Bess that I thought it looked nice. Finally persuading Bess to leave her cleaning chores, we hurried out the door just as Earnest Lee Black came walking by, toting his now-empty mail sack as he returned to the post office. I nodded, but Bess turned the other way, trying to avoid him.

"Afternoon, ladies. Ms. Bess, I don't believe I've ever seen you looking so nice, and...err, you too, Ms. Bee. Nice afternoon for a walk."

"Oh, yes," I answered, and gave Bess a nudge. "Bess, Earnest Lee said 'nice afternoon'."

"Ump. Tell him it was a nice afternoon before we ran into him. And you can tell him he better not leave Mr. and Mrs. Hodges' mail in my box again. I'm getting sick and tired of carrying their mail over to them after he leaves it in my box accidently. The federal government doesn't pay me one red cent to re-deliver mail. I imagine the postmaster would be mighty interested if I complained about my service. And you can tell him he can put a stamp on that and mail it."

"Bess, you ought to be ashamed of yourself. Earnest Lee, don't pay a bit of attention to her. Bess is just a little tired and frustrated today. She's not usually this cranky. She'll be her usual self tomorrow."

"I can hardly wait for tomorrow!"

Bess gave Earnest Lee a pitiful little smile, and he returned the smile as we continued on down the street. *Hey! Could a truce be brewing?*

Mrs. Ricketson must have seen us walk up because she opened her front door just as I put my hand up to knock. She eagerly invited us in with a swoop of her arms.

"Come on in, girls! I'm so glad to see somebody. This old house is as dead as a tomb today. I've wanted to have somebody to talk to all day long. I don't think I've uttered a word to anybody since day before yesterday when

I trapped a door-to-door salesman in the house. He was selling vacuum cleaners, and I invited him in by telling him I was interested in one of his electric sweepers. He ended up staying an hour or so, demonstrating the thing. I didn't buy one, but I did get my front room vacuumed for free."

"That was sneaky, Mrs. Ricketson," I laughingly replied, as we stepped in. "Maybe he'll come back and give you another demonstration. You could get the dining room vacuumed for free next time. You might even consider buying one. It's a lot easier than beating your carpets."

"I doubt that I could ever purchase one. The payments are a little steep for my budget. They make a lot of racket too. Besides, if I bought one, that good-looking young salesman wouldn't ever come back."

"Mrs. Ricketson, you are sly," I smiled and replied, as I glanced around at the dusty room, feeling pity for the young salesman.

"You know, I almost didn't recognize you two. There's something about your hair that's different. You both look stylish. I need to do something about mine before I die." Mrs. Ricketson put her old thin arm up and patted her tiny gray hair bun at the back of her head. "Do you think Thelma could do anything with this thin hair of mine if she cut it?"

"I'm sure she could, Mrs. Ricketson," I replied, "but...your hair looks real nice just the way it is. I wouldn't bother with it if I were you. I think your hairstyle suits you to a tee."

"Do you really think so?" Mrs. Ricketson brightened up. "I've been wearing it the same way since I was a young woman, so I guess there's no reason to change it now. You know I haven't cut it in half a century. My late husband used to love to watch me comb it. He said I looked like Rapunzel. That's not all he said, but I can't tell all my secrets." Mrs. Ricketson's tired old eyes began to glow with the past memory. "Enough about my hair. Come on in, girls."

The front room was small and cluttered with every little whatnot ever sold at the Five and Dime downtown. Mrs. Ricketson gestured for us sit. I sat down on a sagging, faded green settee across the room from a chair I presumed was hers. A puff of dust from the cushions filled the air around me as I settled in. Bess glanced around the neglected room for another chair, but not seeing one, she plopped down beside me on the settee. The old, worn-out springs gave way under our combined weight, and we plunged deeper into the cushions, with another wisp of stale dust filling the air. Mrs. Ricketson didn't seem to notice our sitting catastrophe at all, as she settled herself into her rocking chair by the front picture window. She adjusted the worn, heavy cushion under her bottom and reached for the crocheted afghan that had fallen to the floor. I immediately noticed a set of binoculars and several sets of eyeglasses on the marble-topped table nearby. I suspect she was perched on her everyday throne.

She automatically reached for the curtain, pulled it back, and glanced out at the street. I noticed the curtains were permanently creased where, I'm quite sure, her wrinkled old hands had repeatedly pulled them back, year after year, for a better view of something of interest. *Something of interest was probably just about anything that moved.*

Bess and I squirmed around, trying to get comfortable, but with our knees almost in front of our faces, and with every little movement more dust billowing up, it was next to impossible. Trying not to stir up any more dust than possible, I got right down to business without a lot more chitchat. "You know, I don't remember the last time

I've seen Molly Turner, or Sam, for that matter. Such a nice young couple, with such a bright future. I guess they stay busy like everybody else."

Mrs. Ricketson nodded and answered, "They stay gone a lot, but Sam was at church Sunday morning."

Bess stifled a sneeze and replied, "I don't recall him sitting in their usual pew. Maybe he sat somewhere else for a change, and I just didn't notice him. I usually speak to both of them, but now that I think about it, I might have seen Sam. I hope Molly's not sick or anything."

"Now I know y'all came over here to find out about Molly, so y'all can quit your pretending. Molly hasn't been home for a while now. Just look at that yard. It's a mess. If Molly was at home, it wouldn't look like a tornado touched down to the ground over there. She'd at least have the trash picked up. Molly left on Monday morning, more than a week ago. I saw her when she left. She was carrying her suitcase, walking toward the edge of town." *Molly was alive!* "I suspect she was going to catch a bus at the filling station." *A bus, that's how she got to Waynesville!* "Now I don't know where she went, but she hasn't been back. I suspect she's left Sam, but I really don't know anything for certain. I'll keep a good eye out for her if you want me to. That is, if there's a little something in this for me."

We quickly explained that we worked on a shoestring, and we weren't in any position to pay our informants. Mrs. Ricketson frowned but said she'd do it anyway. She said she had always wanted to be a detective, but nobody had ever hired her before.

"Do you remember what Molly was wearing the morning she left?" Bess asked.

"Oh, yes, of course I do. A beige dress, pink sweater, pink scarf on her head, brown shoes, and carrying a brown suitcase. She was carrying a different pocketbook than what she generally totes. A small black one."

"You certainly are a good observer, Mrs. Ricketson. I believe you remember every detail," I added.

Mrs. Ricketson smiled with pride.

On that note, we stood to leave just as we noticed Sam drive up into his yard. We hesitated and waited by the window, looking out at the poor, dejected man as he opened his car door and got out. Little did he know, but two extra sets of eyes observed his movements that day. Bess finally remarked, "Poor Sam. Nobody at home to greet him, no supper cooked. Every married man deserves that. But I guess you get as good as you give."

We waited to leave after Sam had disappeared into his house. After our stroll back to Bess's, I immediately left for home after explaining to Bess that she could stay up and clean all night long if she wanted to, but I was going to get some rest.

* * *

Elated that Molly was likely still alive, I was expecting a good night's rest, but that was not to be. After continuously tossing and turning, sleep finally prevailed sometime between the time I heard the old clock on the bedroom mantle dong twelve times and the back door slam. I knew without a shadow of a doubt it was Melvin coming in again at the crack of dawn. He was singing "I've Got That Old Time Religion" deep in my heart, deep in my heart.

I lazily lay in the bed listening to all the early morning sounds. Along with Melvin's singing and occasional cussing, crows cawed, roosters crowed, and Hortence mooed. I could hear Vonion hitting the side of the bucket with a stick and the hogs oinking louder and louder as they rushed to gobble up their morning feed. Peacefulness and contentment overtook me as I snuggled deeper under one of Mama's handmade quilts. The morning light spread across my bedroom as my thoughts brought me back to the reality of the case. What were the facts?

First... Molly. Molly was alive. I truly believed that now. She left her home Monday morning, the day before our trip to Waynesville. She and Sam must have had an argument, and she waited until he left for work Monday morning to leave. She probably felt her future with Sam was over, and her marriage was a dismal failure. All the things she held near and dear had been taken away, and she needed somebody, along with Sam, to blame it all on. Evidently Sam had told her about Dixie, and she had a need to confront her. With all her frustrations bundled up inside and nothing to look forward to, she left on her own accord. She took the bus out of town and ended up in Burt County. She was at Dixie's house Monday. We had seen a pink sweater—probably her sweater—accidentally left behind. She probably confronted Dixie and, after that, I had no idea. Did she leave Dixie alive? Tempest saw Dixie later in the day, but it's possible Molly was hiding while Tempest was in the house, or she could have returned later in the day. Everything was possible, but was any of it probable?

Tempest Lamoure...Tempest—that certainly wasn't her given name—was a has-been. She had outlived her profession, and she could see it slowly slipping away. Every time she saw one of her clients enter Dixie's house, she was reminded that her future was bleak, and her income was drying up. In her mind, she probably figured she needed to be rid of the enormous obstacle right next door. It would be easy to eliminate her competition. All she had to do was overpower her and then finish her off with a blow to the head. Tempest had probably been raised to get her way through violence. Bess and I had witnessed that firsthand. We knew Tempest had visited Dixie, and a fight took place.

She had admitted to all that. Was it possible Tempest had ended Dixie's life? Oh yes, it was very possible!

Judge Sam Harmon...a probable killer? Now that was a hard pill to swallow. I would never have believed that he would have anything to do with the likes of Dixie or Tempest. But his name was prominently listed in the ledger many times. He evidently was a regular customer of Dixie's and possibly of Tempest's. According to the ledger, he was scheduled for a visit late that Monday. It had been exactly two weeks since his last recorded visit, and every visit documented in the ledger was exactly two weeks apart. He certainly would have arrived in the evening under the cover of darkness. Dixie would have already had a very eventful day: her school job, a quarrel with Molly, and an altercation with Tempest. And she certainly would not have entertained the judge before she had made herself presentable. The fact that she had already cleaned her wounds made me believe she had fought with Tempest earlier in the afternoon, and the fatal blow came much later. Bess and I had found the bed unmade, and Dixie was wearing a revealing nightgown at the time of her untimely death. More than likely, she had earned her fee, engaging in a pleasurable time with the judge before things got out of hand. Two coffee cups were left on the kitchen table, both with dregs of coffee, but only one with purple lipstick on the rim. Evidently a friendly encounter had turned very violent after Dixie unveiled her blackmailing scheme to the judge, probably as he was about to leave. The indention on Dixie's head was in the front, indicating that the killer was somebody she knew and was face-to-face with her at the time of the fatal impact. In a violent rage, and in fear of being exposed and drained financially by her scheme, Judge Sam Harmon directed the final blow to Dixie's head and left her either dying or dead. He returned home, satisfied that he had eliminated the threat of blackmail and exposure. Was that a possible explanation, or was it just a far-fetched crazy idea I had just dreamed up?

Could I picture Molly killing anybody? Tempest was a fighter. She could have easily committed the crime. Was Judge Sam Harmon our killer? The timing was perfect.

But how do I go about proving any of it?

CHAPTER TWENTY-EIGHT

Hello. Is this Elmo?" I was calling Floyd's filling station on the telephone later that morning to find out about the bus schedule. I had already gotten around Nellie, explaining to her that I needed to speak to Elmo because I might be planning a trip and needed the bus schedule.

"Yessum, it's Elmo all right. What can I do fer you?"

"Elmo, this is Bee Martin. I was wondering if you could tell me a little about the bus schedule. Does the bus come in and go out every Monday?"

"Yep, every Monday morning, just like clockwork. Bus leaves here 'bout eleven A.M. and heads out directly to Waynesville. Gets there about eleven thirty, drops folks off, picks folks up, and heads out again fer Augusta. You can go 'bout anywhere you want to, if'n you don't mind a little waitin' time. After the bus gets into Augusta, there's a whole bunch'a buses goin' a whole lot'a other places. Where you want to go, Ms. Bee?"

"I'm not sure right now, but Elmo, do you have a record of who goes where? If I got on the bus here, could you tell from my ticket where I was going?"

"Well, it's accordin' to where you buy a ticket fer. If'n you buy one to New York City, I could tell that from my records. But a lot of people buy their tickets all along the way."

"Is it privileged information, I mean, where somebody goes, Elmo? I'm lookin' for somebody that might have bought a ticket. Can you tell me where she went?"

"I probably ain't 'posed to, but seeing it's you and all, I guess I could. You must be workin' on a case."

"Monday. A week ago. Monday. Was a ticket to Waynesville bought over there by a young woman, Elmo? Can you check that out?"

"Well, let me see." I waited as I listened to Elmo shuffle papers around, cough a time or two, clear his throat, and yell out to Donnelle to help that customer. "Just a minute, Ms. Bee. I'll be right back. Got to find Donnelle. He's probably asleep in the back." Elmo dropped the telephone. Clang, clang! I was still hanging on. Holding the telephone out from my ear, I could hear him hollering at Donnelle. A horn started blowing. More papers shuffling. Then…"Oh, here it is. You ready, Ms. Bee?"

"Yes. I'm ready, Elmo."

"A young lady that we all know bought a ticket to Waynesville Monday morning, a week ago, and got off the bus in Waynesville. She left from here at eleven o'clock in the morning and got to Waynesville at about eleven forty-five."

"Anybody else buy a ticket for a bus that went through Waynesville that day or the day after? It's real important, Elmo. Maybe the husband of the young lady?"

"No, that's it. Records don't lie."

"Elmo, I'll be down at the station in an hour or so. In the meantime, see if you can trace her bus schedule for the rest of her trip. When she got off the bus in Waynesville, try to find out if she bought another ticket and to where. Do you think you can do all that?"

"Ms. Bee, for you, I can do anything. Just give me a little time. I got to straighten me out a certain young man around here first. He's either got to go to work and quit talkin' everybody's heads off, or he's got to go. He's just about to drive me crazy."

"Thanks, Elmo. I'll see you in a while. Now, keep quiet about this."

"Oh, yes ma'am. I know when you're on a case. Wild horses couldn't make me tell anybody about this."

Evidently Molly did leave town for Waynesville that Monday morning. The pieces fit, and I hoped she had left Waynesville on the bus before the murder occurred. I guess I'd find out soon—as soon as Elmo straightened out Donnelle and checked those records.

I walked over to the window, pulled the curtain back, and gazed across the yard. It was a beautiful autumn morning. The leaves were falling. The blue morning sky stretched on and on, canopying the house and fields. At the farm, all seemed to be right with the world. Sparrows and redbirds were feeding in the lawn around the house, and a squirrel scampered from tree to tree, carrying a nut to his special hiding place. Three old crows marched across the yard as they bravely ventured closer and closer to the house. I could see Vonion out in the orchard, crawling around with a croaker sack by his side, gathering pecans. Ora Lee was sitting near him on an old wooden straight chair with her cane in her lap. Every once in a while she'd point to another spot on the ground and direct Vonion to where more nuts had fallen.

My mind began to wonder as I gazed across the enormous white cotton field near the house. Tears formed in my eyes as I remembered how proud Will had always been of the glorious sight resembling a large white fluffy blanket that had floated down from the heavens to rest near the ground. Tom Wilson would soon start the long and arduous task of picking the cotton and getting it to market. Will, if he had been alive, would be hiring pickers about now with the very same task bearing down on his every thought and move.

The corn in the back field next to the woods was dry and ready for Tom Wilson to pull. Tom would share that bounty with us. The cows and the hogs had to be fed all winter, and we depended on that corn crop for their feed. I had given Vonion so much responsibility since Will passed away. The cows and hogs had to be fed daily, cows milked, chickens fed, and eggs gathered. It was almost time for a hog killing too. Vonion would get a little outside help for that. I depended on Vonion, and now he was taking care of Ora Lee as well. Her health was deteriorating as she aged, and many of her chores around their home had fallen to Vonion. Thank heavens, Roscoe, their almost grown grandson, had returned from Atlanta to live with them. Roscoe worked for Tom Wilson, but he was a great source of help to Vonion as well. Ora Lee couldn't keep all the yards swept now, but she could still shake a stick at anybody who wasn't doing their share.

My house was looking better and better. I had finally gotten used to Melvin and Lambert and all their bickering and cussing. They were rough around the edges but really good-hearted men. Melvin was painting in Bess's bedroom and bathroom this morning, and Lambert was out in the side yard, sawing and nailing on the new shutters for the outside of the house. My mind wasn't set on having new kitchen cabinets put in, but the idea was growing on me. It was over my dead body that Bess would get rid of Mama's wood-burning cook stove, though. She would just have to do her remodeling around it.

Bess would be coming to live on the farm with me soon. The idea had finally started to give me a peace about her future and mine. We could take care of each other. That's what families do. Margaret was seeing Walter, and I had high hopes that she would be headed down the church aisle soon. Yes, life was good! God was good!

And now, back to this mystery. Oh, how it was monopolizing my thoughts...and my time! I better get hopping and get on down to the filling station. Oh, and I better get some gas in the car while I'm over there. Little things like gas in the car seem to always escape my attention.

CHAPTER TWENTY-NINE

Elmo was doing a great job with Floyd's Station. As I drove up later that morning, my mind went back a year or so earlier to the dreadful time of Floyd's death at the hands of our so-called preacher. Bess and I had really wet our whistles in the detective business during that time. Elmo had never been formally charged with Floyd's murder, but had Bess and I not found the real killer, he probably would be serving time in prison right now for a crime he never committed. Elmo was now the proprietor of Floyd's Station. I wish I could say that Donnelle, Elmo's assistant, was doing a good job as well. If he didn't straighten up and fly right soon, I was afraid he was going to be a has-been around here.

The place was bustling today. Donnelle was pumping gas into the hearse for Mr. Lawson, and Old Man Peterson's ancient truck was lined up right behind. Over near the tire racks, a heavy farm truck was parked, and Elmo, standing on a stool, was peering under its rusty hood.

He looked up just as I pulled my car into the line for gas and gave me a wave with his big, greasy wrench. I gave him a smile and a wave back as I stopped the car. I quickly stepped over toward Elmo, careful to avoid any of the numerous oil spills. Elmo gave me a knowing nod and reached into his overalls pocket. He brought out a grease-stained piece of paper, folded into a small square. With a satisfied smile, he handed it over to me. "I think this explains what you want to know, Ms. Bee. I wrote down, word for word, what Mr. McNeely, the guy who runs the bus station over in Waynesville, told me." I smiled as I reached for the note.

"Elmo, you are a jewel. Thank you for doing this for me. This evidence will make a big difference in somebody's life." Elmo was still beaming with pride as I walked over to the drink box by the door to the station and unfolded the note to read it. Word for word, it read: *A Molly Turner arrived in Waynesville on the morning bus a week ago Monday. The same Molly Turner bought a ticket for Augusta on the two-thirty bus the same day. Her ticket was stamped as she left on the afternoon bus.*

I reread the note. It couldn't have been simpler. Molly had left town on the two-thirty bus, and the murder didn't occur until much later in the day. Tempest had not ventured over to Dixie's before two thirty that afternoon. Dixie was alive at the time the bus left town, with Molly in tow. Thank heavens, I could mark Molly off my short list of suspects. She was definitely innocent of murder. Where she was now was still a mystery, but at least I knew now she was alive and well. More than likely, she was with her parents. I felt such relief! I'd head straight over to Bess's with the news as soon as Donnelle pumped my gas. I walked back over to Elmo and thanked him again. "Remember, not a word of this."

Elmo looked up again and smiled. "Oh, sure, Ms. Bee. I'm always happy to oblige you. You'll never know how much I appreciate what you did for me in my time of need. I'd probably be in prison right now if you hadn't figured everything out. If Donnelle don't get to your gas pronto, just give me a holler."

"I'm not in that big of a hurry, Elmo. I'm sure Donnelle will get to it sooner than later. Thanks again now."

"Uh, Ms. Bee, I hope I'm not being too forward, but you surely are looking good these days. You got a new hairdo or something?"

"Or something, Elmo. Thanks for the compliment." *Maybe I needed to keep my hair this color.*

Flushed from the compliment, and all gassed up, I drove straight over to Bess's. She was busy wrapping her china and crystal with newspapers and packing it into apple baskets for the move. Bess was elated to know that Molly was definitely alive. After giving her all the latest details, I left her to her work and drove on back home. As I pulled into the lane, I could see that Vonion had the children picking up pecans in the orchard. With a burden lifted from my heart, I hurried to change clothes and gladly joined the work force. It was after five that afternoon before I walked back into the house, tired and weary, but so satisfied. Melvin and Lambert had left a few minutes earlier, and the house was silent and still. *The house was all mine.* A pleasant relief. A hot bath, a little supper, a call to Margaret, and a good night's rest. That's all I needed, just the simpler things in life. I'd think about the case tomorrow.

* * *

I heard the telephone ring as I was filling the bathtub with warm water later that evening. Two rings—one long, one short. That's me. I hurriedly turned the water off and rushed to the hall. "Hello, Bee Martin speaking."

It was Margaret calling. She was full of school news and all excited about a school conference she had been invited to attend. A substitute teacher would replace her for a few days, and she was to leave tomorrow to be out of town for five whole days. The conference was in Athens, and Peggy, a fellow teacher and friend, was going along with her. Margaret said she had talked with Walter earlier that afternoon, and he was making plans to meet them in Athens on Saturday. They were all going to the University of Georgia football game scheduled for that afternoon. I told her I was delighted for her and hoped all went as planned. After a little more conversation, I asked her to call as soon as she returned the next week, and we said our good nights.

Returning to the bathroom, I stood in the middle of the floor, thinking. How could anything be more perfect? Bess and I could go over to Waynesville tomorrow and wait around at Margaret's house until we could accidentally, on purpose, run into Eli. Margaret would be safely out of town, and we could pretend to be cleaning or making curtains for Margaret's house, or something domestic like that. Maybe it was Eli we needed to talk with first, not the judge. After all, Eli probably kept up with most of the judge's activities—private, and not so private. Unlike the judge, I suspect we could question Eli without him becoming aware he was even being interrogated. It would be a challenge, but I suspect Bess and I were up to it. I hurried back to the hall and telephoned Bess.

"Bess, be ready in the morning to go to Waynesville. I'll pick you up about ten. Oh, and you can be yourself tomorrow. Just dress normally. I'll fill you in on all the details as we drive along."

"Bee, I've got so much to do around here, and every time I think I have an hour or so to do something, you call, wanting me to go somewhere else. I don't know when I'm going to get all this packing done. Can't we wait until another day to go over to Waynesville?"

"Listen, Bess, if we ever get this case solved, and you get moved, you'll be wishing you had something more exciting to do than packing china, or gathering eggs, or picking peas. Now, we've got a perfect opportunity to question a very important person involved in this case, and we've got to do it soon." Relenting a little, I hesitated and said, "I'll tell you what, come out to the farm a little before eleven tomorrow, and you can check over everything Melvin and Lambert have done the last few days. We'll leave right after we eat lunch. I've got plenty of eggs for an egg salad sandwich, and I'll make bread pudding too. Hortence's fresh cream will top it off."

"That does sound good. I'm afraid my weight is going to get out of hand after I move. We'll have to walk around the pond and do a hundred jumping jacks every day."

I agreed with my bossy sister. *Was she bossier than me?* You know, I thought to myself, maybe I would exercise if I had somebody to motivate me and do it along with me. "Good idea, Bess. I'll see you tomorrow. Now don't be late...Oh, and bring an overnight case. We might be gone overnight."

* * *

Bess and I left for Waynesville about one o'clock Friday afternoon. We had eaten lunch, and Bess had inspected all of Melvin's and Lambert's work. She seemed satisfied with everything except the water pressure in her new bathroom. Lambert told her he'd work on it, but he couldn't work miracles. Bess paid them off for the week before we left, explaining to them she never knew if we'd get back alive or not, and she wanted to have her debts paid in full before she died.

I had walked down to visit Ora Lee a while earlier that morning, and she seemed to be feeling pretty well, considering all that doctor medicine was about to kill her, she complained. She seemed very content to sit on the porch that morning, swatting flies as she dozed. Vonion was loading croaker sacks full of pecans into the back of his pickup truck to take to market, and Lambert had Melvin on a ladder measuring the odd-shaped windows to my kitchen for the new shutters as we drove off.

"Now, tell me what's going on, and this better be good. I could be home putting the finishing touches on our new front room curtains right now, or packing my good linens," Bess complained as she drove up the lane. I quickly explained our venture, and Bess said that it was a long shot, but maybe we could get a little something out of Eli. "He's awfully faithful to the judge, but if we play our cards right, we might be able to fool him into saying too much for the judge's good."

Before I realized what I was saying, I replied, "Just let me do most of the talking, Bess."

"Ump, you could've left me at home to finish my packing. You must have forgotten already who got all that information out of Tempest."

"Oh, I'm sorry, Bess, and you did a great job over there. That's what makes us such a good team. We each know when to let the other take over. I never would have been able to get all that information out of Tempest the way you did. You know, I feel sorta sorry for her. She must not have much family, and she really is living in a dream world. I'm just glad we got outta there before a real battle commenced. We could have been beaten to a pulp. Do you think she'll get most of her customers back, now that Dixie's totally out of the picture?"

"Now how on earth do you think I know that, Bee? I only hope most of those men have learned their lessons, but you never know. I do know one thing; she definitely won't get E.N. Frost's business back. His gallivanting days are all over with now. And Tempest better change her disposition a whole bunch if she wants to stay in business."

"Oh, yea, and lose about a hundred pounds. You reckon Biscuit ever recovered? That dog was sick!"

"Poor thing. We ought to be ashamed of ourselves for making that dog so miserable." We both giggled.

My mind was now on Eli. After a long silence in the car, I asked, "Bess, do you think we're barking up the wrong tree? Do you think Eli will give us any information about the judge's whereabouts the evening of the murder without us coming straight out and asking the crucial question?"

"Don't ask me. Remember I'm supposed to keep quiet, and this time I'm glad of it. But you've really got to be careful about what you say because we could be in real danger if he thought we knew that the judge was one of Dixie's former customers."

"Have you considered that Eli didn't even know the judge's whereabouts when he visited Dixie? After all, the judge probably walked over to her house from his office. I doubt he ever drove his car over there."

"Bee, I feel quite sure Eli knows where his boss man is most all of the time, and he's probably covered for him many times in the past."

We soon turned into the judge's long drive. The large two-story Victorian house sat back from the street on a rise like a majestic white iceberg in the middle of the vast ocean. We slowly rode through the spectacular property, past row after row of roses, azaleas and camellias, craning our necks to spot Eli, but the yard seemed totally deserted today. As we pulled into Margaret's parking place beside her little duplex in the back corner of the property, I was beginning to get cold feet about the whole situation.

I was worried. *What in the world are we getting ourselves into? If Judge Harmon is guilty of murder, Eli wasn't about to give away any secrets he might know to us, or to anybody else for that matter. Did Eli know anything about the crime? And could we question Eli in a way that he wouldn't guess we were investigating the murder? Were we putting ourselves in real danger? Mercy, what on earth was I thinking about! We ought to back this car up and go right back home!*

But we didn't!

CHAPTER THIRTY

To keep from being so nervous about questioning Eli, we went to work right off the bat. Bess had me on my hands and knees cleaning baseboards within fifteen minutes after we arrived. "If we're going to be here pretending to work, we might as well be productive," Bess had sternly said, as she placed the empty kitchen canister set into a pan of hot water to wash. I thought she was going a little too far when we started cleaning out from under the refrigerator a little later, but it did keep our mind and body occupied until we could talk with Eli. *Boy, was Margaret going to be surprised when she got home and found such a clean house!*

The afternoon progressed into early evening and there was still no sign of Eli. "Bess, I really don't think we have to clean the whole place today. I'm tired. Let's get some rest and get at it again in the morning. This is the most cleaning I've done since Ora Lee and I did summer cleaning over a year ago."

"I imagine you'll have to get used to it again. We've got to get the farmhouse spic and span before we host the missionary meeting in November." Finally finding it in her heart to allow us a reprieve from our labor, Bess deeply sighed and said, "Oh well, I suppose we've done enough for today. Tomorrow is another day after all."

I suggested we eat our ham sandwich out in the evening air. As I munched on my sandwich, my mind kept going back to the day of Dixie's murder. Why on earth had I thought we could just grab up vital evidence and run with it? I had really put us in a jam. If we turned the evidence in to the sheriff now, we would be charged with tampering with evidence at the scene of a crime, and if we did nothing with the proof, we would be allowing a murderer to go scot-free. We had removed evidence, and nobody, except Dixie's clients and us, as far as I could figure, knew anything about the ledger or Dixie's blackmailing scheme. We were very much aware that Judge Harmon was in the house the night of the murder, and that was the most damaging evidence there could be. Dixie probably produced the blackmailing note to him just as he was about to walk out that night. She thought she had him hooked like all her other less intelligent clients, but Judge Harmon figured he was way above the law and could nip this little scam right in the bud. He wasn't going to be blackmailed, and he wasn't about to give in to the demands of such an insignificant person as Dixie. He thought he was smarter than that. He figured he could eliminate the blackmailing source and a thorn in his flesh all at the same time. In his mind, he was scot-free now and could go on with his life, perhaps finding another loose woman who would surrender to all his sexual desires. But the evidence left behind told the true story.

"Where on earth do you think Eli could be?" Bess asked, as she sipped her iced tea. "We've been here most all afternoon and haven't seen a soul."

"I don't know. I didn't expect to see the judge or Livonia back here, but I'd have thought we'd have seen Eli or Safronia by now. Maybe they've gone off somewhere on a trip or something."

"I doubt that. You know Livonia can't boil water. She's not about to allow Safronia to have any time off. Let's just keep watching for them. They'll have to show up sooner or later. Bee, it's really nice back here," Bess said with a sigh, as she was beginning to relax a bit. "The trees and the flowers are really beautiful, and it's so peaceful. Margaret has been lucky to have such a nice place to stay while she's been teaching over here in Waynesville."

"She has, but Bess, all that might change now. If we ever have that conversation with the judge, he's liable to know we suspect he's guilty of murder just from the fact that we're asking him questions. He's not stupid, you know. We might need to rethink our plan to have that discussion with him. It might be way too risky...Hey, look, Bess, the back door to the big house is opening, and, oh, it's Safronia."

We watched as Safronia untied her apron from around her ample waist and strolled across the lawn. It was evident she was tired from just the way she carried herself. I called, "Evening, Safronia. Come sit with us a spell. Put your tired feet up and rest a while."

Safronia gave us a weak smile and plopped down in the extra yard chair we pulled up for her. After propping her feet on an old stool, she lay her head back so she could stare into the sky. "It's a nice evening. Looks like all the stars are out, and just look at that full moon. I 'spect many a baby will be born tonight. You know what they say about a full moon, don't you?"

"We sure do," Bess answered. "Both of my boys were born when the moon was full. Old Sadie Waller was the midwife back then, and she was running from house to house the night Freddy was born. I think Freddy shares his birthday with three other young men in town, all born the same night under that big, ole October moon."

"Where's Margaret?" asked Safronia. "I don't see her car. Is she off somewhere?"

"She's gone to a teachers' conference. We're doing a little housecleaning while she's gone, you know, as a surprise. Margaret works so hard, she really doesn't have time to do much housework," I explained. "You don't think she'll mind, do you?"

"Oh, heavens no. She'll thank you. I know I would." As if she was aggravated, Safronia looked around and remarked, "That Eli, he ain't made his way home for supper again."

"You know we haven't noticed Eli all afternoon. He must be off gallivanting somewhere," Bess lightheartedly added.

"No, he ain't gallivantin'. He's been working on an addition to the hay barn out at the farm. The judge has a herd to cows out there, and he needs more space to store grain and hay. Eli's been working on it for several months now, and he don't know when to quit. Some nights Eli works till ten or eleven. If I didn't know better, I'd think he had a sweetheart out there." Safronia gave a little chuckle. "Thing is, he's neglecting things around here. If he don't hurry up and get that thing built, the judge is gonna have to hire somebody to help me out. I've been trying my best to do some of Eli's chores for the longest, and it's just about to wear me down. Why, just today, I mopped the front porch and swept the front walks. Mrs. Lavonia had her bridge ladies over, and I could've used Eli to help set up card tables and move chairs. But where was he? Out at the farm again, working on that barn. Me and Mrs. Lavonia are getting right tired of it...Oh, you ladies want some coffee? I'd be glad to make a pot. It'd taste good about now."

"I'll make it," Bess said, and jumped up. "Y'all just sit here and relax. I'll have it ready in a flash. Cream and sugar, Safronia?"

"Yes, thank you." Safronia wrapped her arms closer to her body. "There's definitely a little chill in the air, but it feels good after all that scurrying about I've done all day."

We sat out in the evening air, chatting and relaxing until almost nine o'clock. There was never any sign of Eli. As I closed my eyes for the last time later that night, lying in Margaret's bed, I heard a truck rumble up to the other side of the house. Eli must be home.

* * *

The morning sun spilled in through the bedroom window as the sound of rattling pots and pans in the kitchen woke me. I didn't know if Bess was cooking or cleaning. A little of both, I suspect. Coffee was perking and toast was browning in a cast-iron frying pan as I walked into the cheery little kitchen. As I set the table with Margaret's everyday china, we heard a faint tap at the front door. I imagined it was Safronia. I wrapped my robe a little closer around myself and walked to the door. Eli was standing on the porch with a basketful of brown eggs.

"Morning, ladies. Safronia sent these to you." He handed the basket over and said, "I hope I'm not too late. You haven't had your breakfast, have you?"

"You're just in time. Come on in."

"Oh, no ma'am. Y'all go ahead and eat. We just wanted to be neighborly. If'n you need me this morning, I'll be over by the greenhouse, dividing some of those big ole ferns we keep on the front porch. We try to keep them all winter." Eli tipped his cap, nodded pleasantly, and walked off.

I closed the door. "Well, Bess, it's almost time for that long-awaited conversation with Eli. After breakfast, we'll walk over and pretend to watch how he divides those ferns. We need to know how to do that, anyway."

"I know how to do it, but that's a good idea. Bee, I'm almost too nervous to eat."

"I'm not. Let's scramble those eggs."

We didn't want to appear too anxious, but after a reasonable time, we gathered our nerves and anxiously strolled over to the greenhouse, where Eli was sitting on a bucket with a big kitchen knife in his hand. A wash pot, filled with black soil, was at his side. Several large clay pots sat about, waiting for a few fern fronds with roots to be placed inside, along with plenty of good, rich soil.

"I can make ten ferns from this here one large one," Eli explained, as he chopped away. "I'll give each of you one to take home. Keep it watered and in a warm place all winter, and you'll have a beautiful fern next spring. Just watch what I'm doing, and you can divide yours next year. It's a beautiful thing, nature, and the way it keeps providing for us."

"That's amazing, Eli," I replied. I had never divided ferns, but I knew Bess had been doing it for years. We stood, watching Eli, as I built my nerve up to speak.

"Eli, have you heard anything else about that murder that took place over on the next street the other night? Margaret told us about it. It's just horrible. Something like that, happening so close by and everything."

Eli stopped his work and stared down at his hands as if he was deep in thought. "I really ain't heard too much about any of that, but it was a bad thing. It's an evil world we live in. Wicked peoples everywhere."

"You didn't happen to know that woman, did you? Err, I think her name was Dixie," I said, as I held my breath in suspense as to what he would say. "Or what about the Judge, or Livonia, or Safronia? Were any of them acquainted with her?"

"Oh, me and the judge, we shore didn't know that piece of trash. I doubt Safronia or Ms. Livonia knew her either, maybe just to know what she looked like. I saw her around town a few times. Mostly I'd just see her in the grocery store or walking the streets."

"Margaret said she worked at the school as the secretary. And was quite attractive too. She probably had many a man drooling after her."

"I wouldn't know nothing 'bout all that," Eli sternly replied.

I jumped in, trying to ignore Eli's comment and sudden change in mood. "And Margaret said she was quite forward with the men. A girl like that can get herself into all kinds of trouble," I casually added.

Eli seemed to relent a little. "She probably got just what she deserved. Enticing all those men. Lightening said it was scandalous the way she flirted and carried on, even with him, and him being an old colored man. She didn't have no standards at all...uh...it seems to me."

"Such a shame," Bess added. "I hope she knew her Maker before she died."

"I doubt that. Anybody that carried on like she did and wore all that purple lipstick and stuff, she probably never gave that a second thought. I 'spect the devil's done got his way with her by now. She was just out for what she could get here on this earth. It ain't none of my business what she did, anyway. Ladies, I'll leave the ferns at the door over at Miss Margaret's. Now don't forget them."

Eli resumed chopping at the fern with more determination than before, and we knew it was time to leave him alone with his work and his thoughts. We thanked him again and strolled back to Margaret's house as if we didn't have a care in the world.

"Well, we didn't find out much. Maybe we need to wait around and go straight to the horse's mouth—talk directly to the judge," Bess said, after we closed the door. "He's the one with the firsthand knowledge, anyway."

"I don't know. That might be a little too risky right now. Let's clean a little more. I need to think." Thoughts of blackmail and murder swirled into my mind as I reluctantly reached for the broom.

Did Eli speak the whole truth?

CHAPTER THIRTY-ONE

G rateful we had finished the cleaning, and relieved that we had not blown our cover, we left Waynesville behind in the dust and began our trip for home and security. With the truth about the murder becoming more and more clear in my mind, I knew we didn't need to hang around there any longer.

I had a gnawing, anxious feeling that it might be time to visit the sheriff. The evidence and clues all placed Judge Harmon at the wrong place at the wrong time, and there was no denying that. But was that all there was to it? I had to come forward with the truth, as I knew it, very soon now. And what was to happen when Margaret came back from her trip? With all the damaging evidence we had, and a probable arrest, we absolutely could not let her stay in her home. She would have to move out immediately. *And it was so-o clean now.* She was going to be so shocked to know that someone who had been so kind to her was actually a suspected killer.   We had a few more days before she'd have to be told the truth.

I wondered if it was time for Bess to make her move on out to the farm. I needed the comfort of having someone near right now, and I wanted it to be Bess. I said a little prayer and asked Bess if she'd start spending the night at the house with me now, instead of later. "After all," I said, "your house is so crowded with crates and boxes, you'll probably trip on one and kill yourself when you get up during the night. You can sleep in Margaret's room until your room is completely finished. I think we'd both sleep a lot more soundly if we knew the other was in the next room. Now, I'm not frightened or anything like that, and I don't want you to get the wrong impression that I'm scared, but it just makes good sense."

"I guess you're right," Bess answered slowly, as she stared straight ahead at the road. "You know, now that the time is here for me to make the move, I feel sad in a way. I've lived in my house for over forty years now, Bee. I raised my boys there. Fred died in that house. Tell me I'm making the right decision. Am I going to regret leaving all my memories behind?"

"For goodness sake, Bess, you're not leaving memories. You'll take them with you. And besides, you can visit Jean and Freddy anytime you want to. But if you aren't ready, I don't want to force you. We can put off your move as long as you want to."

"I've been telling myself the same thing all along, but my heart just isn't listening. And I know everything you say is true, except the part about visiting Jean and Freddy. You know I'd have to call and make an appointment before I went over."

Bess seemed preoccupied and didn't say anything else for several minutes. *And that was very unusual for her.* It was in those few minutes that I realized Bess was having as many misgivings and fears about her move to the farm as I was. I had been working toward removing all my doubts about losing a vast portion of my privacy, and I never once thought Bess was having uncertain feelings, also. I was beginning to understand that her fears and concerns about her future were very similar to my own. Only time could really give us all our answers.

"If I'm going to stay out at the farm with you tonight, I've got to run by the house for a few things. You know tomorrow is Sunday, and we are absolutely not going to miss Sunday school or preaching. We've let too many social obligations slide lately." *I told you my life would never be the same. And is church really a social obligation?*

I decided to join the army again and readily agreed to everything Bess said. "Why, of course we'll be in church and Sunday school tomorrow. But right after church, we have to find Sheriff Ledbetter and tell him everything we've learned. He'll probably have one conniption fit about all the evidence we confiscated, but maybe he'll forgive us when he figures out how much time we've saved the law officers over in Burt County. After all, I think we've pretty much solved the whole case for Sheriff Oscar Fay Cornfoot of Burt County."

Bess nodded and silently drove on. As we entered Jeffersonville's city limit, Bess turned off the highway and drove toward her house. We waved at Mrs. Hodges as she walked Mr. Hodges and their big German shepherd dog down the sidewalk with a tight leash on both. Mildred gave us a wave as we rode past her house. She was sitting on her porch on her new porch glider from Sears and Roebuck, with her hair in pin curls, talking with her baby brother, Earl Williford. Bess and I knew Mildred rolled her hair every Saturday afternoon, and you could mark your calendar in ink with that. We returned her wave and journeyed on through the neighborhood. I glanced toward Molly and Sam's little house as Bess drove by.

My heart abruptly stopped when I realized what I saw. "Bess, stop! Stop this car!" I shouted, as I sat straight up in my seat and grabbed at the steering wheel, causing Bess to instinctively react by slamming her foot hard on the brake pedal. The abrupt stop caused us to be jerked forward in our seats as the car engine sputtered and soon died, leaving us stranded in the middle of the street. I quickly glanced into the rearview mirror and saw Miss Effie Belle Sweetwater, the church secretary, in her ancient gray sedan, as it crawled down the street. She must have been in her own little dream world today. She never slowed the car as she motored closer and closer toward us, as we sat like guinea pigs in the middle of the street, waiting for the inevitable collision. Thankfully, she noticed us just in the nick of time. She slammed on her squealing brakes, swerved her car over a few feet, and narrowly missed us. Evidently she was accustomed to near mishaps with her car because, without a wave or a second glance our way, her car kept on going down the street, and she kept powdering her nose as if close calls were everyday occurrences.

"Whatever is the matter with you, Bee? You almost caused us to have a wreck—and with Miss Effie Bell, of all people. Is she blind or something? She acted as if she didn't even know us. And she needs to put that face powder down while she drives!"

Have you ever heard the pot call the kettle black? Now you have.

"She might be blind or something, but thank heavens, she's got good reactions. Bess, listen…I know I saw Molly walk by their front window just then. I'd bet my life on it."

"Well, if you keep grabbing at this steering wheel like you just now did, your life isn't going to be worth a plug nickel, and neither will mine."

"Bess, I know it was her. It was definitely her. Hurry! Back up. There's nobody behind us right now. Go...now."

"Well, I sincerely hope nobody else is back there. I've got to get this car out of the middle of this road before somebody else comes barreling down the street. Are you sure you saw Molly?"

"I'm absolutely, positively sure. Now hurry and back up. We've got to see Molly. Hey, that's Sam's car in the driveway. I'll bet he's at home, too."

"Bee, we can't just go busting into their house right now. They might be doing something...I don't know...you know...something we can't interrupt. We have to be invited."

"For goodness sake, Bess, we're not gonna break into their house this time. We're gonna knock on the front door. That'll give them plenty of time to quit...you know...whatever it is they're doing and answer the door. We're gonna to be invited in this time. We've got to confront Molly and Sam right now. It's way past time for an explanation from both of them. They might claim it's none of our business, but we're gonna make it our business!"

Bess fired the car up again and unintentionally floored it. Grinding the gears, *again*, Bess backed the car down the street, and with one last grind, she shot the car forward and over the cement curbing directly in front of Molly and Sam's little rented house, giving us another major jolt. "Whew," I hollered. I resisted grabbing the wheel but this time grabbed the dashboard for support. "Bess, when are you ever going to learn how to park this thing? And when are you going to quit grinding those gears? You're gonna tear this car slam up!"

"What are you talkin' about? I didn't do a thing except pull the car over a little," Bess innocently answered, as she opened her purse to get out her lipstick and compact. *Bess's driving skills were... oh, you already know.*

I glanced across the street at Mrs. Ricketson's house, and there she was, on patrol duty again, sitting on her throne. With her hand pulling at the curtain, she was watching our every move. *She probably got a big laugh as we zigzagged up and down the street and over the curb.*

"Okay, Bess. Let's see if we can get an explanation," I impatiently said, as we eagerly walked up to the front door—the same front door, I might add, we had entered just a few days earlier without the benefit of an invitation and under the snooping eyes of Mrs. Ricketson as she sat regally on her rocking chair throne. Just as I put my hand up to knock, the door flew open, and there stood Molly, with her arms wide open in welcome.

"Oh, ladies, I'm so glad to see you. Come on in. I'm sorry the house is such a mess. I just got home a little while ago after a short trip to visit my parents." Molly looked at us curiously. "I don't know what it is, but there's something different about both of you. Maybe it's your hair? You both look different..."

We both laughingly gave Molly a hug. Sam stood over to her side and smiled. "Welcome, ladies. Come on in and sit down, that is if you can find a place that's uncluttered. I'm afraid I'm a pretty terrible housekeeper. I've been on my own for a while, and without Molly, I've let a few things slide. But now that Molly's home, I'm sure we'll work together and get this place back in tip-top order." He gave Molly a loving smile and a quick hug. *It seemed as if all was well on the home front.* Molly beamed a smile back at her adoring husband and ushered us in. *Somebody once said, "Absence makes the heart grow fonder." It seems it might be true.*

"Ladies, I suppose I owe the both of you an explanation," Molly sheepishly said, as she moved several newspapers, a Life magazine, and half of a peanut butter and jelly sandwich from the settee and motioned for us to sit down.

"Yes, you do. We've been so afraid something dreadful had happened to you. Child, where on earth have you been?" I asked, in my most motherly stern voice.

"I've been gone for a while, visiting my parents. I, uh, left very suddenly on Monday morning a week or so ago." And with a sheepish glance toward Sam, she continued on. "I didn't even tell Sam I was leaving, I'm afraid. I left on an impulse." She gave Sam another glance and apologized. "I'm sorry for all the trouble I've caused. I shouldn't have left like I did. I should have stayed home where we could have talked all our problems out together." She reached for Sam's waiting hand and clutched it. "I won't ever do it again." A single tear rolled down her cheek. "I promise."

I was so relieved to see Molly again. But I wondered…Had Sam finally been honest with Molly about his mounting problems? Had Molly told Sam that she had hired us to investigate his disgusting actions? Had Molly told us about her visit to Dixie's house? Did Sam even know that Molly knew of Dixie? *So many secrets and so many lies.*

"Well, who wants to talk first? Maybe y'all don't feel as if it's any of our business, but Bess and I have made it our business. Now, what's really been going on?"

Molly hesitated, glanced at Sam, and he nodded. She told us how she had left on the bus after a heated argument with Sam. She said she got off the bus in Waynesville and walked directly over to Dixie's address. "It was easy to find; I just asked the gas station attendant at the bus stop."

After her encounter with Dixie, Molly said she began to realize how her husband had been trapped by Dixie's cunning ways and conniving sexual advances. After being at her parents' home for a few days, she finally came to the conviction that she was only running away from their mounting problems. "We needed to face them, not alone, but together. I realized I had accountability for our relationship, too, and if our marriage was to be saved, I had to return home. I truly longed for my husband and my home. When Sam called me on the telephone, admitting all his indiscretions, begging for my forgiveness and pleading for me to come home, I couldn't get back here fast enough. We're going to work through our problems together this time," Molly added, with so much conviction in her voice. Sam nodded in agreement, and Molly beamed with joy.

As happy as I was for Molly and Sam right at that moment, I knew Molly had to be told the latest developments surrounding Dixie's murder. I hesitated a moment, but asked, "Bess, would you like to tell Molly about the latest developments?"

"No, Bee, you tell her. I'll gladly let you do all the talking this time," Bess firmly replied, justly relieved that she wouldn't be the one to break the horrible news to Molly.

I gave Bess a frown, and then sympathetically looked back toward Molly. "Well, Molly, I hate to spoil your homecoming, and I really hate to be the one to break this bad news to you...but has Sam said anything to you about Dixie's death?"

Molly threw her hands to her face in shock. "Dixie's dead? How? When?"

"She was murdered the same day you met with her in her home, only later in the afternoon. The murderer hit her on her head with some kind of heavy, blunt object. She probably died instantly."

"You don't think I had anything to do with the…?"

"Oh, no. We don't think that you or Sam had anything to do with the murder," I tenderly added.

"I didn't know about it." Molly looked at Sam. "Did you know, Sam? Did you know that Dixie was dead? Murdered?"

"Yes dear, I knew. I was going to tell you. I just haven't had the time yet. And I was sure it was just a coincidence that she died the same day you were in her house."

"Yes, it certainly was," I quickly interjected. "Molly, your bus ticket proves that you had nothing to do with the murder. The murder happened sometime after three p.m. that Monday afternoon, and you were safely tucked on the bus by then."

"So you did believe I could have committed the murder, Ms. Bee!"

"Not really, dear, but Bess and I have to look at the whole picture. In a fit of passion, people will do things they never would ordinarily do, and we knew you didn't go over to that house for a cup of tea. We checked the bus schedule, determined that you were on the afternoon bus out of town, and completely ruled you out."

Molly put her hands to her face again and began to sob those big crocodile tears we'd seen before. Sniveling and crying, Molly mumbled, "This is so incredible. Who…who did kill Dixie? Do you know, Ms. Bee?"

"We think we know, but now's not the time to divulge all of our information. But if it's all right with you, Molly, we'd like to ask both of you some hard questions. Is that acceptable to you, too, Sam?"

"It's okay," answered Sam, "and I'm sure one of the first questions will be, "Who did I throw over the bridge?" Sam smiled.

In our surprise at his admission, Bess and I gawked right at Sam. "Why Sam, how did you know we...?" Bess asked.

"Just as I was leaving, I saw you in the bushes...on lookout."

"Oh, my," Bess muttered.

"I saw both of you. But I think the two of you saw more of me than what you wanted to see," Sam added a little shamefaced. "I went to the bridge that day to throw an old, dead dog into the river. He had died behind the schoolhouse a few days earlier, and I had just discovered him when I went to investigate the horrible odor. I wrapped the stinking dog up in an old drop cloth I found in the boiler room, drove to the river, and threw him into the currents—that is, what the buzzards had left behind. You know school principals have lots of duties that nobody ever thinks about." Sam sternly added, "We need a dogcatcher in this community. I'm tired of dogs tearing into our trash cans and going around having more puppies that grow to be big, hungry dogs. Somebody who has some official capacity in this town needs to do something about that situation."

"As I've been told before," I readily answered. Bess and I gave each other a knowing glance but didn't apologize to Sam for being so sneaky. After all, that's what good detectives do. *You know our motto is "We go where you can't."* We were working on a case the day we witnessed Sam disposing of a dead body into the rushing waters of the river. *And it was a dead body, just not the human kind. Thank Goodness!*

After Sam's admission of throwing a dog overboard, *which was the very least of his recent guilty and not so guilty actions*, I looked at Molly and said, "I'm sure you confronted Dixie about her affair, of sorts, with Sam the day you left home. Can you tell us what happened while you were in the house with Dixie? And please don't leave out any details. Anything you say might be vitally important to the case."

"I'll try to remember everything, Ms. Bee, if you think it's important." Molly sighed and reluctantly continued. "First off, before my stop in Waynesville I had worked up my courage to confront Sam and we had a fight. It started Sunday night, and as Sam started out to leave for work Monday morning, we had more words. Sam finally admitted to me that he had been seeing Dixie for several years and paying dearly for her services. I was really furious. He told me he didn't really understand why he couldn't stay away from Dixie. He said she was like a tick that sucks the blood out of your body and won't let go, or a sickness that just hangs on forever until you die. You know, you just can't get rid of it. He told me he was caught in her vicious web and didn't know how to get out. He said she had used up all the good in him, and she was blackmailing him now on top of everything else. Sam rushed out of the door that morning, slamming it as he went, and left me reeling. Our married life together began to fade completely away after the door shut behind him that morning."

"I decided right then and there to leave Sam and go home to my parents. But first, I wanted to meet the person who had stolen my husband and my future. I called the filling station here in town and found out that the bus out of here went right through Waynesville. I knew right then I was going to be on that bus, and I knew I was going to get off in Waynesville and confront my enemy."

"I left with very little, just a small suitcase and my black purse. I did have a little money, enough to get to my parents' home, but that's about all. I got off the bus in Waynesville and walked the few blocks to Dixie's house. She wasn't at home when I got there, so I sat down on her back doorsteps to wait. A big, sweet dog from next door came over and sat down beside me."

Biscuit?

"I was grateful for its company. Dixie returned home early that afternoon and found me dozing in the sun on her doorsteps."

"She asked me in, without even knowing who I was. As soon as she put her things on the table, I confronted her. I told her I knew who she was, and she had ruined my marriage to Sam. I called her an evil person. She laughed right in my face and said that if I was any good, my husband wouldn't be coming to see her so often." Molly lowered her head and went on. "She called Sam a total pushover and said she could get anything she wanted out of the sorry likes of him. She said he bored her to tears, but his money was good and regular, and she'd keep him coming as long as she wanted to and she even had him paying double now. I still don't understand what she meant by that, but she laughed out loud about it." Molly heaved a sigh, cried more tears, and shook her head. "It's so hard to talk about all this."

"Go on, Molly. Finish the whole story. Get it all out," I encouraged her.

"Anyway, she said Sam was a nobody, and she had a bigger fish to fry that very night. She said she could get big money anytime she wanted it from the big fish. Come hell or high water, she was going to get what was due her after wasting all her good years on jerks like my husband. She told me I might as well leave Sam for good because he was hers, and she wasn't about to let any of her regulars off the hook, now or ever. Ms. Bee, she was so angry at me for coming to her house. She screamed like a maniac for me to get out and never come back. I ran out the back door. I left my pink sweater, but I never looked back. That big hungry-looking dog was still sitting at the back steps when I rushed out. I stopped long enough to pet him one more time and headed back to the bus stop, where I waited for the next bus. I ended up at my parents' home, and that's where I've been until early this morning, when I caught the bus back here. And that's about all I know about Dixie. Even though she was evil, I'm sorry about the way she died. But, dead or alive, she won't be in our future."

Sam never interrupted Molly but sat silently, listening to what a fool he had been. He seemed relieved after we told him that we knew his car was in the shop the day of the murder, giving him an alibi for the day. He was off the hook.

Bess and I never said a word to Molly or Sam about Molly's tearful plea to us to find out what Sam was doing with his time and money. That would remain a secret. We respectfully apologized to both of them for the necessary intrusion into their lives. Surely now, with Dixie completely out of the picture, and with a big effort on both their parts, they could work out their problems and become a family again.

We left them then, knowing we were right on target with the investigation. Judge Harmon had certainly been a big fish in Dixie's little pond, but I'm afraid he had made too big of a splash to swim out unnoticed.

CHAPTER THIRTY-TWO

More determined than ever to talk to the sheriff, we decided to go on by the station before leaving town that evening. With Molly's admissions, the evidence was mounting. I was now surer than ever I knew exactly who the killer was.

"He's gone out into the county to serve some court papers on some poor dirt farmer who won't pay his accounts. He'll be back directly, in an hour or two," Vernon, the deputy, replied after Bess and I charged into the station. He leisurely handed us a sheet of paper. "Fill this out and sign both your names on the bottom line. Make sure you put down all the details of your complaint, and I imagine he'll see about it Monday morning, bright and early."

"Can't you radio him that we're here, or tell us where we can find him or something? It's vitally important for us to talk with him right away," I anxiously said to Deputy Vernon, as he sat behind the desk, taking out big chunks of an apple with his big front teeth and chewing noisily. I figured I was up against a brick wall here that even a blast of dynamite couldn't tear down.

"Now, Ms. Bee, you know yourself, I can't tell you the sheriff's whereabouts. That's privileged information. Anyway, he told me not to bother him tonight unless it was a life or death situation. He did say something 'bout going off coon hunting later on tonight with Earl Williford. Somewhere back in the swamps behind Earl's house."

"Well, this could be a life or death situation. *I fibbed a bit.* And since when did his coon hunting take preference over performing his duty? I 'spect he doesn't even eat those coons after he kills them."

"Me and Earl eats them." *I wasn't surprised.*

I scratched out a message on the paper: "Call or come by." I ended it with "the sooner, the better" and signed my name. Exasperated with Sheriff Ledbetter and with Vernon as well, I motioned to Bess for us to leave. "We've never been able to count on Sheriff Ledbetter in time of emergency. Just tell him he better call or come out to the house as soon as he can, and I don't mean maybe." I handed the paper to Vernon, as apple juice ran down his chin, and we haughtily pranced out. As we neared the car, I asked Bess in my most irritated tone of voice, "Have you ever thought of running for sheriff, Bess? Anybody would be a better choice than what we've got now."

"Don't even think about it. I can't even keep you in line, much less a whole county. Anyway, you'd be better at it than me."

We hurried by Bess's house, where I waited in the car as Bess gathered a few things, and then we headed straight for home.

* * *

Darkness was beginning to fall around us as we rode down the lane toward the house. I could hear a hoot owl in the distance as the lights from the car shone ahead, illuminating the porch. I was beginning to calm down a bit, and was so thankful just to be home to my sanctuary again. Bess stopped the car in the yard.

"I can never remember to leave the porch light on when I leave in the daylight. Bess, leave the car headlights on until I can get the porch lit up. I'll hurry." A sudden chill in the air caused me to shudder as I grabbed my bags out of the backseat of the car and then headed up the steps for the porch. Suddenly, right ahead of me, a stray black cat jumped out from behind a potted plant on the top of the steps, scaring me so badly that I jumped and had to grasp the handrail to keep from falling over into the dark, overgrown shrubs.

Bess called out from the car, "You all right?"

"I'm fine," I called back. "That old stray cat scared me. It's been hanging around lately. I think Vonion's feeding it. We might as well give it a name and keep it to kill rats. I'll have the porch light on in a second."

Going into an empty house at night by myself is not my favorite thing to do. Relieved that Bess was with me tonight, I pulled the porch light chain hanging from the ceiling, and Bess switched off the headlights to the car. I called out, "All seems to be just as we left it, Bess. I'm glad to be home."

"I'm glad I'm here with you too," Bess answered, as she hurried up the steps. "Mama and Daddy would be so relieved to know I'm going to be living with you now. There really is no place like home! And I feel as if I'm finally here." *Those few words of Bess's were like music in my heart.*

"I hope Melvin and Lambert have finished with your bathroom. Go on into Margaret's room and put your bags down, and then we'll check out the progress in the rest of the house. At least that turpentine odor isn't as strong as it was earlier. Hey, I'm hungry. Let's get a little something to eat, too. I think there's some more of that good vegetable soup I made a day or so ago. I'll heat it while you get settled in."

"I could go for that. We haven't eaten in hours. I'll be just a few minutes."

"Take your time."

I put my bags down on the bed in my bedroom and walked into the kitchen. I quickly turned on one of the back eyes to the stove and opened the refrigerator for the soup. It wouldn't take but a minute for it to heat up. Bed sounded pretty good right now; it had been a long and eventful day. As I dipped some to the cold soup into a boiler, I heard Bess talking to somebody. Their voices seemed to be coming from the direction of the porch. I stood by the stove and silently listened. Maybe Vonion had walked up to the house to check on us. No, it didn't sound like Vonion's low, raspy voice. I placed the boiler on the stove and turned the eye down lower.

Curiously, I followed the voices out to the porch and stood in the doorway of the house. Bess was standing over by the screen door and speaking to a shadowy figure on the steps. I cleared my voice, and Bess turned my way. She called out, "Oh, Bee, it's Eli. We forgot our ferns today, and he's brought them over. Isn't that nice of him?"

I froze! I absolutely knew Eli wasn't here about ferns. *Oh, dear God! What to do?* "Oh, uh, yes, Bess, that's nice. I need to turn the stove off. I'll be just a minute." I turned to go back into the house as I heard Bess tell Eli to come on into the porch. *What to do? What to do?* I stood in the middle of the kitchen floor, stunned, frightened, and knowing. I had made the horrible connection earlier but was still grappling with the truth behind it. Now I knew, I just knew, all my instincts were correct. I grabbed a kitchen knife, stuck it under my belt, and headed for the bedroom where I kept Will's rifle behind the door. I reached for the gun, checked to see if it was loaded, and walked all the way through the house into the front room, not even thinking, or caring, that the floors might not be quite dry yet. I opened the other door that led out to the porch and stood in the threshold. Bess was standing at the other end of the porch, and Eli was standing directly between us under the solitary lightbulb which dimly illuminated the porch. Bess was thanking Eli for the ferns, and Eli answered that they were still in the back of his pickup truck.

I raised the rifle straight toward Eli. With my finger on the trigger, I said, "Hello, Eli. It's mighty late for a visit."

He turned toward me, and the gun startled him. He stepped back and replied, "You going hunting, Ms. Bee?"

"Bee, put that gun down, for goodness sake. It's Eli."

I motioned with my gun. "Bess, move toward the other door right now." Confused, Bess slowly began to move.

"Bee, what is the meaning of all this?"

Eli thought fast, quickly rushed me, and reached for the gun barrel. As he pushed the gun upward toward the ceiling, I fired. The blast of fire hit the ceiling as Eli quickly grabbed for the gun. I staggered backward and called out for Bess to run. Eli turned toward Bess with the gun in his hands and stepped backwards. "Don't you move!" He waved the gun directly toward me. "Ms. Bee, get on over by Ms. Bess now, and Ms. Bess, if you move one muscle, I'll shoot Ms. Bee's head clean off!"

"Let's do what he says, Bess. He's killed before, and he'll do it again. He doesn't have anything to lose now."

"Eli? Oh, dear! Eli, please don't kill us. Please!" Bess began to cry. "Leave, just leave!"

Eli clinched the rifle firmly and aimed it directly at us. Slowly, with his right hand, he reached for his pistol that he had concealed in his overalls pocket. He aimed it directly at us as he dropped Will's rifle onto the floor. He moved closer and looked squarely at me. "I knew today when you was questioning me, you'd figured me out. I didn't want to kill Dixie, but she never would have left the judge alone. She was eventually gonna take him down into the gutter. There wasn't no good in her, just meanness and greed. It was just a matter of time before she would be demanding more and more of the judge's money and threatening him more. The judge just got caught up in her evil and kept digging himself deeper and deeper into her shameful ways. I had to protect the judge, and now I don't have no choice but to keep protecting him. He's got a good name and a good reputation, and the likes of that harlot was destroying him."

"You don't need to keep on killing, Eli. The judge wouldn't want that. He'll represent you in a court of law, and a jury will understand. Please, put that gun down," I begged. "I know you don't want to kill again."

"I've got to protect the judge. It's the only way. He's been so good to me all my life. He was my bestest childhood friend. We went off to war together, and he saved my life. He was my commander and shielded me with his own body from enemy grenades, saving me from the brunt of an explosion. He stayed in the army hospital for weeks, recuperating. Never complained. Always took care of me. When Safronia was sick, he paid for her operation and all her medicine and doctor bills. He educated my son, gave me a place to live and work..."

"He wouldn't want you to murder. I know he wouldn't," I desperately argued, realizing Bess's and my life depended on it. I slowly moved my hand toward the knife stuck under my belt.

"He'll never know. He doesn't know I killed Dixie, and I'll never tell him. After you're dead, nobody can destroy the judge's reputation ever again. Dixie's gone now, and you'll be gone soon. Nobody else on earth knows how that sinful woman manipulated and used my boss man. She was blackmailing him, and he didn't have no choice but to give into her demands. He was too weak when it came to women. He'd have eventually been back for more from that no-good, rotten floozy. "

I reached out and grabbed Bess's hand. "I'm sorry I got you into this, Sister. I'm so-o sorry. I love you." I quickly pulled the knife from under my belt with my other hand and lurched toward Eli.

Eli instinctively shielded his body from the knife with his arm and easily knocked it to the floor. He quickly regained his composure. Bess grabbed me and I clutched her for support.

"I've got to kill you. I don't have any choice. I wish it could be another way, but..."

Out from the shadows of the overgrown shrubs by the steps, a figure moved. "Put the gun down, Eli. You've killed enough."

The figure stepped closer into the light. He held a gun and aimed it right at Eli. He took another step closer and said again, this time louder and more demanding, "Eli, throw the gun down. I don't need that kind of protection. I can face what I've done, but I can't face any more killing. Now, throw the gun down! If you kill again, I'll turn you in, or you'll have to kill me to keep me quiet."

"No siree, you ain't goin' down now. You got too much good in you. Too many people's countin' on you. I can get rid of these women just like I got rid of that Jezebel.

Nobody will ever know what happened to Dixie or to these ladies. Get outta here and go home. Let me handle this my own way. I'll put an end to everything right here and now."

"No, Eli. Enough is enough. No more killing. I can't live with myself now. Now let's go!"

"Git outta here, Judge." Eli cocked the hammer to his pistol and began to squeeze the trigger.

One bullet, meant for Eli, was all it took to take him down. Eli fell hard to the porch floor. I crumbled, as Bess fainted dead away.

* * *

"Mrs. Bee, are you okay? It's all over. Eli's dead. I had to kill him." Judge Harmon was leaning over me. The dim light of the porch bulb was enough for me to see Eli a few feet away, lying on his back with a red bloodstain seeping into the denim fabric of the bib to his overalls. "I'm sorry for everything. Do you think Mrs. Bess's all right? Let's try to wake her."

I gave Bess a little shake, and she hesitantly slit one eye open. She immediately realized we were still alive and grabbed me. I held her as we cried together. Judge Samuel Harmon fell to his knees beside us. Through my tears, I watched as he put his hands over his face and wept uncontrollably.

CHAPTER THIRTY-THREE

It had been about two weeks since the dreadful incident on the front porch. It was late afternoon, and I was standing at the kitchen sink, washing turnip greens. Thanksgiving was just around the corner, and I was beginning to prepare some of the food for our meal. With the turnips cleaned, blanched, and frozen, I'd be that much closer to having the food ready for our day of thanks. Vonion had his eye on a gobbler back in the woods behind the pond. With my list of family and friends growing, I knew we'd need two turkeys this year. I knew the Lord (and Vonion) would provide. I'd instructed Vonion to pull Will's old hay wagon, minus the side bodies, into the yard a day or two before the big day, and with everybody's help, we'd load it up with turkey and dressing, chicken and dumplings, vegetables, casseroles, and desserts.

Bess was so excited about the prospects of showing the place off. She'd invited her sons and a good many of our friends from town and about. I hoped the weather would be nice and Bess and I could hold out to get ready for the day, and then have the energy to enjoy it. I had so much to be thankful for: my health, my family, my home, and most of all, my faith that the Lord was always watching over me. A new son-in-law seemed to be in the works too, and you know how much that excited Bess and me. Ora Lee was feeling better every day and had finally resigned herself that the doctor medicine was good for her. I think just having Walter prescribe it made all the difference.

Bess had not left me overnight since the incident on the porch. Oh, of course, she went back to her house in town to pack and clean, but she never stayed past dark. We had made the transition of living together as smooth as could be. Oh, and did the house look terrific! All Bess's nice furniture and glassware were a lovely addition to our décor, and the new front room curtains Bess had seamed together were outstanding. Melvin and Lambert had finished all the floors, and they just shined. By the way, they had been completely dry the night I had to walk over them, brandishing my gun. All the painting was complete now. Bess's bathroom was beautiful, and Melvin and Lambert had even repaired the hole in the porch ceiling and repainted the whole thing. You would never know that a bullet had splintered through the wood and was lodged somewhere above. I told them not to worry about trying to dig the bullet out. I got some comfort knowing that bullet was hidden away, maybe for somebody, years from now, to find and wonder why a bullet was lodged into the timbers of the old house.

I smiled, but actually I was very melancholy about the results of our investigation. Margaret had returned to her little duplex at the back end of the judge's property. She believed, as I did, there was nothing to be frightened of now. Safronia was still there, caring for the house and

Livonia, but her heart was shattered. Margaret called last night and said Safronia would be moving soon to stay with her son and his wife in South Carolina. Her and Eli's son was a lawyer and was quite capable of caring for his aging mother for the duration of her life. I didn't attend Eli's funeral, but from all accounts, it was a small service with just a few people attending. Margaret said Judge Harmon and Livonia paid for the whole thing but respectfully stayed away. I truly hoped they could mend their marriage, and the judge would continue to do some of those good things with his life that Eli had been so sure he was capable of.

As I reached for a large boiler, my mind went back to the night of Eli's death. Judge Harmon had called the sheriff's department as soon as he'd covered Eli's body with a blanket. Vonion heard the shooting from his house and had rushed up the lane. He and Roscoe, and even Tom Wilson, had sat on the steps guarding the body until the law arrived. Bess made coffee for everybody, and we waited well over an hour for Sheriff Ledbetter to arrive at the house. The Judge, Bess and I had stayed in the kitchen away from the others where, despondently, Judge Harmon had explained that Dixie had been a terrible thorn in his flesh. He was like an alcoholic, he had said. He just couldn't stop seeing her. He said he had been seeing her regularly for four years, every two weeks, just like clockwork. *We already knew that; the ledger told us that story.* That last night, after his and Dixie's last rendezvous, he said he was leaving to walk back to his office when Dixie handed him an envelope with a note inside, and asked him to read it later. He said he couldn't wait and read it as he started out the door. It was one of those mimeographed blackmailing notes. Livid, he said he tossed the note on the floor and left, vowing never to return and never to give Dixie one penny of her request of one hundred dollars in return for her silence about their arranged meetings. He walked to his office, got in his car, and drove home. After arriving home, instead of going into the house, he walked around to the backyard and sat out under the stars to smoke awhile, hoping to calm his nerves. Eli must have noticed the light from the cigarette and stepped out into the darkness to join him. He told us that Eli had known of his wayward visits to Dixie's for years and had covered for him many a time. "I expressed my torment to Eli, and relinquishing my determination to ignore Dixie's demands, asked Eli to carry the blackmailing money over to Dixie first thing in the morning. I told Eli I just didn't know how to rid myself of the canker that was embedded deep in my flesh. As long as Dixie was available, I knew I couldn't resist the temptation."

"I knew this wouldn't be the last time I'd be blackmailed by Dixie, but I didn't know how to stop it. I believe Eli didn't waste any time. More than likely, he walked over to her house soon after I left him to go into my house that night. I really don't think Eli meant to kill Dixie but just wanted to frighten her. Perhaps an argument between the two of them occurred and he probably reacted with violence. With no other way to silence her for good, he must have resorted to taking her life." Judge Harmon closed his eyes and beat his fist on the table in anguish. "I should have realized what Eli was capable of. Maybe I did know…and…I'm just as guilty as Eli."

He paused, and then went on, "I knew Eli would go to the limit for me. He had demonstrated it many times in the past. At the farm, he had once jumped between an angry bull and me. Another time he stepped on a rattlesnake just before it was about to strike out at my leg. Many times he's covered for me with Livonia when I'd be out somewhere that I had no business. When the news of Dixie's death became public the next day, I became nauseated and sick. I absolutely knew in my heart Eli had committed the crime, probably shortly after our conversation the night before. I knew that the blunt force to Dixie's head must have come from Eli's hammer—the same hammer he kept stuck in the tab of his overalls. I had no doubts, but didn't say a word to Eli, or to anybody. A secret, I thought, to be carried for the rest of our lives and would remain unmentioned between the two of us. I'm so ashamed of myself now. I'll be tormented for the rest of my life...and rightly so."

Judge Harmon said that he had watched from the window of his house as Bess's car left the yard that very afternoon, and then, a few seconds later, he witnessed Eli's truck pulling out right behind us. He said a strange, dark feeling consumed him. "I suspected Eli was following you. You know, the two of you have a reputation for being crime solvers, and I just put two and two together. I remembered Sheriff Cornfoot laughingly mention that two old ladies from Jefferson County were investigating the crime." After apologizing for calling us "old ladies," he went on. "According to Sheriff Cornfoot, Zeniss Coleman, a prisoner in the county jail, had snitched on you two about your true mission the day an ornery old lady landed in jail with him." *You know, Aunt Dora's most thrilling adventure.* "I was afraid that Eli could be considering more violence as a means of keeping our horrible secrets and quickly decided I would follow Eli's truck and see what he was up to. I followed him all the way into your county. I waited and watched as Eli did the same. Y'all visited someone in a little house in town, went by the sheriff's office and then by another house. I followed Eli all the way out to your place, Mrs. Bee. Since becoming a Superior Court judge, I've received several threats on my life, and I've resigned myself that I must carry a gun in my car for protection, so I took my Saturday night special from the glove compartment and left my car next to the highway. I walked the last leg of my trip, down the dark lane here to your house. The rest you know."

* * *

A few days later, Bess and I traveled back to Burt County to relinquish the stolen ledger, as well as other bits and pieces of evidence we had stolen. *Minus the green shoe, of course. Bess fussed at me about burning the other shoe. She said she could probably repair the one Biscuit chewed on and get some more wear out of the pair. I told her not to worry about them. I had already put them down in the ledger as an expense.*

We gave our statements to Sheriff Cornfoot. After a stern scolding about tampering with evidence, he told us the milkman had come forward earlier in the investigation with a description of us. After a call to his first cousin about some ladies in a car from our county rounding up Aunt Dora from the jailhouse, both sheriffs figured we were on the case. Sheriff Ledbetter told his cousin not to worry, that we'd solve the murder sooner or later, just be patient.

With an amused expression, Sheriff Oscar Fay Cornfoot asked us, as we were about to leave his office, "Have y'all ever considered joining the F.B.I.? They need some good bloodhounds." We chuckled at the thought.

How foolish! But...then again? I smiled as I remembered the conversation.

* * *

A soft tap on the porch screen door. Who could that be? Bess or Vonion don't ever knock. Ora Lee always comes right in through the back door without ever a thought to knock. I rinsed my hands in the cool water running into the sink and picked up the drying cloth. "Coming," I called. I ran to the bathroom to check my hair, now almost back to my natural, unnatural color. Quickly glancing at myself in the bathroom mirror, I thought, *not too bad for an old country woman.* Maybe that exercise routine Bess had us on was working faster than I ever thought it would. "I'm coming," I called again, and hurried out to the porch.

There on the top of the steps, he stood. Low and behold, Bess had a suitor, and after all this time of saying she was absolutely through with men. *I knew she didn't mean it. And here was the living proof.*

There he was, such a familiar face. Standing all stiff and erect, not relaxed at all. His stomach was tucked in, and his shoulders were back. All shined up and polished in the daytime. Clean and pressed. His hat in one hand and a pretty bouquet of yard flowers in the other. Waiting to begin a courtship, I assumed. I suppose I should ask him in. After all, our freshly decorated parlor was ready for our first caller.

I walked closer to the screen door and pushed it open. Expecting him to ask for Bess, I quickly blurted out, "Bess is in town right now, but I expect her back shortly. Come on in and wait for her in the front room."

He timidly answered, as he held the bouquet out toward me, "Bee, these flowers aren't for Bess. They're for you. I came to call on you. I think it's high time you started socializing some. After all, you've been by yourself far too long."

Not really "The End."

22886189R10192

Made in the USA
Charleston, SC
06 October 2013